HIDDEN AGENDA

THE ELLER SERIES, BOOK 2

KATHRYN HALBERG

GenZ
The Future of Publishing

THE ELLER SERIES

KATHRYN HALBERG

1

"...*A*re now welcome to board flight 1124 with service to Chicago."

Rolling her eyes at the barely audible announcement, Carlie triple-checked her boarding pass and progressed toward the gaping doorway, slipping between the clustered hordes of passengers. Most people used digital passes now, but she preferred the security of a printed pass. A quick scan of the paper and she was ready to flee the past, the pressure, and the family. At least for a week.

"Thank you, Ms. Eller," the bored airline attendant read her name off the ticketing scanner without looking up, waving her through the gate. Carlie hefted her bag over her shoulder and ducked into the aircraft. She inched down the narrow aisle, shuffling to the last row of what passed for first class on this hop-skip-and-jump plane that connected Cincinnati and Chicago. At five foot ten, being tall had its advantages, but not in air travel. Carlie stowed her carry-on bag and slid into her seat, searching for her earbuds before another passenger tried to spark a conversation.

"Where are they?" she muttered, rummaging through

her purse. Sensing the arrival of her seatmate, she heaved a sigh of relief as her hand closed around the elusive things.

Cinching her belt, she tried not to notice the light, pleasant cologne wafting toward her as the new arrival worked on his seat belt. Once he, too, was settled, he glanced her way and she froze, her slate blue eyes held hostage by his brilliant, bright gaze. She sucked in her breath and turned away. Crap. Why had she made eye contact? That was like sending a green light to chat. Carlie dipped her chin forward to swing her curtain of pale caramel-colored tresses between them, hoping it disguised most of her flushed face. She focused on her earbuds and made a show of checking them and the connection to her phone.

Tilting his head to the side, the man watched her as he brushed back his wavy blonde hair. "Hi," he said at last, his voice friendly.

"Hello," she mumbled back, casting him a definite 'I-don't-talk-to-strangers-on-an-airplane' frown.

"Outbound or homeward bound?" he pressed.

"Um... Out?"

"Me too. Continuing, actually. Last flight of the day, thank God."

Chatty. Great. Carlie nodded once and succumbed to her signature awkward silence. She was such a stellar conversationalist. For a moment, she felt his inquisitive gaze linger on her, but he finally gave up. The plane took off and Carlie drifted into a more comfortable purgatory, slipping from dreadfully awkward to dozily aloof.

A light tap on her arm brought her back to reality. Seriously? He clearly couldn't take a hint.

"Look," she snapped. "I'm really not interesting in talking ri—" Her words skidded to a stop.

"Would you like something to drink? Pretzels?" the flight attendant inquired.

"Oh." Carlie's cheeks burst into flames. "Thank you. Ginger ale?"

Jesus. What a total bitch move. Carlie mumbled an apology to her handsome neighbor.

"It's okay. I debated whether or not to interrupt, but these really are the best pretzels in the sky," he teased, popping one into his mouth. "I'm Kurt," he managed around the twisted carb.

She blinked, smothering her annoyance. "Carlie."

"So, that's out of the way... Shall we resume ignoring each other?"

His spring-green eyes watched her with interest, dark blonde hair falling carelessly over his forehead. Kurt was long and lean with well-formed muscles on his forearms. His skin was warmed by the perfect permanent golden tan only achieved by a pairing of lucky genes and spending a significant amount of time in the sun. A rich burgundy polo contrasted perfectly with his skin tone, and also seemed to make his unusual eyes glow. He was incredibly attractive and vaguely familiar, but she couldn't place him. Carlie squinted out the window and took a deep breath, remembering her promise to her best friend Kim. Talk to a man, someone new. She could do that. She had to. She could not let the past continue to torment her.

"Your call." She shrugged, leaving it to fate. And Kurt.

"We have a good twenty minutes or so before landing. Want to tell me your life story?"

"I'm afraid it wouldn't take that much time. I was born. I went to school. And now I'm on a plane," Carlie said.

"Ah. I'm going out on a limb here... You're a glass-is-half-empty kind of person. Am I right?"

"I could be now," she retorted, leaning away from him.

He held up his smooth hands, smiling. She guessed him to be around her own twenty-four years. "No offense intended."

Just talk, Carlie. Get it out of the way. "Mmhmm. So, what's your story?"

"Oh, just your garden-variety mile high club wannabe," he deadpanned.

She choked on a laugh. "Funny guy, aren't you?"

"I try. Is it working?" Kurt asked, one eyebrow dancing.

Her cheeks warmed, but she didn't give in to his charm. "I don't think so, but I'll keep you posted. Are you staying in Chicago or passing through?" She was uninterested in his answer, but it seemed like a standard kind of thing people ask.

"Staying in Chicago for a work thing. You?"

"Same. Perhaps we'll bump into each other." She smiled and slipped her headphones back on with relief.

Cranking up the volume, Carlie almost missed his reply. "I hope so."

They landed in Chicago, and Carlie took off for the restroom to shake Kurt. He seemed nice enough, but she didn't want to send the wrong message. As far as she was concerned, she had met her initial quota of conversing with a man. Kim would be proud—task complete before she even hit the ground. A definite win.

After hailing one of the many idling taxis at the terminal, she settled in for the slow ride to the downtown hotel. Rain trickled down the windows and drenched the Windy City. Pedestrians were huddled deep into their raincoats, and one man fought a black and silver umbrella that had flipped inside out in the strong city gusts. Thank God she wouldn't have to shuttle all over the city this week; the weather forecast was not promising. She sighed with satisfaction as the cab pulled to a stop at her destination. The simple pleasures of an all-in-one venue.

"April showers," joked the elderly cabbie as he deposited Carlie outside her home for the week. "Could be worse—could be snow!" Giving the man the socially required and expected exaggerated groan, she thanked him, juggled her bags, and turned to her home for the next five days.

The Splendor Hotel and Convention Center rose majestically in front of her, blotting out the rest of the city skyscrapers. It was far taller than her family's EHL Global corporate office building in Cincinnati. The wet, muddy color of the tower hinted at what was probably a pleasant neutral façade in the sunshine. Multiple columns of the same stone-like material graced the exterior, and she paused for only a moment before diving out of the rain. She tripped over her feet as she got caught up in a revolving-glass-door-and-luggage entanglement and barely regained her footing as she passed through to the cool marble luxury beyond.

Smooth, Car. Way to make an entrance.

Head high, walk with purpose, she admonished herself.

"Reservation for Carlie Eller."

A stately brunette in a standard-issue fitted hotel suit smiled in welcome. Her brass nametag read *Emily*. "Welcome to The Splendor, Ms. Eller. Here for the United Marketing Association convention, correct?"

Carlie mumbled in the affirmative while the woman clicked away on the computer. The clerk's expression turned apologetic. "Unfortunately, your room is not quite ready. I'd be happy to hold your bags for you and send a message when your room is available."

Carlie handed over her luggage and scanned the pristine lobby, noting the plush sofas and the darkened bar entrance across the way. A hint of lemon polish filled the air. "Is there anything open—maybe a restaurant nearby—where I can wait? And is the conference registration open?"

"Yes, ma'am. While the bar doesn't open until three"— Emily gestured to her left—"Sammy's is still serving lunch on the second floor. As for the conference, if you take the elevators to your right, you'll find the registration desk in the fourth-floor lobby."

"Thank you."

The mirror-paneled, brass-accented elevator was fast and smooth, and the doors quietly parted open to the fourth floor. Carlie stepped onto the white marble floors specked with gold and admired the circle of white Tuscan columns decorating the conference center lobby. Strategically placed potted plants and small tables added warmth and vitality to the open space.

Behind the trussed table with the bold United Marketing Association logo, two attractive corporate-type women glared at each other, the hostility tangible even from a distance. The elevator doors swooshed closed behind her, so Carlie approached directly; there was nowhere else to go now without being obvious.

"Is this where we check in for the Digital Marketing Convention?" Carlie inquired, politely ignoring the simmering friction at the table.

"Yes," said the coiffured redhead with a blink, a polite mask dropping into place. "Welcome! I'm Lane Gray, and this is Melanie Addams with United Marketing Association. Your name, please?"

"Carlie Eller, EHL Global."

"Oh, Ms. Eller! We're so pleased you could join us," she purred, smoothing her tailored suit jacket and pointedly ignoring the woman at her side. "I hope you're ready for a week of learning, networking, and fun! Here's your conference lanyard with all the information you'll need. The drink tickets are color coded for each evening, so please refer to the program. The presenters' lounge is down the hall to the right, and you'll be able to go over your deck in there. Should you need anything else, please come find me."

"Or me," added Melanie, a younger perky blonde in a dark blue suit. "I look forward to attending your session, Ms. Eller."

"Thank you. I hope it lives up to your expectations," Carlie said over her shoulder while escaping to the elevator. She tucked the weighty red lanyard and attached pouch under her arm and tried not to bolt into the enclosed space when it was revealed.

As the doors slid closed, Carlie spied the two resuming their battle poses. Well, that was interesting. It's not like all coworkers got along, but that display was a bit juvenile.

Stepping off the elevator to the second floor, she crossed the expanse of marble to the Sammy's bistro entrance. Mellow jazz and a couple's laughter greeted her, and dim light from the rainy day filtered in through the wall full of windows. Carlie took a deep breath, mouth watering at the warm scent of fresh bread. A buffet along the wall stood empty, the exposed metal gleaming in the overhead lights. The hostess showed her to a small table with crisp white linens. A server materialized, depositing a breadbasket, menu, and glass of water.

Carlie selected a warm roll and chewed slowly as she surveyed her surroundings. She counted twelve guests scattered about the large central area in groups and pairs and three others eating alone along the perimeter. These fellow solo diners intrigued her. The first, a middle-aged woman in black capris and a colorful button-down blouse, sat at the table closest to her own. She was slowly picking apart her salad, building an impressive pile of greens on her bread plate. She caught Carlie watching and gestured to the plate with her fork. "Why do they put all this rabbit food in a salad? What happened to good old crunchy iceberg lettuce?" A burbling laugh escaped Carlie as she picked up her water glass to salute the stranger.

After ordering, she turned her attention to the second table, where a studious, grandfatherly man in a beige suit was buried in a book, absentmindedly spearing chunks of salmon. He chewed slowly and wiped his chin with his cloth napkin after each bite, though from where Carlie sat, there didn't appear to be any food on his chin. Curious.

The third table's lone occupant was a terribly attractive man, perhaps a few years older than her, with dark, closely cropped hair. He clutched a tall draft beer in one hand, his cell phone in the other. Whatever was on his device must have been compelling, as his eyes never strayed from it. As he was oblivious to his surroundings, Carlie continued to analyze him, noting his high-end clothing and leather shoes. He was the kind of man women would chase after. One she'd never have the nerve to approach, but who captured her attention, nonetheless.

The waiter returned with her soft drink and deli sandwich, and she happily discovered it was devoid of any mayo or pickles. The little things in life. Catching the eye of Salad Lady, Carlie fished out the lettuce from beneath the toasted top and held up the dark green leaf. The woman wrinkled her nose in distaste and shook her head, then smiled approvingly as Carlie set it aside. In this instance, she fully supported Salad Lady's opinion. The wilted leaf shriveled into itself on the plate.

The elderly Mr. Salmon had finished his fish and moved on to a baked potato. He didn't dab his chin after these bites.

Carlie's attention returned to Beer Man, now working on a burger and fries, his gaze still arrested by his phone. What could possibly be so enthralling? Perhaps he was watching the news. Stock prices. Or a movie. Reading about the history of beer. Who knew?

Setting aside the ridiculous conjecture, Carlie dug out her own phone and scrolled through the groan-inducing, nonstop stream of wedding-concept photos her sister flooded her inbox with, as well as a text from Kim that read, *This week... just do it!* followed by a GIF that was suggestive enough to perhaps warrant an R or possibly NC-17 rating. Either her best friend was now working for Nike or she persisted in her one-track mind, currently residing in the gutter. Carlie's guess was the latter.

"Ahem."

For a bizarre moment, she was convinced everyone knew the contents of that last text exchange. Face heated, Carlie looked up from her phone in confusion. It was the hunky Beer Man. Stunned, she could only stare mutely.

"Sorry to intrude. I was wondering if you dropped this on your way in?"

He held out a red conference lanyard, his cool blue gaze holding her frozen for a long moment. She glanced at her belongings, and sure enough... How had she managed to lose it in the short time she'd had it in her possession?

"Oh! Yes," she said, trying to not look as uncoordinated as she felt. "Thank you."

"I'd be at a loss without mine. Figured you might need yours," he added with a slight smile.

He left it on her table and casually exited the restaurant.

Her fingers toyed with the edge of the lanyard as she stared at the space he had occupied.

Later, as Carlie waited for her check, Salad Lady paused as she walked by Carlie's table. "If I were twenty years younger, I think I'd try to get to know that young man," she said with a wink before continuing on her way.

Indeed.

2

*A*lone in her room on the twenty-second floor, Carlie plugged in her drained devices and slipped away for a long, hot shower to erase the travel—a personal recharging of sorts. Bundled in a plush hotel robe, she settled into her new accommodations. The panoramic view of the crowded city buildings was pleasant enough, and she could just make out Lake Michigan through the gray haze. Too bad it was raining; it would be great to stroll along the water's edge, so very different from the murky Ohio River back home.

Staring into the mist, Carlie couldn't stop her mind from journeying back to Cincinnati and reliving Friday's miserable dress shopping outing with Rachael. Running into *him*.

~

"There's something wrong with this one. There is absolutely no way this is a size four," her sister complained from the dressing room.

"That's because you're a size six," Carlie muttered under her breath in the brightly lit walkway.

"Do me a favor, Car? Tell her this was clearly mislabeled. She can bring the other one," Rachael's melodic voice called through the private room's curtain. A dainty hand shot out, fingers clutching yards of creamy satin and lace, followed by a wide wooden hanger. "Honestly, things would be much easier if there was a consistent sizing standard. Perhaps I should..."

Carlie shook out the offending fabric and ignored her bossy sister's continuing monologue as she emerged from the dressing room hell. Working the dress right-side out and stuffing the lace shoulders over the hanger, she paused to look for the saleswoman. When her gaze landed on the man who stood mere feet away, her stomach plummeted. Carlie closed her eyes and sucked in a breath, her senses alert.

Him. Shit, shit, shit. Flustered, Carlie mentally grasped for calmness and tried to pretend nothing was amiss. She continued shoving the flimsy dress shoulders over the wooden hanger, desperately praying he hadn't noticed her.

"Hey, Carlie," he greeted, his voice like honey over her rattled nerves.

"Hey," she echoed, a knot forming in her gut as she waved the wedding dress toward the bored shop clerk. Pausing to snag the next soon-to-be-discarded option, the hopeful saleswoman collected the latest reject with a polite nod and drifted away with a firm smile plastered in place.

Task complete, Carlie glanced his way.

Brent. For how long had she both hoped for and dreaded this moment?

Her heart stuttered as she drank up the familiar sight. So confident, so self-assured. From the trendy, artfully mussed brown hair to his perfect smile and tailored casualwear, he was so painfully perfect. Except for the designer handbag dangling from his fingers.

"Nice bag." Carlie hoped her smirk disguised the trembling frown that threatened. That specific buttery leather bag had been purchased at the outlet mall. Carlie would know; she had been with her friend when she bought it. *Ex-friend*, she mentally corrected.

He frowned at the accessory in his hand before turning his smile back to her. "Uh, yeah, thanks."

Did his smile falter the tiniest bit? Shaking her head, Carlie retreated, wishing the floor would split wide open and swallow her whole.

"Wait a minute, Car. Please?"

Cursing under her breath, she pressed her eyes closed and debated her options. Unless she wanted to make a scene, which had never been her thing, there wasn't much to consider. Slitting her eyes open, Carlie scanned the area around them, searching for the little raven-haired traitor. Where was she? Gina never left her playthings unaccompanied for long. She must be in the dressing room. Fan-freaking-tastic. Talk to him or chance running into her. Inwardly groaning, she turned back to Brent.

"What?" Carlie snapped, unsure if she was more upset with his presence or with herself for being so flustered.

"Damn, you look good." He eyed her appreciatively.

Her jaw dropped open before she could stop it. "That's it? That's what you wanted to say?" She shook her head, incredulous.

Nine months. After their disastrous split, she'd spent nine freaking months worrying about running into him, and *that* was what he led with? "Unbelievable," she muttered under her breath.

"Look, I..." He hesitated, thrown off by her uncharacteristic response. He cleared his throat then pushed onward. "It didn't end well, and I'm sorry. Things fizzled out. We had become glorified roommates. You saw it too."

It wasn't a question.

But it also wasn't a topic she was ready to revisit.

Unwilling to think back over the four years they'd spent together, Carlie clamped her jaw shut, not trusting herself to answer. His hand traced the air and his mouth—those perfect lips she knew so well—as he summarized the shortcomings of their relationship. As if from a dream, she briefly recalled those lips begging her to return home with him, that it had all been a mistake. Her eyes tracked his hand through the increasingly thick air and zeroed in on the small familiar scar across his knuckles, a lasting mark from their first wretchedly wonderful Thanksgiving together in college when he carved his hand instead of the turkey and they spent the holiday at the emergency room. Carlie curled her hand into a fist to keep from reaching out as the memory dissolved.

"And Gina, well, we didn't mean to, you know..." He rubbed his hand along the back of his flushed neck. "It just happened."

Too lost in her own musings to put together a meaningful response, she stared at him, through him. She imagined what would happen if she threw caution to the wind and kissed him. A curveball. Maybe he'd realize how much he missed her. She missed him. And she didn't. Maybe she missed being with him. Damn it, this was such a mess. Why wasn't she over him already?

"Anyways, I just wanted to tell you that I'm sorry. For everything. Christ, this isn't coming out well, is it?" His nervous smile was charming, reminiscent of their early days when he used to make an effort.

Say something, Carlie. Open your damn mouth!

"No, Brent, you're screwing this up, like everything else," accused Rachael as she strutted out of the dressing room. A furious Italian trailed in her wake, both women hellbent on separate missions.

"Ah, Rachael. Always a pleasure to see you," Brent said, voice dripping with newfound sarcasm.

Carlie shook herself and watched Rachael and Gina stalk toward them. Her old friend refused to meet her eyes.

"Come on, Carlie, we're out." Rachael tugged at her sister's hand. "No luck today." She paused to toss a pointed glance at Gina. "And recent additions seem a bit...beneath us."

Her heart-shaped face lit with anger, Gina stormed up to Brent, ignoring the dig. "What's going on out here? I thought we talked about this?"

Brent brushed off Gina's words. Staring over her dark head, his unreadable hazel eyes tracked Carlie's departure.

Without waiting to see how their drama played out, Carlie allowed her sister to pull her from the store. Rachael was unusually silent as they marched down the crumbled sidewalk to the parking lot. Judging by the press of her lips, she was struggling to keep her mouth shut. Quite considerate of her, actually.

They chased the shadows before them, and Carlie attempted to tune out the various groups of laughing bridesmaids gushing over the glowing brides-to-be.

Brides-to-be.

No, no, no.

"What were they doing there?" Carlie muttered, casting a sideways glance at her petite older sister. "I mean, it's a wedding shop. Are they...?" The sharp stab of betrayal plunged deep.

"Oh, please. Let them have each other. He's a first-class dick, and she's not worth your time. What kind of friend steals your man? She's got some serious issues. Cheaters gonna cheat again. And I saw the way he was looking at you, Car. He knows he messed up," Rachael rattled on, apparently having memorized a lecture on the psychology of a cheater.

"Besides"—she wagged her eyebrows up at Carlie— "you, little sister, are hot, single, and ready to mingle. You don't need him. What you *do* need is to step out of your shell and give one of your hot-to-trot fellas a chance. It's time."

"Oh, sure," Carlie laughed despondently. "And who should I choose; one of the guys looking for an in with Dad? Or maybe one of the creeps who slither around town looking for their next conquest? Or perhaps one of your heartbroken hopefuls, devastated that you're off the market?"

"You left out the nerds," she teased.

"I *am* a nerd," Carlie glared.

"Please." Rachael rolled her eyes and started her black Lexus sedan. "You are not a nerd; you're an Eller."

Her groan didn't even faze Rachael. The curse of having a legendary sister and a famous family was a burden Carlie rarely discussed, let alone dwelled on. But having experienced the single life post-Brent, she was already sick to death of the social and financial climbers.

As the city streets gave way to the suburbs, she glanced at her sister—as Kim called her, a grown-up Alice in Wonderland—who was chattering on and on about possibilities and blind dates. Sorry, Rach. That was so not happening.

∾

BLINKING BACK TO THE PRESENT, Carlie turned to the luxurious suite and tried unsuccessfully to stop the looping confrontation with Brent. Seeing his beautiful face, those arms that she desperately wanted to lose herself in. Imagining a whisper that she longed to hear, him saying that the last nine months were just a bad dream, that she was still his one and only.

With bitter amusement, Carlie considered how she must have appeared to him. It definitely did not match the way she had hoped their first public encounter would go. She was supposed to be polished, sexy, and nonchalant. She would say all the right things and make him remember how much he wanted her—but no, he couldn't have her! She was clearly so over him. She had moved on.

But reality was cruel.

Instead of the confident strength she had promised herself to draw upon, Carlie was a passive, wordless coward. Oh, and the sex appeal was off the charts, as she had stood before him in her old black leggings, a shapeless T-shirt, and sneakers. She was hopeless.

Pulling the towel off her clean hair, she shook out the damp, wavy mane and crossed to the mirror. Marie had done a great job with the color; it would dry to rich caramel waves, a blend of dark blonde and soft brunette. Carlie was taller than most and kept fit. Her blue eyes were nothing special—not the pale blue you see in eyeglasses ads but a dark slate blue, fringed with naturally dark lashes with the tiniest upward slant to the corners. Nose average, lips on the fuller side. With some makeup she could make it work. And, of course, she hadn't been wearing any when she saw him. Whatever.

Self-deprecation complete, Carlie blinked away her run-in with the past and admired the soft king-sized bed covered in a fluffy down comforter, a handsome solid desk and dresser, and a bathroom too large for one person. The mini fridge was stocked; an attached note encouraged her to enjoy herself, *compliments of EHL Global.* "Thanks, Dad," she laughed to the empty room.

After college, Carlie hadn't been sure she wanted to work in the family business. She felt the need to earn her way, prove her worth. Her dad—The Great Charles Eller, as the media called him, founder and CEO of EHL Global— assured his youngest daughter she could start at the very bottom if she wished. Well, perhaps she didn't need to start at the *very* bottom. Through consistent effort and innovations, Carlie had made her mark, earning a position reporting directly to the digital media senior director for the company. Like her dad in appearance and behavior, Carlie was quiet and studious, analyzing each problem until she could manipulate it and work it to EHL's best advantage.

Her mother, on the other hand, was all things legal and procedural. She and Dad complemented each other well. He created, she protected and expanded. Then there was Rachael, the ultimate saleswoman. Carlie had no idea where her sister got that from. If Dad and Carlie could make it, Rachael could sell it. And while not quite family, Brian Henderson and Brian Lyles—the Brians—rounded out the C-suite. Henderson was a finance genius and Lyles kept the place running.

Selecting a cold flat water from the fridge, Carlie contemplated what to do this evening. As much as she preferred to stay in, she needed to get out of this funk and stop reliving the past. She chewed on her lip and looked outside at the continued rain that was now coming down in sheets.

"Definitely not going out there," she mumbled, spotting

the conference lanyard on the foot of the bed. She flipped through the schedule in the lanyard's badge holder and saw that an early bird meet-and-greet was planned for that evening in the lobby bar. Sounded like a plan. If nothing else, she could grab a drink and bite to eat before hitting the sack tonight.

She pulled on a pair of black slacks and a knit top and descended to the lobby lounge. The piano in the corner was unaccompanied, but the bar was staffed and well-stocked. She took a stool at the bar, ordered a vanilla vodka and diet soda, and watched for signs of this supposed get-together.

The bar slowly filled, several people wearing the red pouches around their necks. *Smooth move, Car. Of course, they're wearing them,* she thought. She debated going back to her room to get her lanyard but elected not to when it became obvious that virtually everyone here was with the conference.

Mr. Salmon from the hotel restaurant was at the entrance, and she scanned the room, wondering if Beer Man was going to make an appearance. Not that she was hoping, of course. Of course not.

"Is this seat taken?" a warm voice inquired behind her. A shiver worked its way down her back.

"Oh, hey, you," she greeted Kurt, a.k.a. Airplane Man. She hoped she didn't sound disappointed.

"Hey, yourself. Charlie, right?"

"Carlie," she corrected.

"That's right. So, you're here for the marketing conference? Small world!"

"Getting smaller by the second."

"I don't know about you, but I'm ready for a drink. They messed up my reservation and now I'm on the sixth floor. Terrible view," he complained. "You could come check it out sometime," he added with a cunning smile, green eyes twinkling.

Carlie smothered her groan. "Thanks, but I'm good."

"If I had known you were coming here, we could have shared a cab from the airport."

"Oh, that's okay. I had some errands to run before coming here," she lied—with no shame. "I would have hated to keep you from your wrong room."

Looking over Kurt's shoulder, her breath caught as Beer Man entered the lounge. She was really going to have to find out his name. For propriety's sake. He paused at the table near the entrance, chatting with a redhead holding a camera. Was that the conference host? Carlie idly wondered if the woman's check-in table nemesis was here too.

"I wouldn't have minded in the least," he continued before ordering his drink.

Contemplating Kurt's profile, she wondered if he always tried this hard. He was quite handsome with those clear green eyes, intelligent face, and wavy, dark blonde hair. If he took it down a few notches, he'd fare much better. She wondered how he'd take it if she suggested that. Probably not well. His type usually didn't.

"Do you think there will be live music this evening?" Carlie asked, changing the subject.

"Good question. Hey, barkeep," he hollered, a tad too loudly. She suspected this wasn't his first drink of the evening. "Music tonight?"

The seasoned bartender strolled over and nodded. "Should be here soon."

"There you have it," said Kurt, looking to all the world like he'd pulled a rabbit out of a hat.

Behind him, Beer Man approached the bar, and a look of recognition passed over his face as she entered his line of sight. He joined them, and Kurt hovered a little closer to her side.

She smiled hesitantly. "Thanks again for finding my badge earlier. I would have completely missed this event without it."

"No problem. Glad to help. I'm Alex." He extended his hand.

"Kurt and Carlie." Kurt intercepted Alex's handshake.

More than a little annoyed, Carlie leaned away from Kurt to offer her hand as well. "Alex, very nice to meet you. Now I won't have to call you Beer Man." *Shit, shit, shit.* Did she really say that out loud?

"Beer Man? That's a new one," he said, puzzled. "You two know each other? Work together?"

"We traveled here together," replied Kurt.

"We had the same flight. We met this morning," Carlie corrected with a reproachful eye toward Kurt. She did not like the way this was going.

"Hello, everyone!" The greeting came from the bar's entrance, loud and not entirely unwelcome. The perky blonde from the registration table was holding court.

"I'm Melanie Addams with United Marketing Association and am honored to unofficially welcome you to this year's Digital Marketing Convention. I see many familiar faces and several new ones," she crowed as she surveyed the gathering. "I hope you are all prepared for the wonderful week we have in store for you!

"Now, before the music starts, I want to highlight a few of the people who will be speaking this week. At the table with my colleague Lane is the legendary Bernie Bartlett, who will deliver the opening keynote tomorrow."

Lane and Bernie both waved politely.

"At the bar," Melanie continued, "I see Alex Williams, author of the bestselling *Marketing Done Wrong*."

A gnawing sense of recognition at both the name and the book rose in Carlie's mind, but she pushed it away. Her dread mounted as the perky host's eyes continued down the line and lit on Kurt, then her. *Please don't say my name*, Carlie pleaded mentally. *Not yet.*

"And next to Alex is Kurt Hunter, who many say is fast on his way to becoming the next Charles Eller! And speaking of The Great Eller, we are fortunate to have his daughter Carlie Eller with us. Carlie is the force behind EHL Global's soon-to-be-released, much-anticipated marketing platform."

Closing her eyes to the stares, Carlie wanted to melt into her chair and become invisible. As a murmur made its way across the room, their little trio quickly became a source of fascination. Fan-flipping-tastic.

On the plus side, however, she now had a real name for Mr. Salmon. So *that* was Bernie Bartlett. Huh.

3

*A*s soon as the announcement receded and the music began, Kurt puffed up like a damn peacock. Clearly, adoration agreed with him. As a surge of attendees moved toward them, Carlie's anxiety crept higher. She needed an out. Fast.

Alex was smooth and took it all in stride. He frowned briefly at Kurt, then glanced her way and arched his eyebrows, shrugging as the tide made its way toward them. She saw a small opening and excused herself before they were inundated.

The crowd allowed Carlie to sneak across the room. Heaving a sigh of relief, she found herself face-to-face with Mr. Salmon, Bernie Bartlett.

"Very nice to make your acquaintance, Mr. Bartlett," she said, grasping the back of an empty chair.

"Please, call me Bernie." He gestured for her to sit.

"Thank you, Bernie. Carlie Eller at your service," she automatically offered, feeling like dork of the year.

"Ms. Eller, tell me something," he inquired with a gentle smile. "Why are you joining an old man like me, who doesn't know the first thing about computers these days, when there is a veritable feast of superstars in this room?"

Carlie looked at the sea of unfamiliar faces.

"I don't do well in crowds," she confessed.

"Yet you're here to speak to hundreds of attendees?"

"That's different. I can talk about my work all day long, but when it comes to being in a crowd and not having work to fall back on... I just can't do it."

"I see. Well, I'm delighted to have you join me. I'm afraid I was not very good company for our hosts." He tilted his chin toward Lane and Melanie. "They barely spoke a word to me."

"Oh, that? That's not you. I think there's bad blood between them," Carlie said. "I don't know what, but they were definitely having some words at the registration table earlier..." She trailed off, aware that she was dangerously close to gossiping with a renowned media magnate. He must think she was so immature. Carlie could practically taste her mother's disapproval.

"If that's all it was, then I am relieved. Perhaps I'm not quite as intolerable as I feared."

They passed the time pleasantly talking about his career, from his early days as a typesetter and his rise to media superstar, to his more recent incarnation as a philanthropist and humanitarian. It was a humbling experience to share a table with him.

"We have company," he said, smiling over her shoulder.

Glancing behind her, Carlie was pleasantly surprised to see Alex standing there.

"Carlie? I think this is yours?" He held out her black handbag.

"Well, look at that. You're becoming my personal valet. Need a job?" she joked, a blush painting her cheeks.

"I do believe this is my time to exit gracefully," said Bartlett, rising to his feet. "I look forward to talking with you again, Ms. Eller. Have a good evening, young man."

"Thank you. Nice to see you again, Bernie," said Alex.

As Mr. Bartlett—Bernie—left the bar, Carlie turned back to Alex, a delicious male specimen who, incredibly, was still standing at her side.

"So...Alex Williams?"

"Carlie Eller?"

They stared at each other, letting the recognition set in. "You know Bernie?" she asked, trying not to make a big deal about it.

"Yeah, I interviewed him for a book a few years ago. Great guy. He really knows how to build confidence and inspire a person," he said.

"I sat with him for only a few minutes, and I already want to change the world," she agreed, her mind racing with possibilities.

"Did you see him earlier at Sammy's? I thought about joining him, but he looked lost in his book."

"I did, but I didn't know Mr. Salmon was Bernie Bartlett!"

Alex's brow furrowed. "Mr. Salmon? Ah! Now the beer guy comment makes more sense." He smirked. "Did you notice his napkin habit? He does that with all meat. Guess we all have our quirks."

"What's mine?"

"Besides the food names—which, trust me, that is a quirk—you seem to have a penchant for leaving things behind for me to find.

But," he added, leaning toward her, cool blue eyes boring into her own, "I don't mind having an excuse to find you." He smiled before turning and strolling casually back to the bar.

This conference was a win. And it hadn't even started yet.

~

"YOU MET HIM? BERNIE BARTLETT?!" Rachael screamed into her ear.

"Yup. Sat right at the table with him."

Carlie grinned, knowing her sister was probably seething with jealousy.

"And you talked to him?!"

"That's generally what one does when sitting at a table together," she teased.

"Car, that's incredible! What was he like? Did you tell him about me? About our work? What did you talk about?"

"He was pretty quiet and easy to talk to. We mostly talked about him. It was awesome." Carlie paused. "And it made me realize that we need to talk to Dad and the Brians. I'd like to see us get more involved in giving back, Rach. Corporate responsibility—"

"Sure, sure," Rachael cut her off. "I wonder what would happen if I sent him an invitation. Do you think he'd come?"

Carlie rolled her eyes. Of course, it was back to the wedding. Five minutes later, her sister was still dissecting every minute detail that was in question. How did this happen? How did her sister go from a ballsy sales expert to a bridezilla full of anger and frustration? Rachael was now harping on the unforgivable behavior of a florist who had questioned her choices. The florist was no longer part of the planning process.

Her sister was going to drive herself into an early grave from wedding planning.

Audibly clearing her throat, Carlie cut into the verbal assault of the poor florist who never knew what hit him. "Did I mention the other people here? Get this, Kurt Hunter —as in Hunter Industries—was next to me on my flight, and I didn't even know it. He's at this conference. And I'm pretty sure he was flirting with me."

"Oh. Em. Gee. Don't tell Rick, but good lord. Kurt is gorgeous! If I were you, I'd be all over that!"

"And he knows it. I tell you, Rach, he was kind of annoying. But the interesting one..."

"Wait. You had *Kurt Hunter* hitting on you, and you found him annoying?! What's wrong with you, Car? This is why you're single. I cannot believe it."

"I said there was another guy, an author."

"I don't fucking care who the other guy was. Kurt Hunter! I just can't even right now. I have to go. Text you later, Car. And for God's sake, give him a second chance!"

Carlie stared at her dark phone. What was that?

Carlie dropped the phone on the nightstand and considered the last few months. Ever since Rachael met Rick and got engaged—in the span of two heartbeats—her sister had been driving her batty. Home, work, here. Marie, her most favorite person in the world outside of her family, continued to urge Carlie to be patient with her sister. She also said something about the highway of life. Chewing on her lip, she thought about the stylist's words at the salon yesterday morning.

~

Torture. Somewhere along the line, Carlie had missed the "essentials of womanhood" package other women seemed to be born with. As she fidgeted in the salon chair, Rachael continued to blow up her phone with pictures of centerpieces. As if she had an opinion on these that would ever align with her sister's grand vision. Carlie didn't understand the purpose of a centerpiece. Maybe they should make donut-like tables, that way they wouldn't need centerpieces. Then a donut-shaped tablecloth...

"You sure you don't want to try a new style, hon?" Marie pulled Carlie out of her breakfast-deprived thoughts.

"No, thank you. Just a color and highlight, please," she said. Again.

It wasn't that Carlie didn't like change; she just knew what worked for her. And...maybe she didn't like a lot of change. Her phone vibrated again. More damn pictures.

"Did Rachael set a date?"

"Late August. Should be beautiful. And hot."

"So lovely, your sister. My little bluebird. She'll make a picture-perfect bride."

Carlie smiled at the familiar nickname. Mom, Rachael, and she had been coming to this same salon for decades, listening to Marie's stories and telling her theirs. In some ways, Carlie felt closer to her than her own mother.

"Yeah, well, the beautiful blue bird has some crazy talons right now," Carlie muttered.

A soft chuckle filled the air. "Be patient, honey. Rachael only has two modes: Drive and overdrive."

There was truth to that. It was part of her sister's personality that Carlie would never share. Maybe Rachael had cold feet and this was how it was manifesting. She couldn't blame her. After how things had imploded with Brent, Carlie was full of anxiety for her sister. And herself. What if it was her lack of drive, her more quiet life that had pushed Brent away?

"Marie?"

"Mmhmm?" She looked up from her work, the dye brush raised above the plastic container.

"For four years of my life I was convinced I was with the right guy. Everything seemed so right."

"Yes," she murmured. "I know."

"Rach and Rick have known each other for no time at all."

"Mmhmm. It's sudden, but when you find the one, when it's real love, the timeline doesn't matter so much."

Carlie fiddled with the fray at the edge of the protective cape while her thoughts wandered. She glanced up at Marie, then back to the fringe.

Marie caught and held her eyes in the mirror. "Honey, you're bobbing about like a hula girl on a dashboard. What has you all stirred up? The wedding? Something else? You know you can tell me anything."

Fingers still working at the loose threads, Carlie took a deep breath and spilled. "Do you think I'm distant? Or cold? Or, I don't know, off?"

Marie's brows drew together. "What? No. Why would you think that?"

Smoothing the edge of the cape, Carlie confessed her insecurities. "I can't help but wonder why I wasn't enough. That there's something wrong with me."

"You? Oh, sweet girl. You are enough. More than enough. And someday someone will be lucky to discover that. *He* wasn't enough. A man like that is a man who doesn't deserve you. Good riddance!"

"But everything seemed so perfect."

Folding another piece of foil around her comb handle,

Marie glanced at Carlie's reflection and frowned. "Perfect? No, no, no. Perfect is not real; it is not a relationship. A relationship is ugly. It can be beautiful, but it's full of fireworks. All the happiness and anger, good times and heartbreaking times. When you know the worst there is to know and still decide to make a go of things, that's a relationship. You decide every day that you will keep working on it. Keep trying to make it better than the day before. Some days you will succeed. Other days you may need a glass of wine." She chuckled and patted the piece of foil-wrapped hair in place. "But you know when it is right."

Marie made it sound so simple, so defined. "How long have you and Rob been together?"

"Oh, I was seventeen, and he was nineteen. Handsome as could be, and you know I was smitten from the start. Let's see, that would have been... almost forty years ago! My mother of course didn't approve, but here we are—still together!" She smiled and collected another piece of foil. "Still working things out, still figuring things out. Still having those wine nights. But still right together."

"Forty years? That's amazing."

"It is. But it goes by in the blink of an eye." Marie shook her head with a misty smile. "Of course, things were different back then," she continued, lost in time. "It was the early '80s, and the women, we were changing the world. No more staying at home to cook and raise the babies. We were strong and in control. We had *Cosmo*, short skirts, and money of our own. We had big hair and even bigger colors. You would laugh to see what my hair was like then! Oh, but I was young and in love, and we knew we could make it work. And we did. Not without struggles, but we managed."

She filled the time with the familiar stories of her and Rob's wealth of odd jobs and raising their boys.

"But why all this talk, young lady?" Marie asked.

"I don't know. Overthinking, I guess."

"You're still a baby. No need to rush. You had one bump in the road, but there is a whole highway ahead of you."

"I love you, Marie."

"And I you, honey. Now you sit there while this color sets," she said, depositing a handful of magazines in her lap. "Maybe you look in these and find yourself a distraction!" She patted her hand and greeted another regular. Carlie forced a smile, then actively shut down her train of thought.

Dutifully, she flipped through the glossy covers. Garbage, all of it. As her phone buzzed again, Carlie noticed the last issue in the stack was *Modern Bride*. Great. Slumping in the chair, she set about learning what was trending for the sake of Rachael's wedding spectacular.

RETURNING TO THE PRESENT, Carlie snagged her charged laptop and prayed the new length of highway she was starting down would be kinder than the last. She didn't think she could survive another Brent in the road.

4

*L*aptop open to go over her presentation slides, Carlie reviewed the notes Rebecca had made. As far as managers went, Carlie had lucked out with her. Her boss knew the company's vision and direction and was dedicated to elevating their department, yet still allowed Carlie the creative freedom to experiment with data visualization and automated audience segmentation—two of the components that were going to make the new marketing matrix a success.

Flipping to her email, Carlie saw an unfamiliar email address. Curiosity piqued, she opened the missive and saw herself. The email contained a photo from earlier tonight—Kurt and her at the bar—and a message: *Hope to make this a regular thing, Carlie. See you tomorrow. – Kurt.*

She'd had her fair share of admirers over the years, but this was just... weird. How did he even get that? And her email? She searched Kurt Hunter and Hunter Industries on Google, looking into who this guy actually was. Hunter Industries was a hodgepodge of communications and tech—buying, developing, and selling smaller companies that showed promise. Kurt, thirty-one years old, was an Ivy Leaguer who had begun with one small company and built it into a behemoth of sorts. He had been romantically linked to some serious headline makers and sat on several boards. She begrudgingly admitted he was rather interesting and impressive.

Carlie flipped back to her email, examining the photo. In the corner, she could see what looked to be Alex walking into the frame.

Okay, Google—spill about Alex Williams. It pulled up an excerpt from his latest book, *Marketing Done Wrong*. It read, "One of the greatest travesties of this generation is the large-scale minimization of the individual. Marketing automation and the bottom line have partnered to bring ruin to a marketplace of the average Joe and Jane, their unique needs and wants replaced with the equivalent of a cookie-cut Lunchable presented as a custom bento box."

Well. That was more than a little demoralizing.

Going back to the original email, she hit forward and sent it to Kim, replacing the subject line with "Does this count?" *Let's see what she makes of this.*

After all, it was her doing that Carlie was even making the effort to be more social. After the disastrous dress shop incident with Brent, Kim had met her at their favorite hangout, Pam's Diner, and promptly served Carlie the cold splash of reality she hadn't known she'd needed.

∼

Nodding to the familiar hostess, Carlie requested a table for two. She'd drop dead if Kim ever beat her here; her friend operated in her own time zone. After ordering a coffee, Carlie opened Instagram and immediately saw her sister's smiling face. She and Rachael were only four years apart and had grown up doing everything together, but her sister's no-holds-barred attitude toward life, as well as her tiny stature, golden-blonde hair, and bright baby blue eyes, made them about as different from each other as possible. Her post read, "Brunch with the dogs and bae! XOXO." Gag.

"Don't you look happy," Kim drawled as she slid into the booth.

"What is 'bae'? Like, who even says that? Or at least, who over the age of sixteen says that?" Carlie amended without looking up.

"Rach?" At her nod, Kim made a face. "I heard it means poop or something in Denmark."

"Good God. That's just great. Now I'll picture a pile of shit every time she uses it."

"You're welcome, sunshine." She grinned. "Coffee please, extra creamers," Kim requested of the passing waitress.

"Want to guess who I ran into?" Carlie asked.

Annoyed gray eyes flashed at her. Kim hated guessing games.

"Him," Carlie said.

One black brow raised, Kim's impatience visibly mounted as Carlie stirred her coffee. "And?"

"And..." Carlie blew out, "*she* was there."

"I hope you put that bitch in her place."

"I didn't exactly say much." *Understatement.* "He apologized. I think." Carlie wrinkled her nose trying to recall. It was funny how such moments could be so clear and frustratingly fuzzy at the same time. She took a sip of scalding coffee before continuing. "We were out dress shopping, and there he was."

"Damn. You *think* he apologized? A little late for that," Kim growled. "You did everything for that bastard, and what'd he do? He screws your friend in your own bed. As far as I'm concerned, he can go to hell."

"The worst part was, I couldn't think of a single thing to say. It was awful." Carlie dropped her head onto her arms in defeat.

Kim's drawn-out silence caused Carlie to look up.

"Look at yourself, Car. Look at the control you are still giving him over your life. That is not you, and you know it! Do you think he sits around pining away, hoping you'll waltz back into his life?"

Carlie glared at her. "No."

"Then why are you?"

Drumming her fingertips on the table, she fought the urge to be defensive, to bring up Kim's relationship issues. "I don't know," Carlie finally sighed. "So, what do I do now?"

"It's been what, eight, nine months? It's time to move on. Find someone new. Get yourself a rebound man. Fuck your way back to healthy."

Her ribald suggestion was greeted by their shocked waitress. "Your coffee?"

Carlie laughed until she cried.

After lunch, they took advantage of the warming weather to walk in the park. Kim caught Carlie up on all the drama in her currently on-again relationship with Owen. Carlie nodded at the right moments and made appropriately noncommittal comments. He was a nice enough guy, a talented artist, and they got along famously, but their explosive personalities were way too much combined. It had taken a couple of back-and-forth spats before Carlie realized that Kim was going to do whatever the hell she wanted to do when it came to Owen. Someday, they would break up for good, but that was not going to be anytime soon. For the sake of their friendship, Carlie had become a Swiss sounding board.

"You should totally double with us for dinner and drinks soon," Kim slipped in. "Owen has a really hot friend I think you'd dig."

"Kim, I don't think it's the right time for that. I'm not in a good place."

"Oh, puh-lease, girl. You don't have to marry the guy. Have a little fun. You remember fun, right?" she prodded.

Carlie huffed. Fun. Kim's version of fun required a pit stop to the corner store, little foil packets of pleasure, and ten minutes in the bathroom while your dinner companions pretended not to notice the conveniently mutual absences. Not that Carlie had learned that example from experience or anything. Ahem.

And it wasn't that Carlie was terribly opposed. She just wanted something more. Or nothing. She didn't even know anymore. The last thing she needed was to waste more time on a selfish jackass.

"I'll think about it, okay? Give me a little time."

"Sure, sure. Five minutes good?"

"Kim!"

"Nah, I get it. But I'm worried about you. You need to get out there and live a little. You're twenty-four and acting like you're sixty. When's the last time you got laid? I'll bet it was Brent, right?" She held up her palm to stop Carlie's indignant reply. "No, don't answer that—I see it in your face. Honestly, Car, just do something. Or someone," she added with a devilish gleam.

Spoken as only Kim could get away with.

"I appreciate what you're saying"—Carlie nudged her friend's shoulder—"and I'm going to think about it. But for most women, our lives don't revolve around sex and hot guys. We may enjoy them, but they're not priority number one."

"They should be. And I don't want to live in a world where they're not near the top of the list," Kim said. Knowing her, she was only half joking.

They moved to the edge of the path as a group of joggers ran through. One of the men sent an appreciative whistle. Kim obnoxiously whistled back, causing Runner Boy to briefly lose his footing. Red-faced, he hurried to rejoin the rest of his flock.

"Now *that* is someone we can agree is in the 'don't do' list." Kim smirked.

Carlie stopped walking and watched the group disappear around the bend before turning back to Kim. "Tell you what, I'm going to Chicago next week for my conference. I'll keep an eye out and maybe even talk to a guy," she offered.

"Talk? As long as it ends with a satisfied smile on your face, I'll call it a win."

WONDERING AGAIN what Kim would make of Kurt's email, Carlie changed and headed to the twenty-four-hour fitness center.

Running on the treadmill was no substitute for the outdoors, but it worked in a pinch. After miles of running to nowhere, she slowed the machine and began to cool down, her mind finally ready to process recent events.

The redhead with the camera (Lane?) had probably taken the photo and shared it with him. And their email addresses were listed in the conference materials. The simplest explanation was usually the correct one. It was still weird, though. Perhaps some women would be thrilled that he had sought them out like that, but Carlie wasn't one of them.

Now, to the other problem. Apparently, everything she had worked on for the last two years was, to Alex, a major issue. He may as well have written that EHL was a blight on the human race. And her work in particular. Why couldn't he understand that she was generating ways to present more relevant information to consumers? Carlie was trying to remove unnecessary clutter from their lives, making their online experiences *more* personalized, not less so.

This was not good on many levels.

One: Kurt. Pretty boy needed to chill. Not sure what to do there yet. But, according to her sister, Carlie needed to give him a chance. Hmm...

Two: Alex. Why did he have to be so damn attractive but her polar opposite in work philosophy? She was completely drawn to him, but she couldn't imagine spending time with someone who couldn't respect her work.

Three: Why was she behaving like some hormonal teenager? Maybe it was the result of seeing Brent again, or Kim's overenthusiastic pep talks. Whatever the cause, she needed to shake out of this and focus on what mattered. She had to deliver a killer presentation. This was her family's work and reputation. *Her* work and reputation.

Which brought her to number four on the list: She needed to figure out Rachael. What was going on with her sister? True, Rach only operated at one speed—full throttle —but the snappish retorts and moodiness were bizarre. Could she truly be getting cold feet? That would be under- standable, considering how fast things had moved with her and Rick. But how did you help someone with cold feet, if that's what it was?

Good grief. Mind tripping over too many topics to sort through, she flipped off the treadmill and returned to her room to shower and get some shut-eye.

5

*I*t's dark, and I'm standing in my opulent hotel room. I'm not alone. His breath is warm on my neck, his hands possessive as they grip my shoulders and slide down my arms, pulling me back against his chest. One hand teases up my arm and works its way into my hair. His mouth presses gently to the sensitive spot behind my ear, sparking a fire beneath my skin.

Softly moaning, needing this, wanting this, I try to turn to him, but his hands hold me firmly in place. I close my eyes and lean my head to the side, wordlessly encouraging his progress. A shiver races down my spine and I brace my hand against the wall in front of me. His hand slowly moves across my abdomen, heat searing through my night shirt. He gently bites my ear, then nibbles along the underside of my jaw as his hand slips beneath the hem of my shirt, his long fingers searching and caressing.

Releasing his hold, he turns me, sealing his mouth to mine, bringing my back up against the wall. His tongue teases the corner of my mouth, and I surrender, opening and giving him access. Warmth spreads throughout my body as the kiss deepens.

The closeness. The possessiveness. The togetherness. God, how I have missed this.

I blissfully wrap my arms around his neck and mold my body to his. I open my eyes and tilt my head back, needing to explore his face, his eyes. Brent's hazel eyes could never hide their passion, not even toward the end. The fire burns, turning his eyes darker. My fingers thread through his hair and his features shift. Instead of Brent, I'm now caught in a different gaze. I pull back and Alex watches me, a blue storm swirling in his eyes.

CARLIE SHOOK HERSELF AWAKE, sweat and desire clinging to her. Holy hotness. Staring into the darkness, she slowly breathed in and out until her pounding heart began to calm.

Five o'clock in the morning. Ugh. She lay still for a few moments longer, felt her limbs relax and her body cool off. Her thoughts raced, trying to pinpoint when her head had decided to play games with her. They said dreams were full of hidden meanings. Her whole life she'd been analyzing her vivid dreams. Carlie smirked... This one wasn't hard to figure out.

Alex Williams, what were you doing in my dreams?

Carlie could just imagine his reaction if she asked him that tomorrow. Or in a few hours, she supposed. She grabbed a pillow and stuffed it over her face. This was awful. How was she going to face him after that?

Car, you're being crazy.

He wouldn't know she had dreamt about him. *Play it cool, and don't be a complete idiot.* Tossing the pillow across the room with a frustrated grunt, she flung the sheets aside, grabbed her laptop, and got an early start to the day.

Don't be an idiot. Don't be an idiot. Don't be an idiot.

The mantra wasn't just coming at Carlie in her own voice; Rachael and Kim took turns in her mind, too. As the elevator door slid open to the fourth floor, she repeated the phrase to herself one more time, then stepped out to the conference lobby.

A sleepy buzz filled the air, and she joined the shuffling line passing through the continental breakfast and coffee tables. After selecting some chunks of melon and a bagel, Carlie frowned at the commercial-grade coffee dispenser, missing her Keurig at home. All the luxuries at this hotel, and they still had crap coffee in the conference wing. At least it was caffeine. She poured as much as would fit into the dainty cup without spilling, then made her way to a round table in the staged ballroom.

"...and the sales calls! It's enough to make me want to get rid of my office phone altogether," said a smartly dressed young professional. The bright blue permanent marker script on the white adhesive nametag said *Rita*. She glanced at Carlie as she joined the small group. "Am I right?!"

"Totally," agreed Paul, another perky morning person. *Fantastic*, Carlie groaned into her coffee cup.

Leaning over the empty seat between them, Rita glanced at her nametag. "Hi, Carlie! Help us settle something. In a digital display campaign, do you go per click or per view? I was telling Paul that unless you're Pepsi or something, you should always go with cost per click. Brand awareness only gets you so far, am I right?"

Carlie smiled, gulping down the last of the weak contents in the miniature cup. Search engine marketing was a good topic, but not at half-past seven in the morning after the night she'd had. Or dream she'd had.

"I would say it depends on your budget, goals, and call to action," Carlie offered, putting down her now-empty cup and forking a piece of melon.

"I told you! There's no one-size-fits-all answer," Paul declared. "She didn't believe me. Newbie," he said affectionately. "I'm just messing with her," he directed to Carlie as he adjusted his black-rimmed retro glasses. "Rita and I are both here from Clyo Marketing. Our first time here."

"You know," said Rita, gesturing to Carlie's empty cup, "there is a Starbucks just outside the front lobby, two doors down."

"Rita, you're my new best friend," Carlie laughed, finally finding a bit of enthusiasm. "If you'll both excuse me."

Making quick work of the stairs, she exited to the street level and slipped into the gray morning. She joined the Starbucks queue, inhaling the familiar coffeehouse smells.

"Good morning," came a deep timbre.

Carlie turned to the same blue eyes from her dream.

Don't be an idiot, don't be an idiot...

"Good morning," she chirped, a little too brightly. Her face heated as she heard her voice. "Sleep well?" Oh, good grief. The blush was becoming a full-on flush.

Alex either didn't notice or chose not to remark, instead answering with a nod.

Carlie turned the corner in the line, now in a better position to face him. His hair looked darker, a glossy black, wet from the morning mist or an early shower. She fought the insane urge to touch it, to see if it felt as silky as it appeared. Standing next to him, Carlie noticed how tall he was. Alex was a good three or four inches taller than her. She could even wear heels and still be shorter. This appealed to her latent vanity. She and Brent had been close in height, and it had always made her feel a bit less-than-feminine. Was that part of Brent's attraction to Gina?

"Come to Chicago often?" Alex interrupted her thoughts.

"Not really," she answered. "I'm usually so elbow deep in work and meetings that I don't get out much."

"Well, if you'd like a guide, I'd be happy to show you the sights. I'm a regular to Chi-town. What kind of stuff are you into?"

Right now? You.

"Oh, you know, the usual. Music, food, touristy stuff, I guess," Carlie rambled as they inched closer to the counter.

"Have you had any Chicago deep dish yet? There's a great place nearby." He gestured down the street. "We could grab lunch?"

"Sounds like a date," she answered, cringing inwardly. *Date?* He probably didn't mean it that way. Too late now. Carlie approached the counter and ordered her latte. "Venti, please." She was going to need it.

Armed with real coffee, she and Alex returned to the hotel and conference center.

"Hey, Carlie. And Alex?" called a voice she was coming to recognize.

"Good morning, Kurt," she offered, feeling a little more generous now that real coffee had been secured. And some one-on-one time with Alex. Not that she had any clue what they'd talk about at lunch.

"I have a seat open at my table if you'd like to join me. And you too, of course, Williams," he added as an afterthought, a vague nod lobbed in Alex's general direction.

Carlie glanced at the table she had joined earlier; her seat was still available. "Thanks so much, but I already have a seat. I'll catch you at the break, though." She walked away, leaving the two to find their way.

"Glad you made it back in time," Rita said, smiling.

She waved her green-logoed cup and smiled back. "You're a lifesaver, Rita. A true American hero."

They settled into the usual introductory chatter before

Lane and Melanie took the stage, both in a better mood than yesterday. Or at least acting as though they were.

"Good morning and welcome to the tenth Annual Digital Marketing Convention. I'm Lane Gray, and this is Melanie Addams. We're thrilled to have you with us this year," the redhead evangelized in her throaty voice. "I hope you are all prepared for a great week!

"Now, a bit of housekeeping. Please make sure you keep your lanyards on and watch those drink tickets—I know those can be a hot commodity." She paused, waiting for the sparse laughter to spread. "As you've gathered, our large group sessions will take place here in the ballroom. The breakout sessions will take place in here, as well as in the two smaller rooms on either side of the ballroom. Also, if you'll download our conference app, please complete the evaluations after every presentation. We want to deliver the best experience possible, and the only way we improve is through your feedback."

All around the room, attendees were picking up their phones, surfing the app store for the right one, showing their phones to each other. Carlie frowned at the confusion. They should have had the app info and Wi-Fi password on the tables already. Her sarcasm lifted its head. *Guess I'll have to submit a survey.*

Lane handed the mic over to Melanie, whose teased blonde hair added an extra two inches to her height. "As Lane said, we are so thrilled to have you with us. And I imagine this next speaker is part of the reason you all got here on time this morning. It is my distinct privilege and honor to present our opening keynote speaker, the legendary Bernard Bartlett."

As she rattled off Bernie's accomplishments, the man in question climbed the short flight of stairs to the stage. He graciously thanked Melanie and Lane, then began his lecture.

While he spoke of covering some of the biggest events of the previous decades, Carlie desperately tried to pay attention. What she definitely was not doing (and definitely doing) was looking to see where Alex had ended up. She casually scanned the room in front of her, not seeing his gleaming black hair and blue eyes. Slowly craning her neck, her gaze passed from table to table, finally finding what she sought. *Oh, merciful heaven.* He was staring right at her.

Carlie broke eye contact and resumed watching Bernie, feeling a bit like a child at a Sunday sermon; she knew she would learn much from it, be a better person for it. But she could feel his eyes on her. The temptation to turn, to return his stare, was overwhelming. *Lord deliver me from temptation.*

And Alex was temptation itself.

*a*t long last, Bernie returned to his seat to a rousing ovation. Carlie stood as well, nearly lightheaded at the relief flooding her system. Her neck relaxed by degrees, the tense muscles overjoyed to be permitted to move again at will.

"We'll take a fifteen-minute break. Then please follow your guidebook for the breakout session information," Lane directed from the stage.

Carlie joined the throng of attendees streaming toward Bernie to thank him for his vision and words of wisdom. At least she imagined that that was what he had offered. While waiting, she glanced around and saw Alex hovering close to the lobby, hooded gaze fixed on her. He stood with an air of confidence and self-assuredness. And sex. The man looked like a damn god. Shaking her head, she turned back to find Bernie's amused smile. "It is good to see you again this morning, Carlie." He clasped her hand and nodded toward the doorway. "Though it does look like Alex is hoping to steal some time with you, too. I will see you at the speakers' dinner, yes?"

She stammered some kind of response, wondering if she was so obviously infatuated.

As Carlie crossed the room, Kurt waved and jogged over to join them.

"That was something," Alex murmured as she came to a stop.

"It was," she agreed, not sure if he was talking about Bernie.

Kurt, oblivious to the tendrils of connection forming between Carlie and Alex, wrapped an arm around her shoulders and missed the twitch that pulled at Alex's mouth. Perhaps she wasn't too far off in calling their lunch a date?

"Which session are you attending next, Kurt?" she asked, gently extracting herself from his loose embrace.

"Mobile marketing. How about you?"

"Oh, you'll have to share notes on that with me. I'll be in the omni-channel breakout session."

After chatting for a few minutes, Carlie excused herself to check her messages. From Kim: *Holy shitballs. Who sent you that email?* Carlie quickly typed back, *Kurt Hunter.* No immediate response. She couldn't wait to see what Kim said to that.

Returning to the lobby, her steps slowed as she observed Lane and Melanie heatedly talking in the corner. Carlie didn't mean to eavesdrop, truly, but when they were bickering right there...What could she say? She was no saint. When she heard them mention Kurt, Carlie all but stopped and stared. Apparently, she wasn't the only one Kurt had been chatting up. Shocker.

Examining her program, she located the breakout session and walked toward the side room, seeing rows of padded maroon-and-brass chairs starting to fill. Just before she reached the doorway, a hand grasped her elbow. Startled, she looked up to see those cool blue eyes.

"What would you say to an early lunch?"

Carlie regarded the room before her, which suddenly held much less appeal, then nodded. She might not have been hungry yet, but she was working her way there.

Alex and Carlie ducked into the late morning rain. Her thoughts fled back to high school, to the *one time* she had let Kim talk her into skipping school to go hang out with the college guy she'd been seeing. Kim never got caught; Carlie got detention. It was the first and last time she ever ditched school.

Now, as she skipped out on the conference she'd prepared for all month, Carlie felt a lightness that even the rain couldn't dampen. She was in a new city with an interesting man. Something new was *finally* happening in her life. A change was coming. And she was breathless with anticipation.

As they hurried down the crowded streets of Chicago, fate decided she'd had enough giddiness. Her heel slipped on a discarded wet newspaper, and she began the agonizing, slow-motion descent into busting her ass. Just as she felt the first kiss of pavement, Alex wrapped his hands around her upper arms, hauling her back to vertical.

"There you go. Are you all right?"

After she regained her balance and time returned to normal speed, Carlie stood stunned, then burst out laughing. It was that or cry. "Did that just happen!?"

"Glad to know you can laugh at yourself." He grinned. He released her arms but kept a firm hold on her hand as they walked the rest of the way.

Alex held open the door to Angelo's, and she peered into what looked to be a total dive. Her skepticism must have been written across her face. "Trust me," he said, escorting her to a booth along the wall.

Carlie slid into the booth, her slacks catching on the cracked red upholstery. A chipped gray tabletop spanned the distance between them. "If the menu's sticky, I'm not eating here," she stated, not quite joking.

"No sticky menus, I promise." His accompanying boyish smile stole her response, and she simply sat and stared at him. His shoulders were broad, his dark hair cut short but stylish, and his face was chiseled in a way that made her want to explore the angles with her fingertips. His cool blue eyes danced and his mouth twitched at the corners. He clearly enjoyed watching her watch him.

A bored, young waitress appeared, interrupting Carlie's visual inspection. "Drinks? You two want some pie today? Deep dish will take forty-five minutes. We don't take short-cuts here."

"Water, no lemon," he said, then gestured to Carlie.

"Diet Coke, please."

The waitress disappeared and Carlie eyed the stained ceiling tiles and scarred, but clean, floors. "Charming place, Alex."

"Like I said, we all have our quirks. Even this place does. It may be shabby, but it's the best you're going to find around here."

Having settled on the Angelo's Deep Dish special, they began the forty-five-minute wait. Carlie fiddled with her straw, mind awkwardly blank. She continued to sneak peeks at him, wondering what a guy like him saw in a klutzy computer geek like her. He leaned against his seat and watched her, finally leaning forward and grabbing the straw from her drink, the smooth plastic gliding out of her fingers.

"Did you see the video about the turtle and the straw?

It'll change your mind about using these things," he said, twirling it between his fingers.

"No, but did you see the video about the guy who took the straw from my drink? It didn't end so well for him."

He stopped twirling the straw and met her eyes, trying to decide if she was kidding. He slid his wrapped straw across the table. "Sorry," he mumbled.

Carlie tried not to laugh at his contrite expression. Quirking her lips, she took a long drink without the straw. "For what it's worth, I prefer straws. But I'll try it your way today. Just don't push me to accept paper straws. That's a firm line in the sand."

"Duly noted."

The waitress reappeared with a basket, dropped it on the table, and disappeared again without a word. Carlie folded back the red-and-white-checked parchment paper to reveal steaming hot breadsticks. She tugged one out and sniffed it before taking a nibble from the end. She hummed with satisfaction at the perfect ratio of buttery goodness and garlic salt.

"I forgot to thank you." She gestured to the window with her breadstick. "I can't believe I almost wiped out."

"You do get points for style." He winked.

"That was some Superman stuff, though. It seems you keep rescuing me and my belongings. And here I always pictured myself as being totally independent."

"Oh, you're still independent, Lois Lane, you just get some extra backing with me around."

"And you plan to be around, *Superman*?"

"It's possible," he said, swiping a breadstick from the basket. "Do you want me to be?"

Carlie pinched off another bite of her breadstick and mulled over his words. Was that rhetorical? Stealing another look at him through her lashes, she saw him frowning at the door. Carlie glanced over, surprised to see that the light rain had become a true downpour. The wall of water outside the door and windows encased the restaurant in a cocoon, isolating them from the rest of the world.

"That depends," Carlie replied. He cocked his head expectantly. "Let's see how good this pizza is."

7

*W*hen Ms. Cranky delivered the pizza, Alex took charge of the pie server. He scooped up a slice and dropped it onto a plate, cheese bridging the gap, clinging to the silver edge. Accepting the plate, Carlie admired the thick pool of toppings. No wonder they called this pie.

"What's the best way to eat this thing?" she asked, analyzing all possible delicious points of entry.

Alex dropped a slice on his plate and picked up a fork and knife. "If we need to return to the conference sauce-free, I suggest silverware."

Carlie savored her first bites, surprised at the rich meat and seasoning and the thick, sweet crust.

"So, perhaps I was a bit hasty in judging the place," she admitted, closing her eyes to chew another bite, releasing a sigh.

She opened her eyes to find Alex watching her, completely amused. "Enjoying yourself?" he asked.

Carlie winked and took another bite, laying it on thick with the moaning and earning a hearty chuckle from across the table. Alex stabbed his own pizza, and they ate in silence for a few minutes.

"Tell me something," Carlie said.

"What?"

Don't be an idiot, don't be an idiot...

"Do you hate what I do?" she asked.

"Why do you ask that?"

Her nose scrunched up as she answered. "I looked up your latest book, and it seems like an exposé on my work, indirectly."

Way to kill the mood, Car. She mentally facepalmed herself. Subtlety was not a strength.

He studied her as he chewed his pizza. She swirled her plastic soda cup in her hand, wondering if he was going to answer.

"I think you take a lot of pride in your work, and I appreciate that," he hedged.

"But what I do...?"

Stop digging, Carlie!

"Look, what you do is..." He paused and looked skyward for inspiration before continuing. "It's not what I would choose to do. But you do it well."

"Fair enough." Carlie let it go. For now. "So, tell me about your family," she said.

He gave an audible sigh of relief. "There's me, my sister, and my folks. They're divorced, but still friendly."

"How old's your sister?"

"Allie? She's twenty-seven."

Allie and Alex. Cute.

"Mine's twenty-eight; my sister, I mean. Almost the same age. You guys close?"

"Not as close as we once were." He frowned and

narrowed his eyes. "She's a teacher and likes to lecture me a little too much. You?"

"We're close. We're not much alike, and she drives me crazy, but I love her. She's my best friend," she explained with a shrug.

"You're lucky."

"I am."

"And you're beautiful."

I am? Where did that come from?

"Oh." Carlie swallowed another bite and glanced up again. "You're not so bad yourself."

"I know."

"And you're *so* humble," she laughed, tossing a napkin at him.

He finished his pizza and pushed his plate aside. "Ready to head back? It's probably getting close to the next set of sessions."

He flagged down the waitress for a box and the check. "My treat," he said, snagging the bill as soon as it hit the table.

While he settled the tab, Carlie watched the wet streets beyond the window. Thankfully, the rain had stopped. They strolled back to the hotel, seeing others in red lanyards standing outside, enjoying the break in the drizzle. As they stopped at the main lobby elevators, she nodded to the box. "What are you going to do with that?"

"I was going to drop it off in my room. Care to walk with me?"

She shrugged. Why not?

The door stopped and she looked at the number, surprised. "You're on twenty-two also?"

"It would appear that way."

They walked past her room, stopping three doors down. He slid his card in the slot and opened the door to an identical suite. He tossed his jacket on the chair by the door and walked to the fridge, depositing the box. Carlie stood with her back to the closed door and met his eyes as he came to a stop halfway across the room. They remained like that for several heartbeats until he walked over and tugged her hand, pulling her closer.

Carlie nervously took a half-step forward as he lifted her chin, tilting her face up to search her eyes. "Is this okay?" His voice was low, husky. She didn't even think before giving a small nod.

His eyes dropped to focus on her mouth, and he closed the distance, touching his warm lips to her own. A tingle worked its way down to her toes, and he pressed a hand to her back, bringing her closer. Carlie moved her palms up his firm chest and let them rest on his broad shoulders while he cradled her jaw in his hand, his fingertip drawing a line of heat behind her ear.

Alex slid his tongue across her lips, drawing a giggle from her. He pulled back and smiled at her reaction, before returning to claim her mouth, delving in and teasing seductively, sending waves of desire swirling through her body. All too soon, he retreated, and the kiss was over.

Closing his eyes, he brought his forehead to rest against her own. She took a deep breath and shakily exhaled.

Alex pulled away, his blue eyes darkened with hunger. They stared at each other for a moment before Carlie shook herself. "We should go back."

He nodded and collected his jacket.

"I've wanted to do that all day," he murmured as they walked to the elevator. "It was worth the sleepless night."

Guess she wasn't the only one.

Refusing to release her hand, Alex stood close by her

side on the way down. Carlie smiled shyly up at him. The doors slid open on the twentieth floor, admitting a pair of young women. They glanced at Alex with interest, then looked away when they saw her watching. She couldn't help but feel a little smug. *Not today, ladies.*

Back at the fourth floor, he released her hand as they exited the elevator. Carlie excused herself and headed to the ladies' room.

What was happening? Carlie shut herself in a stall to sort out her emotions. She and Brent had ended last summer, which seemed both forever ago and all too recent. How could she be feeling all this... desire? And for God's sake, she had just met him!

But the chemistry was undeniable. Like the moon to the earth, she felt a constant gravitational pull to be near him. It was compelling and terrifying.

Pull yourself together, Car.

It was a kiss. An amazing, earth-shattering kiss, but still just a kiss. It wasn't even like she would see him again after this week.

Just a kiss. Just a kiss. Just a kiss.

Deep breath.

Carlie exited the stall and washed up, splashing cold water across her face. She touched her lips, scarcely believing what had happened. Somewhat restored to normalcy, she emerged to face whatever the next part of the day would bring.

As she crossed the conference lobby, pretty boy Kurt sidled up. "I was looking for you. You okay?"

She forced herself to focus and pasted a smile on her face. "Absolutely," she responded, allowing him to take her arm. He walked her to a round table off to the side of the ballroom and pulled up a chair next to her.

"You disappeared before I could find you for lunch. Did you go back to your room?"

She nodded. Close enough. They did go to that floor. Not exactly a lie, but she had no desire to go into that conversation.

"Oh, that's too bad. I wish I had caught you first. Join me for a drink this evening? You will be attending the social before the speakers' dinner, right?"

Seeing no way to politely decline, Carlie nodded and agreed to a drink. Across the room, she noted the moment Alex walked in. His face darkened when he saw Kurt hovering. She winked to let him know it was all good. He inclined his head, then turned away.

Oblivious, Kurt continued to talk about the morning's sessions and the latest news.

"So, uh, did you get an email from me?" Kurt asked. An anxious look clouded the clear green of his eyes.

Ah. The email. She had nearly forgotten.

"Yes."

"Were you surprised?"

"You could say that."

He lapsed into a story of sweet-talking Lane into sharing a link with him of her photo feed. "From there, it was just a matter of piecing together your email, which wasn't terribly difficult."

Pretty much what Carlie had expected.

"I hope you don't mind. I enjoy talking with you," he said. "If I'm coming on too strong, say the word."

Word, word, word! Her lips twitched at the thought, but she soldiered on. "It's fine, Kurt. Maybe scale it back a little, okay?"

"Done. But we're still on for a drink this evening?"

"Sure."

8

"*Y*ou try to focus after a kiss like that," she wailed to Kim over the phone.

"I like the sound of this guy. Tall, dark, and handsome. Like a fucking fairy tale."

Carlie rolled onto her stomach as they talked, having already spilled the details of the eventful trip thus far.

"And Kurt Hunter, huh?" Kim said.

"Yeah..."

"I can't believe you didn't recognize him! His company is always making headlines, and he's been on the cover of *Time*. The last woman he dated was on the cover of *Newsweek* for her work with the World Health Organization."

How did everyone know this? Rach was forever talking her ear off about the up-and-comers, the "it crowd." But, honestly, who would have thought she'd ever need to know? Carlie was a number-cruncher, not a celebrity-watcher.

"By the way, I ran into Rachael. I mentioned your text, and she told me you blew him off. That's epic." She could hear Kim's grin over the line. "I was planning to tell you off and encourage you to give him a go, until you mentioned Alex. What are you going to do?"

"Question of the day, right?" Carlie paused before continuing in a near-whisper. "I think I could really like him, Kim. He's smart and so hot and, unbelievably, he seems to like me, too. It's freaking me out."

"Oh, sugar. You know that's allowed, right? You've done your time with an ass, now it's your time. Let him wine and dine you."

"What if I never see him again after this week? I don't think I can do this."

The line was silent as they both thought over failed relationships of the past.

"You know what? What if you do? You can't know the future, babe. Just play it out. And be safe. I'm a phone call and a short flight away if you need me."

"I know. Love ya, girl."

"You too, Car. Now, get a move on. I want details later. The juicier, the better."

Get a move on? If only she knew what move to make.

Dressed in a simple, low-cut black dress and pumps, Carlie slid a silver cuff bracelet onto her wrist before snagging her handbag and the red lanyard. Glancing down the hallway, she wondered if Alex was still in his room. *Always best to not look too eager, girls,* she heard her mother's voice in her head. With a resigned sigh, Carlie turned back to the elevator.

The elevator door swished open, and Carlie stared at her reflection in the floor-length mirrored wall. She might not emit the come-hither signal many of her female acquaintances had perfected, but Carlie could definitely pull off this look. The black A-line dress skimmed her curves before flowing out to end above her knees, and the heels made her muscular runner's calves seem both defined and leaner. She mused that her sister would be thrilled to see her wearing pumps—she was always pestering her to not be afraid to own her height.

Carlie far preferred comfort to style, especially since she had two left feet. She frowned at her reflection. "No tripping tonight, Car," she whispered to herself. Moments later, she stepped into the busy hotel lobby. Crossing the open space, she felt exposed and worried she was overdressed. But when she entered the bar, she relaxed, seeing several others dressed to the nines.

The same bartender was keeping shop. He shot her a flirty smile and asked, "Absolut Vanilia and diet?"

Grateful, she nodded before digging into the lanyard pouch, trying to figure out which drink ticket she was supposed to use this evening.

"It's the green one," said a smoky voice over her shoulder. She turned to see Lane Gray, the statuesque redhead and host.

"Thanks." Carlie smiled. She slid the ticket and a tip across the bar and turned back to her.

"Enjoying yourself?" Lane asked.

"So far, so good," she replied.

Lane ordered a chardonnay as she adjusted the camera bag on her shoulder. "I saw you talking to Kurt and Alex yesterday," she murmured, not even bothering to look her way. "Both at once. Quite a step up, I imagine, from the farm boys of Ohio."

Excuse me?

Carlie took a sip of her drink, eyes narrowed as she wondered what Lane was getting at. "I do enjoy making new friends," she replied evenly.

"Friends, is it? From the way Kurt was talking, it sounds like you might be a little more than that." She paused, looking Carlie up and down. "Not that I see the appeal."

What?! Carlie gave her a sugary smile. "Well, I'm sure you know him better than I do. If you'll excuse me." She brushed past Lane, snagging a seat at an open table. She took a deep breath, shaking off that catty weirdness, chalking it up to the irrational behavior some people got around her billionaire family, assuming the Ellers were monied hicks from the cornfields of Ohio, modern-day *Beverly Hillbillies*. Rolling her eyes, she pulled her phone out, thankful for the distraction of two new text messages.

Rebecca, her boss, wanted to know how it was going. Carlie glanced up at the bar to see Lane flirting with the bartender. *The conference is going well, met a few interesting people*, she texted in response. Carlie gave Rebecca some quick tidbits about Bernie and Kurt, though nothing too personal. Let her mull over those opportunities. She would probably devise some new project to work on next week.

The next text made her smile. *Sorry to flip out on you, Car. Had a rough day and the caterer flaked on me. On to plan B*, wrote her sister.

Another caterer bites the dust. Wonder what this one did? Probably told Rachael that asparagus was out of season or something. Smirking, Carlie messaged back, *No worries. Everything else going well?* She saw the telltale waving dots and got an instant reply. *Yup. Rick says to tell you hello. Hope you're having fun!* She hit the message's like button and closed the app.

"May I join you?"

Heat climbed her neck, and she looked up into his cool blue eyes. Alex stunned in a sharp, tailored black jacket, white shirt, and dark jeans. He pointed to her phone. "Care to share your number with a hack writer?"

Smiling, she reopened the text app. "Tell me yours, and I'll text you mine."

Reciting the number, she sent him a simple message, *Carlie Eller, straw fiend.*

His phone chirped and he checked the screen, a crooked smile warming his face. He shook his head and sunk into the seat next to hers. The scent of his aftershave, a warm and woodsy masculine scent, tickled her senses. He caught the attention of a passing waiter and ordered a pint of Guinness before turning his lazy smile back to her.

The rest of the world might have had a crush on Kurt, but his pretty and playful looks couldn't compare to Alex's broad shoulders, square jawline, and Roman nose. She thought again that he looked like a god. It was easy to imagine him with a toga and sandals, or maybe a trident. Hmm. Definitely more of a trident god. A beer-drinking trident god. A beer-drinking trident god who was sitting here, his attention completely focused on her. Quiet and unassuming Carlie Eller. Wow.

His beer arrived, and he took a deep drink, his throat working above his collar. Not that she was watching.

She couldn't look away.

Alex settled the glass on the table and eased his arm along the back of her chair. "So...you come here often?" he teased.

Laughing, she relaxed into the seat and his arm. "What did you do after today's closing plenary?"

"Hit the gym and the shower, caught up on some work. The usual. You?"

"Work. It never seems to sleep."

They fell into a comfortable silence as the musician in the corner played the piano. This was nice.

"Don't you two look cozy."

*a*rms crossed over his chest, Kurt frowned at them.

Carlie sat up, feeling like a wayward teen, and gestured to the chair on her other side. "Kurt! Come join us," she offered, remembering too late that she had agreed to meet him.

Kurt's expression lightened a little at her invitation. "Let me grab a drink. Can I get you another?"

"I'm good for now, thanks," Carlie answered with a smile.

She watched him walk to the bar and glanced at Alex, who was studying Kurt with a guarded expression. Lane crooned a greeting to Kurt and soon the bar came alive, energy radiating across the room with him at its center. The redhead slid her arm through his and tossed a smirk at Carlie.

Rolling her eyes at the overt display, she glanced back at Alex and said, "She's so annoying."

He watched Lane and Kurt a moment longer, expression lightening. "I thought he liked you," he said.

"He likes a lot of people."

"And you?"

"And me, what?"

"Do you like him?"

Interesting. Was that a hint of jealousy?

"He seems nice enough, but I don't think he's my type. I find myself more drawn to darker, moodier writers these days."

Ego appeased, he relaxed and slid his arm down the back of her chair, caressing her upper arm. "Glad to hear it. I myself am into annoying redheads."

She elbowed him in the side, then leaned back again.

"Tell me more about you," Carlie asked. "Where do you call home, for instance?"

"Home is a lot of places these days. I have a place outside of the city in New York but have been spending a lot of time traveling, living out of suitcases."

That didn't sound enticing. "Do you like traveling?"

"I do, but it gets a bit tiring going from city to city to promote my books, speaking at colleges, bookstore and library signings, doing the conference circuit. But I'm glad my agent suggested this one."

They sipped their drinks, and Carlie pondered their locations.

"I take it you're in Cincinnati?" he asked, clearly following the same wavelength.

"Just outside of it; I live a little north of the city."

"Your family's there, right?"

"Mmhmm. I'm a few blocks away from my parents. My sister and her fiancé bought a place in the neighborhood, too. We didn't stray far from the coop." She grinned.

"Must be nice to have your family close."

"Yes and no. I adore being able to see them, spend time with them, but it can be a little overwhelming at times, too. It's like I'm always in the crosshairs. An easy target."

"Have you ever considered moving away?"

"Not until recently. I went through a pretty rough breakup last summer," Carlie said, swirling the drink in her hand. "But I have too much going on with my work and my family. My sister's getting married in August, and I offered to help with the planning."

"I see."

They let the subject die when Kurt returned. He carried a basket of pretzels and plopped into the seat next to her. "You guys still going to the dinner with us at The Rat Pack Club?"

She had promised to see Mr. Salmon, er, Bernie, at dinner. "Yes. Is it far from here?"

"No, it's just a few blocks away. We can walk if the weather holds," said Alex. He reached under the table and squeezed her hand.

"I'll get another round for here, then we can take off?" she offered.

"Sounds like a plan," agreed Kurt.

Such a happy little trio, Carlie laughed to herself as she squeezed up to the now-packed bar.

After the drinks were downed, the group strolled to the restaurant together, the awkwardness of earlier becoming a thing of the past.

The dinner was relaxing and entertaining. Carlie sat between Bernie and the evening's host, Melanie, the perky blonde. Without Lane around, she was quite easy to talk to. Alex grabbed a seat across from Carlie, sitting in front of a larger-than-life painting of Old Blue Eyes himself, Sinatra. Kurt ended up a few seats away, being pelted with questions by a terribly overeager agency rep. He turned large searching eyes her way, and Carlie replied with a shake of her head and an encouraging smile; it would do Kurt some good to spend time with someone he didn't want to sleep with.

Their wine glasses stayed full as Bernie delighted and inspired them with tales from his career, including a run-in with an up-and-comer, Carlie's father. "Charles was a very quiet but very smart young man. I'm not surprised to see he's come so far. And it would appear that young Carlie takes after him," he added, lifting his wine glass to salute her.

Carlie blushed at the praise, raising her glass to him in return. "I can only hope to make him proud."

Bernie nodded and took a small drink. "I expect you do so already."

"I admire all the work your charity has done, Mr. Bartlett," said Melanie. "How do you decide which endeavors to pursue?"

"To tell you the truth, I let my board determine much of that these days, though the wife and I do have a few causes close to the heart," he replied. "Helen and I have found that our greatest enjoyment comes from helping children develop a passion for learning. Our inner-city reading programs are our pride and joy."

"I'd like to get involved, Bartlett," said Kurt. "It's one thing to buy and sell companies, but I want to do something that makes a difference. This sounds like a great project."

Bernie looked down the table, assessing him. "I think that's a fine offer, son, and I would enjoy having your assistance."

Looking pleased and surprisingly excited, Kurt raised his glass to Bernie with a genuine smile.

Right there. That is the real Kurt. Why didn't he drop his flirtatious act more often? This was a Kurt Carlie could see herself being friends with.

"I'm disappointed that I cannot stay in Chicago longer. Your presentations sound fascinating," said Bernie, directing his attention to Alex. "Your new book has made some waves, Alex."

Alex looked up from the wine glass he swirled between his fingers. "You know I'd be happy to meet with you anytime to talk more about it. In fact, I'll be out your way again soon."

As they discussed future plans and downed far too much pasta, Carlie listened to Dean Martin croon "Volare" and considered these new friends, so quickly endearing themselves to her. It was good to get out among a new crowd. No one asked about Brent or shared their overly sympathetic reactions when they found out they had broken up. There were no uncomfortable questions about what happened. It was a fresh beginning.

The rest of the dinner passed too quickly as they discussed work and mutual acquaintances. Carlie spoke a little about her project for EHL, Pendulum, and how their early case studies were panning out. Melanie was especially interested in learning more about how the proprietary platform could work for her growing division at the association. Overall, it was a pretty amazing evening.

10

_T_he party said their farewells in front of a likeness of Sammy Davis Jr., bid adieu to The Rat Pack Club, and spilled out onto the streets of Chicago. A fine mist drifted from the sky. Some of the more adventurous of the crowd continued to another bar, and Melanie took off with Kurt in a taxi—probably to go heat things up, Carlie figured. Eventually it was just Carlie and Alex, leisurely walking back toward the hotel. The wine and food worked their magic, leaving her light and happy. She twirled around in a circle on the sidewalk. Alex laughed and caught her arm, pulling her in for an embrace, before she spun herself out of his grasp again.

"You do that pretty well for someone who wiped out on a newspaper today," he teased.

"I did no such thing! I'll have you know, Superman himself came and caught me," she volleyed back, continuing to dance just out of his reach. The air was crisp and cool, slightly damp from the earlier rains, but she felt warm and bubbly.

"Superman, eh?" He laughed and watched her with

unconcealed amusement. "Tell me more about this man who caught you."

"Well, if you must know, he's quite handsome. And strong. And passably smart—"

He gasped and held his hand to his chest in mock horror. "Passably? That doesn't sound good."

"Mmm. But he makes up for it with his impeccable timing and grace."

"Like this?"

He took two long steps and trapped her in his arms, allowing for no escape. "What else does this Superman do?" he asked, his voice lowering as he swayed with her in his arms.

"I can't say for sure, but I believe he also smells divine."

"How do I compare?"

Carlie wrapped her hands in his coat lapels and pressed herself against him as she inhaled his scent. "Passable." It came out less teasing than she intended, her voice dropping to chase his.

"And his kiss?"

"Pass—"

He smothered whatever words she might have prepared with his kiss, slow and gentle, as he danced her across the sidewalk. They settled back into the depths of a shadowed, vacant storefront's doorway. He deepened the kiss, his hand at the back of her neck, his hips pressing her back against the recessed bricks. Alex moved his mouth against hers, his tongue sliding in and out, and she matched his strokes, giving as good as she got. He tasted of red wine and spice.

Winding her arms over his shoulders, she combed her fingers through his dark hair, teasing the short locks above his jacket. He lowered a hand to her waist and moved it up her side, cupping the curve of her breast. Carlie nipped at his lip as he lowered his other hand to grasp her backside, pulling them closer together. Through her thin black dress, she felt the stark ridges of his jeans and belt, the bulk of him swelling beneath. He reached lower and caressed her thigh beneath the dress, massaging the backside of her leg.

She shivered as Alex cupped the back of her knee, lifting her leg to curl around his slim waist. "Are you cold?" he asked as he trailed his mouth away from her lips, kissing along her jaw and behind her ear before dipping lower to her collarbone and exploring her cleavage.

"No," she whispered, closing her eyes as desire flooded her system.

"Good," he mumbled. His heated breath and kiss delved deeper, and she gasped into his ear. Moving both hands up the backs of her legs, his fingers dug into her rounded backside and urged her tighter against him. Her hands roved over his back, feeling the taut muscles and tension building in him.

Carlie rolled her hips and felt his answering moan. She thrilled at the power she held to make him respond like that. He tore his lips from her chest and captured her mouth again with a fierce possession. Spreading his fingers, he lifted her so her upper back was supported by the wall, leaving her sensitive juncture to ride his clothed erection, circling and rubbing as the sensations built. The thick seams of his jeans penetrated the soft black material of her dress as he pushed closer. One hand in his hair, Carlie stretched her other arm out to provide leverage against the roughened brick at her back. His kiss robbed her of breath as his tongue plunged deeper in her mouth, working in time to the movement of his hips. Sensations blurred and a fiery heat built, bringing her closer to the edge. A ball of sizzling electricity spooled ever tighter at her core, and coils of heat radiated throughout her body.

A whimper escaped her throat, and she felt his lips quirk up as he tightened his hold on her hips, tilting at a deeper angle while he ground harder, all the while devouring her mouth. Carlie scratched her nails along the back of his neck, and he growled, biting her lip. Curving a hand between her legs, he sought out and expertly teased her pulsing bud through her damp panties, and she exploded, shattering against him in the open air, coming in shuddering waves of welcome relief.

He slowed, easily supporting her weight as he pulled her against his chest, a satisfied smile curving his perfect mouth. He lowered her, sliding her down his body to find her feet. Alex pressed a soft kiss to her lips.

"And was that passable?" he asked.

Carlie shook her head in a daze, not believing what they had just done. That was unreal and had seemingly come out of nowhere.

"No?" he said.

"No. I mean yes. Passable." She glanced down at his excited state. "Are you okay?"

"More than okay." He chuckled and pressed a kiss to her temple, then took her hand as they resumed the walk to the hotel.

They entered the hotel lobby, and Carlie grew nervous. Crossing into the lights and refinement, the blood drained from her face. Mortification took hold. She couldn't believe her brazen behavior. On the freaking streets of Chicago! Anyone could have been looking. She could barely look at him by the time they got to the elevator.

"Carlie? What's wrong? Are you okay?"

She forced her chin up, willing him to understand. "This

is so not me. I can't believe we..." She trailed off, covering her face with her hands.

Alex pulled her hands from her face, holding them between his, his eyes filled with concern. "I'm sorry, Carlie. I didn't think...I mean, I didn't plan..."

Taking a deep breath, she nodded. "I know. Me neither."

"But I did enjoy it," he added softly, massaging the inside of her wrist with his thumb.

"Me too," she whispered. Carlie consoled herself, knowing they didn't actually do anything worth regretting.

They were quiet the rest of the way up. When they exited the elevator, Carlie stopped outside her door. "Do you...?" Her hands fluttered toward her door.

He stared at the door then shook his head, grasping her hand. "We both had a bit to drink, and—Christ, I can't believe I'm saying this—but I don't want to rush things with you, Carlie. I don't want this to be something you regret."

Bringing her captive hand to his mouth, he pressed a warm kiss to the back of it. "I will see you in the morning."

He released her, and Carlie slipped into her room. "Good night, Alex," she murmured as the door closed between them.

What a night.

She changed into her favorite flannel pants and a loose tank top and spread out on the bed with her laptop, scrolling through her email before jumping over to Facebook. Carlie sent a few birthday wishes and responded to some messages. Nothing new there. Frustrated, she closed the laptop and lay back, wondering what *he* was doing now.

Her phone vibrated and hope soared as she recalled giving him her number earlier.

Not him.

Damn.

Still, she was happy to hear from Kim: *How's it going with mission Just Do It?*

How's it going? That's a good question. Carlie stared at her phone, not seeing it as she replayed the events of the evening. Kim was her oldest friend, essentially her sister, but she couldn't bring herself to disclose what she and Alex had done. In the freaking street.

Going well, she replied. *Alex is really great.* Really, really great, she amended. In fact, one might say super. She groaned at her own cheesiness.

I looked this guy up. Alex Williams. Does he look that good in person?

Better, Carlie replied, adding a devil emoji.

That's my girl! How's the conference itself?

It's okay. Just came back from dinner with some of the other speakers and sponsors.

She rolled onto her side and cradled a pillow under her head.

Sounds thrilling *yawn* Anything going with Hunter?

No, I'm pretty sure Kurt moved on to another woman, which is fine by me. Carlie wondered if that was true. He and Melanie did leave together.

Owen is not answering my texts, Kim interrupted her runaway thoughts.

That time again? Carlie waited to see if Kim was going to add more, not wanting to say the wrong thing.

I haven't heard from him since Saturday, she added.

It's only Monday, Carlie consoled.

I think he's seeing someone else.

This wouldn't be the first time. One of these days Kim was going to realize she would be better off without him. Carlie sighed and replied, *And if he is?*

If he is, I'm done. I mean it this time. I can't keep doing this.

If Carlie scrolled back far enough in her texts, she would find an exact replica of this conversation.

What are you going to do?

I'll give him until tomorrow night. If he doesn't reply by then, we're through.

Are you going to give him a chance to explain?

I haven't decided yet.

Nope, definitely not done with him then. Carlie shook her head, sad for her.

Does he still make you happy?

Not lately, that's for damn sure.

Thinking back over all the years Carlie had spent with Brent, it dawned on her how their last year together had been filled with more frustration and loneliness than happiness. Carlie wanted to tell Kim to move on from Owen, find someone new. But her BFF was not ready to hear it.

I know you're going to do what is best for you, Carlie typed and hit send. Please let her figure it out before she continued down this road too much longer.

I have an early morning tomorrow, new product launch. Keep me posted about your Alex. Miss you!

Will do, Carlie replied. *Miss you too.*

She stared at the screen—"your Alex" jumped out. Was he *her* Alex? Could he be? He lived in New York, didn't agree with her work, and traveled all over the place all the time. Oh, God, what if she was just another number to him? Did he do this everywhere he went? A sick feeling took hold and she stared numbly into space.

Stop it, Car! You're overthinking this! She crossed her arm over her face and closed her eyes, remembering the feel of him against her, his breath hot and hands deliciously greedy.

So, what if it was just a fling. She could do this, right?

She was twenty-four years old—a damn woman, not a child. *Live a little*, she heard in Kim's voice.

Carlie's phone buzzed again, and she lifted it to see what else Kim had to say. Instead, she found a short text: *Good night Lois Lane. See you in a.m.*

She hit the lights, fussed with the pillows, and fell asleep wondering if and how she should reply.

11

*I*t's raining. My footsteps echo as I walk alone down the eerily empty street. Glancing up at the silent buildings, I grow uncomfortable, sensing the eyes of the masses watching me. I'm not supposed to be here, but I don't know where else to go.

I begin walking, unsure of my destination. Ahead I hear a bird cawing, warning me away. Perhaps it thinks I'm a scavenger, competition come to steal its meal. I keep going anyway.

Scattered newspapers and fast-food wrappers line the quiet city street. An empty cab sits at the curb. Passing it, I note the door is open and keys dangle from the ignition. That's odd. Am I supposed to get in the car? I look around, knowing I am being watched. I close the door and keep walking, rain soaking through my clothes.

The awning of the next skyscraper looks inviting, offering a break from the rain. I shiver as the cold and chill seep into my bones. My relief in the portico is short-lived; a liveried man emerges from the entrance, asking if I'm checking in. I shake my head no, and he tells me to move on. I can't stay there. He disappears into the building as if he'd never been there.

Dismayed, I lift my face into the rain, scanning the surroundings for another shelter.

What am I doing here? Where is everyone?

Somewhere deep inside, I am aware that I am dreaming, but I continue, curious to see where I'm going.

The blacktop of the next cross street appears to be moving. As I approach, it becomes apparent that the road has been washed away, replaced by a rush of dark, deep water. A flood. It has become a river. A wooden dock grows out from the sidewalk I stand upon, and I step out onto it.

Across the street-river, solid footing continues, but I'm not sure if I can make it across the tumultuous, raging waters.

I take another step farther out onto the dock, and the timbers begin shuddering, fighting valiantly against the current.

You can do this, *I tell myself.*

I take another step and scream, feet flying out from beneath me. I cling to the aged wooden boards as they come apart beneath me.

Tumbling into the raging river, I gasp, trying to keep my head above water. I cling to the remaining weathered pillars of the dock, struggling against the current.

"Let go," a voice says.

Head thrashing to find the source of the voice, I see no one. I'm exhausted from holding on so tightly, fighting the violent current. My hands hurt. My arms are sore. The rushing water rips at my body. But I can't let go. I'll be swept away and drown.

"Let go," a voice calls again.

Taking a deep breath, I unclench my arms from the wooden post and am immediately pulled downstream.

I fight to stay afloat. Debris in the water scratches at my legs. The water is roaring in my ears, and I'm frightened. I'm going to die.

I keep drifting downstream, gaining speed, seeing no end in sight. A bird soars above me, cawing loudly. Is it the same one from the street?

At long last, the water begins to slow, and I along with it. Eventually, it stills, and I realize my feet can touch the bottom. I stand and look around me, noticing I'm no longer in a city.

Where am I?

The water has all but vanished, and I'm now standing in a small puddle. The puddle seeps into the ground, and the ground itself begins to collapse. I try to run, but my feet are now trapped, and I am sucked deeper and deeper into the ground.

JERKING AWAKE, Carlie gulped down air and shivered in her bed. The room was dark and cool, and she was trembling like a leaf. She flipped the nightstand light on. The clock read five thirty. Wrapping her arms around her legs, she waited for the shaking to cease. That was insane. Her adrenaline at full throttle, she gave up on sleeping and again got an early start to the day.

Workout clothes on, she headed to the gym, hoping for solitude and quiet. She had learned early in life that such dreams demanded either a punishing workout or deep meditation to prevent another breakdown. She was stronger now and would no longer give in to the anxieties that haunted her psyche. Carlie did some light stretches in the elevator until the doors slid open to the fifth floor, where she discovered she was not the only early riser. Two others worked out their demons on the equipment, though thankfully no one she recognized. She needed to breathe, to think of something other than the wacky dream and what it might or might not mean. Pausing to snag a bottle of complimentary water from the fitness center's mini fridge, she climbed aboard the elliptical, ready to race herself to nowhere.

Thinking about Alex, she wondered what she was going to do. Part of her wanted to pack up and run home, pretend last night never happened. But she was not a coward. Carlie increased the resistance and kept moving.

Another part of her wanted to go back up to floor twenty-two, pound on his door, and ask him what he was thinking. Sounded like the plan of a crazy person. Groaning, she dismissed the thought.

Okay, so no running away and no rogue kamikaze action.

What did that leave?

A fling, she had told herself last night. Could she do that? If she was honest with herself, she was not a fling kind of person. And the way her body responded when Alex entered a room, when he looked at her with those blue, blue eyes...when he held her...

Car, you are not allowed to fall for this guy. It. Will. Not. Work. She slammed her hands on the handlebars for emphasis.

"Hey, now, what did that machine ever do to you?"

She nearly fell off the elliptical and swung her head around to see Kurt watching her, clearly amused. "I mean, I know it can make you sweat, but so can I," he teased.

She rolled her eyes. Back to being the macho man again, huh?

"Morning, Kurt," she huffed out, focused on regaining her stride.

"Good morning to you, too."

He stood watching her for another moment. Carlie glanced at him, not failing to notice his trim, muscular physique. "Is there something you wanted?"

He gave a devilish grin. "You could say that."

"Ha. Ha. Guess I set myself up for that one."

He remained still, watching her.

"Actually, I do have a question for you," he said, stepping closer to her machine, his voice quieter.

She raised a brow and waited as he gathered his thoughts.

And waited.

And waited.

"Is this a question I'm supposed to hear?"

He batted her sarcasm away. "So, I'll be blunt. What is it about Alex? I mean, you and I theoretically have so much more in common. We talk the same language. We operate in similar circles. But you won't even give me the time of day. And he..." Kurt killed whatever he was going to say and gave a grunt of frustration instead. "You don't know him. Have you ever cracked open one of his books?"

Continuing to focus on her stride, she watched the little tracking boxes on the machine's display inch across the screen, pixel by pixel. "Kurt," she began. Then stopped again. What could she say?

He waited, and when it became obvious that she wasn't going to continue, he sighed and prodded her. "What?"

Pressing her eyes closed, she took a deep breath. "I don't know what's going on here, but I am in town for a conference. I need to focus on my work. Whatever is or is not happening with me and Alex—or you—is...immaterial. We're here for one week. One. And who knows if any of us will ever see each other again." Frustrated, she stopped her machine and gulped down some water.

"Hand me one of those towels, will you?" she said, gesturing to the metal table behind him.

Kurt tossed a clean hand towel and spray bottle to her.

Wiping down the machine, Carlie took advantage of the

distraction to think over what she had just rattled off, realizing it was true. She didn't know if they would ever see each other again. The thought of not seeing Alex again... She couldn't think of that right now. Especially not with Kurt watching.

She turned back and tossed him the towel.

"So that's it? You're not going to give me a chance?" Kurt asked.

Throwing her hands in the air, Carlie growled and shouted at him, "What are you even talking about?"

He muttered something under his breath, then stormed up to her, pinning her to the machine. Stunned, she stood still, her breath uneven from the workout.

He watched the sweat run down her chest before raising his eyes, staring intently. Holding her face between his hands, Kurt lowered his lips to hers. He wasn't gentle; his kiss was designed to conquer, to claim ownership. Carlie gripped the equipment behind her, shock stalling her thoughts before her mind began to race. She tried to piece together what the hell was happening. Regaining her wits, she shoved him away, breathing harshly.

"What was that?!"

"I figured I should at least give you something to think about before you wrote me off."

"Jesus! You don't just do that to someone! And what about Melanie?"

Kurt's incredulous look was almost comical. "Melanie? What are you talking about?" He shook his head and stared straight into her eyes. "Tell me something, Carlie. Have you read his books?"

She was confused. But she knew where he was going with this; she'd had this same argument with herself. But what business was it of his? Carlie glared at him and stalked away.

"Read them, Carlie!" he called after her.

12

_S_he escaped to her room, showered, wrapped her hair in a towel, and collapsed onto the bed. What was happening here? Carlie wanted to discredit Kurt, badly, but she kept hearing his voice, telling her to read the books. She'd read the excerpt; she knew where Alex was going with it. But how much did that matter? It was just a book.

A soft knock sounded on the door.

Perfect. What now?

She shrugged into a hotel robe and stalked to the door, swinging it open. "What?" she demanded irritably.

Alex stood in the hallway holding two Starbucks cups, eyes wide with shock.

"Alex! I'm so sorry. I was... I don't know what I was expecting," she stammered.

"No, no, it's okay. I shouldn't have surprised you. I figured you might want a treat for the morning," he said, looking at her robe-shrouded figure. "Should I leave?"

Following his gaze, Carlie became aware of her state of dress. Undress.

"Give me a minute," she said, blustering through her

self-consciousness. "Come on in and have a seat, if you'd like."

She snagged clothes and fled to the bathroom to dress and pull her hair back into a knot. Tossing all the damp towels in the corner, she gave herself a mental shake, took a deep breath, and rejoined him in the bedroom.

"Thank you," she said, nerves calming as she inhaled the soothing scent of coffee. Carlie noted the name on the cup —Lois. Cute.

"You're quite welcome," he replied. "Want to talk about it?"

"Not just now," she said, grateful for the choice. If only others were as understanding. Damn Kurt.

Alex looked around the room, eyes pausing on the bed, then returned his focus to her. "Sleep well?" he asked, echoing her question from the morning before.

She nodded vaguely. "Then got up early to work out."

"Which put you in a *great* mood," he noted.

"Yup. Endorphins, you know." She laughed, lightening up some more. She held up the cup. "But this will do me more good than a treadmill."

"Did you eat breakfast yet?"

"No, I was planning to grab a bagel from the conference lobby."

"Well... I was going to see if you wanted to go down to Sammy's with me. They have a great breakfast buffet."

"Give me five minutes." She smiled, tossing him the remote. She giggled to herself, remembering Lettuce Lady and her first glimpses of Alex on Sunday in the hotel's bistro. If anyone had told her she'd be back there in two days for a breakfast date with him, she would have laughed.

Carlie returned to the bathroom to finish getting ready

while he clicked on the morning news. "Big accident on I-90," he called.

"We should try to avoid it," she hollered back, teasingly. This was nice, being with someone in the morning again. Doing normal stuff. The banality of domestic bliss.

"Ready," she said, grabbing her bag as he turned off the television.

She smelled the syrup and waffles as they stepped off the elevator and entered the restaurant. The table linens were a happy yellow this morning.

"Coffee?" asked the waiter. Carlie nodded and turned over the mug on the saucer before heading to the buffet.

"What's good?" she asked.

"What's not good? Bacon, sausage, eggs, waffles. Definitely try the waffles," Alex said, dropping half of a Belgian waffle on her plate.

She accepted the waffle and added some eggs and fruit before heading back to the table. Alex returned, and they dug in.

"Holy shit, these waffles are divine," she hummed, chewing the sweet and crusty treat as pancake syrup dripped down her chin.

"Told you," he said over a mouthful of the same.

They ate in comfortable silence and her mind drifted back to Kurt's comments. And what else had happened. That kiss. She kept her nose buried in her breakfast, hoping Alex didn't notice her sudden flush. It was ridiculous to be embarrassed by it. It wasn't like she had something going on with Alex, right?

"What's wrong?" he asked, and Carlie realized she had been holding the same bite of waffle on her fork for far too long.

"Nothing. I'm just thinking; spaced out." She forced a laugh.

"Hmm."

Damn. *Change the subject, Car!*

"Tell me about your books..." she began, then cringed, doubting she wanted to hear this.

Alex paused mid-chew, surprised. Swallowing his food, he grabbed his coffee cup and molded it between his hands, staring into the java as though looking for inspiration.

"I write about people," he started. "People the way they used to be, how we used to have stronger community values."

That sounded harmless enough. Quaint even.

"I also review current economic and business trends and break them down into how they impact our lives as individuals."

"How long have you been writing?" she asked.

"My first book was published six years ago, and I've been on the writing, editing, touring loop ever since."

"How many books have you published?"

"Four, with two more in the pipeline."

"All before thirty? I'm impressed," she said honestly. "One more question before I end this, uh, interrogation. Have you ever written about my family? Or EHL?"

Say no, say no, say no...

Alex continued to fidget with his cup, rolling it between his hands. "Yes."

Damn. Carlie processed this and raised her eyebrows, waiting for him to continue.

He sighed and put his cup down. "Carlie. I like you. A lot. And I don't want something I wrote years ago to come between us now. Is it important?"

"I don't know," she answered. "You tell me."

Alex leaned his head back and stared at the ceiling. When he returned his gaze to her, his face was devoid of emotion. "There is a strong correlation between the rise of your father and EHL Global and the decline in morality of the marketing communications industry," he said flatly.

She split hairs in his statement, looking to make sense of it. "Correlation? I can correlate anything if the parameters are wide. Are you saying it's causal?"

"The numbers are there, Carlie. There is direct evidence that your family's business has manipulated our perception of norms, systematically desensitizing the average American from the shocking images and language that tear down the traditional values this country was built on."

If a mind could blink, hers did. "What are you talking about?" she blurted.

"Let's just change the subject, please."

"Let's pause a minute, please," Carlie countered, not ready to roll over on this one. "Let me see if I have this straight. Are you saying that *my family* has something to do with demoralizing this country?"

"Said. It was five years ago. And it's not quite that clean-cut."

"My family—my Midwestern, heartbeat-of-America, country-living family who still meets regularly for dinners together. You're saying *we* are ruining America?" She dropped her napkin on the table.

"Carlie, calm down. It's not like that."

"Please," she spat. "You're going to judge me? Judge my family? Judge what we do? You know *nothing* about me. Or my family. You have no idea how hard my mom and dad have worked to create this vision. You have no idea how hard I've worked."

His face was blank.

Carlie jumped up, knocking her chair over in her haste. "I have to go, Alex. I'll see you later."

Grabbing her things, she stormed out of the restaurant, leaving a trail of diners and staff staring after her. She crossed to the elevator, jabbing the button, willing it to open.

Heavy footsteps followed her across the marble floor. "Carlie," he called.

She hit the up button again, hoping it would summon the elevator faster.

"Look at me, damn it," Alex said.

"Go back to your breakfast, Alex. I need to go. Just leave me alone," she said, not bothering to disguise her anger. "I'm sure I'll see you later at the conference."

The door opened, and she turned into it, Alex studying her as the door closed between them. She paced in the confines of the cube, praying the elevator would continue up without company.

One prayer answered, she made it back to her room and felt like screaming. Last night was so perfect. How did everything go to hell today? And it was not even eight o'clock yet.

Ripping open the mini fridge door, Carlie selected a split of wine and twisted off the top, dumping the contents into a glass on the counter. She dragged it over to the desk seat and stared at it glumly. *It's five o'clock somewhere, right?*

She contemplated calling Kim, then remembered she had something going on this morning. Besides, she had her own drama going on with Owen. Carlie briefly considered, then quickly ruled out, her sister and mom. She finally grabbed her phone: *S.O.S. Do you have some time to chat?*

Marie wasted no time texting her back. *Of course, honey. Now?*

Carlie took a big gulp of wine and punched the call button.

"What's going on, my girl? Are you okay?" She heard the worry in the older woman's voice.

"Oh, Marie, I'm so sorry. I didn't mean to scare you." She took another drink before continuing. "I need advice. I'm in a crash-and-burn pattern right now."

"Tell me what's happening."

Carlie told her about Alex, skipping over a few of the details, then Kurt and their encounter this morning.

"I hope you slapped him good for that, Carlie! If I were there—"

"Oh, I'm pretty sure he got the message," she interrupted. "But he made me wonder, so I couldn't help but ask Alex about his writing when we had breakfast just now."

She spilled to Marie about the conversation and his comments about the Eller family and their company. Returning to the fridge, Carlie grabbed a second mini bottle of wine and added it to the remaining sip of the first.

"I'll be there soon!" Marie hollered a little more loudly. "Sorry, honey, my first appointment just arrived. I have a few minutes, though. Now you listen to Marie. First, we all do things we wish we could forget about. I've known you long enough to know a few of yours, young lady. Second, most of us don't have those things published for the world to read. And finally, my dear, if he has you this upset, I suspect there is something going on that's worth pursuing between the two of you. I want you to put down that wine—yes, I can tell —and drink some water. Go to that conference and focus on your work. Let the rest happen as it will. The Lord is watching. He'll make sure you do the right thing.

"Oh," she continued, "and I want you to give that other

young man a slap from me. That boy needs to learn some manners!"

Carlie's eyes grew misty at the conviction and love pouring through the phone line. "What would I do without you, Marie?"

"You'll never have to know, my dear. Now, you let me go do some hair, and you go take care of business."

"Love you, Marie."

"And I you, sweetheart. Go dry them tears and be the strong woman I know you are. It'll all work out the way it's supposed to."

After hanging up, Carlie debated her wine glass.

What Marie didn't know wouldn't hurt her.

13

*A*fter finishing the last split of wine and a bottle of water, she pulled herself together and changed into a suit. *Dress for success*, her mother always said. Carlie felt the difference as she slipped into her heels and slung her lanyard around her neck. She looked into the mirror, swinging up her finger guns. "There's a new sheriff in town, partner," she said to herself.

Laughing at her foolishness, Carlie wondered if she maybe shouldn't have had that last glass. Too late now.

She strutted to the elevator and prepared to face the music.

"Good morning," greeted Melanie in the conference lobby. "We've just started in the ballroom. Please grab a coffee and head on in."

Nodding as she passed, Carlie made another ridiculously weak coffee in the petite white cup and dropped into an empty seat toward the back of the room. Queen Bitch Lane was on stage, introducing the next speaker. Fab.

Her phone buzzed, and she looked at the screen. *I'm sorry, Carlie. I can't change the past*, Alex's text read.

Humph. Slapping her phone face down on the white linen, she attempted to focus on her coffee and the lecture. From the corner of her eye, she saw someone approach the table. She tilted her head and watched Kurt slide into a seat at her right. He said nothing, just focused on the speaker alongside her. After a few minutes, he leaned over and whispered, "I'm sorry about this morning, Carlie. I had no right. It was wrong, and I hope you can forgive me."

She turned to look at him and was so tempted to slap him for Marie that she sat on her hand and giggled. Oh, she really should not have had that last glass of wine. The confused look on his face made her giggle more, and soon she was rushing out of the room in a full-on laughing fit. She ran into an empty breakout session room and sensed Kurt following.

"Are you okay?"

Carlie wiped the tears from the corners of her eyes and gulped in air, trying to get ahold of herself. She leaned over and braced her hands on her knees as she focused on her breathing. In...out...in...out.

After another moment, Carlie straightened up and narrowed her eyes at him. "What you did was wrong. I know it, you know it, and Marie knows it, too."

His face scrunched up in confusion. "Marie?"

"And let me tell you something else. I choose who I kiss...or maybe I kiss who I choose. It's not up to you, not Alex, not anyone. Got it?"

He frowned, then realization dawned. "Have you been drinking?"

"Maybe a little bit, but that's none of your concern, either."

Frustrated at this whole day, she gave up on the conference and marched back to the elevator. Kurt continued to follow her. "I'm fine, Kurt. Go back to your Melanie and your groupies."

"What the hell, Carlie? What did you drink? I'm seeing you back to your room. Which floor?"

She punched the elevator button for twenty-two and sulked in the corner of the elevator, crossing her arms over her chest and glaring at him. *How can someone so cute be so annoying?*

"Want to tell me what is going on?" Kurt asked.

"I told you. I'm over this whole day."

"You said nothing of the sort, but that's neither here nor there. What is this about Melanie? That's the second time you've mentioned her to me."

"Well, you two left together last night. Didn't you...you know?"

"No. I also don't have any groupies, at least as far as I'm aware. And I think I'd know."

Carlie stared at him in silence, refusing to comment or acknowledge the frisson of relief that may or may not have run through her.

"Wine," she said. "Lots and lots of wine. All of it, in fact."

"I see that."

The elevator door swooshed open, and she stumbled out onto her floor.

"Care to tell me why you are drunk at"—he checked his phone—"nine-fifteen in the morning?"

"Like I said. I'm over this day."

"Carlie, I said I'm sorry for this morning."

"Always about you, isn't it, Kurt? This happens to not be about you, buddy. Mostly."

Realizing she'd passed her door, she swung around and narrowly missed colliding with him. He followed her back to the correct door, and she hunted for the keycard.

Swinging the door open, she kicked off her shoes and paid no attention as they flew across the room. Flinging open the mini fridge, Carlie glanced over her shoulder at Kurt. "You look like a bourbon guy. Is that right? If so, sorry to disappoint. All out. But I have vodka!"

"Carlie, stop. Sit down." He grasped her upper arm and walked her over to the desk chair. He turned back to the fridge and rummaged before pressing a cold bottle of water into her hands. While she drank the water, she watched suspiciously as he collected her shoes and put them together in the closet. Then he wandered into the restroom and straightened up there, too.

"What are you doing?"

"I'm trying to make sure you don't trip and crack your head open."

"Oh." She frowned. "Why?"

"Why don't I want you to crack your head open?"

"No, why are you here, helping me?"

"Contrary to popular opinion—or yours, at least—I happen to be a somewhat nice guy. Or try to be. I don't know what has you all riled up, but I'm not going to sit here and watch you get even more drunk."

She considered this as he straightened the bedspread and cleared away the empty wine bottles. He then reached for the room phone. "Room service? Yes, we'd like a couple orders of toast and a pot of coffee. Thank you."

He stood watching her, frustration (concern?) pulling a corner of his mouth down. "Are you going to make me guess what happened?"

Carlie groaned and set the half-empty water bottle on the desk. "I talked to Alex about his books." She glanced quickly at him, checking to see his response.

His face neutral, he urged her on. "And?"

"And he told me what he wrote."

"He *told* you?"

"Yes." She hesitated. "You were right."

They were both quiet as the words hung between them. Carlie stood up and dove onto the bed, laying back and closing her eyes.

She heard him continue to shift through the room. This was so weird.

"Want me to leave?" he asked.

"No, you may as well stay and keep me company. Unless you want to get back to the conference?"

"Not at the moment," he said, walking over to the chair she had just vacated. He sat and leaned back into the seat, tilting it back on its rear legs.

"And you were worried about *me* cracking my head," she snarked.

He dropped the chair back to all fours at the same time they heard a knock at the door. Carlie leaned up on her elbows, wondering if she should bother getting up. "Room service," Kurt said, walking to the door. She collapsed back onto the bed as he carried a tray back to the desk. He dropped a plate of toast on the bed. "Eat," he commanded.

Saluting him, she rolled over onto her side and picked up a triangle of barely toasted white bread. Carlie chewed on the corner of it and watched as he stirred a pack of sugar into his coffee. "What's the deal with you and Melanie, anyway?" she asked, trying not to sound overly curious.

He grinned. "I figured you'd circle back to that again." He set the spoon aside and picked up the cup, inhaling the bitter aroma. "Her brother and I went to school together. She's like a sister to me. I may have played a small role in helping her land this gig with United Marketing Association"—he looked at her sharply—"which I will deny if brought up in her presence."

Absorbing this, she took another bite of soft toast. "And when you left the restaurant together last night..."

"Not that it's any of your business, but she wanted to warn me about a certain redhead who had plotted to, uh, spend some extracurricular time with me."

Lane. That did not surprise her.

"When we got back here, she dragged Lane to the bar while I slipped in and got back up to my room."

Oh.

"What about you and Alex? Stay out late?"

Eyes closed, she thought of their stolen time on the street. "We walked back to the hotel, and he left me at my door." That part was true, at least.

"Mmhmm," he murmured.

"Toss me that water, please," she requested. "This is so dry."

He obliged, and then a comfortable silence dropped over them. Carlie worked on her water and toast; Kurt sipped on his coffee. Her phone vibrated on the table next to him, and he glanced down, a slight frown marring his handsome face. "I should go," he said, standing up and handing her the phone.

A text from Alex. *Are you in your room? I'm coming up. Please let me in.*

Swallowing another gulp of water, she watched as Kurt gathered his things and straightened up the tray. He had genuinely surprised her. Yet another side of this enigmatic man.

"Kurt?" He paused at the door, not looking at her. "Thank you. I mean it. I'm glad you were here for me."

He gave a terse nod, then closed the door behind him.

*C*ollecting Kurt's still-warm cup, she topped it off and tried a sip. Not Starbucks, but fresher than the stuff in the conference lobby. Carlie freshened up before plopping down on the chair. Waiting for the knock.

Ask not for whom the bell tolls, she thought, tapping her fingers on the padded arms of the chair.

Finally, the knock sounded. Too late to run now. She took a deep breath and swung the door open, looking at him. Good God was he hot. Leaning one arm along the wall, his other hand was raised, primed to knock again. Was he not expecting her to answer? He dropped his hand and stood up straight. "May I come in?"

Carlie stood aside, allowing him to enter. Closing the door behind him, she debated where to go next. She settled on the desk chair, not wanting to sit on the bed with him right now. She took a seat and watched him pace back and forth across the room. Silence ensued.

"You didn't show up at the conference this morning," he noted.

She shrugged. It wasn't true, but she didn't bother correcting him. What difference did it make?

"I was hoping I'd get a chance to talk to you." He kept pacing, running his hands through his hair. "You have to understand, it was nothing personal. My books are meant to encourage thought, dialogue. I want people to open their eyes, see how things are changing. Understand it."

He stopped pacing and dropped to the corner of the bed facing her. "I didn't know you; I didn't know your family. What I do know is my research. History, trends, revenue and expenditures, surveys, market research... Those are solid. Those I can analyze. Those I can write about. I don't regret including EHL or your dad. But I do regret how it's made you feel. I would never do something to intentionally hurt you. I'm sorry. Please don't let that be a reason to stop talking to me. I would like to further explore this." He gestured back and forth between them.

Her whole life, Dad—and Mom and Rachael to an extent—had made headlines. EHL Global was as much a part of her family as her sister. She and Rach grew up with mayors and bigwigs stopping by, fancy dinners with corporate boards, whirlwind trips to major cities while their parents conducted business. They didn't shield their daughters from it; the girls were invited to be active participants to see how they could help change the world. As a child, it felt like a game. As Carlie got older, she saw it as an unparalleled opportunity. Alex wasn't the first person to write about them. Nor would he be the last.

But...

"You should have told me," she said.

"What should I have said, Carlie? 'Hey, I'm the writer who said your dad's the antichrist, and EHL is sending this country to hell in a handbasket'?"

"Did you say that?!" she gasped, horrified.

His eyes flared wide open. "No! Of course not. I'm trying to make a point," he said, soothingly. "I do my job, you do yours. But our jobs don't have to define who we could be together, do they? *How* we are together?"

She shook her head slowly. "No, they don't. But I can't be with someone who doesn't respect what I do, doesn't respect my family."

"Carlie, listen to me. I respect you. I respect your intellect. I respect your reputation. I respect your dad, his vision and ability to turn a small agency into a global machine. I can appreciate that. I can respect and appreciate you but still not like parts of your business. Hell, I don't like my fucking publisher! But some things we can't choose; we can't control them as easily."

Her head was throbbing as the effects of the wine wore off. She got up for a fresh water and rummaged through her bag for a couple of ibuprofens. Carlie tossed them back and gulped down some water. "I don't know what to say right now, Alex."

"Then don't say anything." He walked over and loosely wrapped his arms around her. "Let's just see how this plays out." He placed a kiss on the tip of her nose, and she laughed in surprise.

"Did you kiss my nose?"

"Well, I wasn't sure you wouldn't throw me out if I did anything else." He caressed her cheek affectionately. "Should we start over?" he asked.

She nodded.

"Hi, I'm Alex." He smiled.

"Carlie."

Not wanting to press their new start too much, they returned to catch the second half of the morning's sessions.

They parted ways in the conference lobby, he to discover the latest in content marketing and she to the email marketing drip campaign breakout session. "Carlie! Come join us!" her new friend Rita called. She smiled at her two favorite over-enthusiastic newcomers.

"Rita, Paul, good to see you again," Carlie greeted. "How are you enjoying your first convention?"

"Oh, my gosh, I'm getting so much great info. I'm already making lists of project updates to implement when I get back to the office next week," said Rita.

"Same," replied Paul. "I'm going to jump over to the other session, so we can double up our takeaways. Catch you ladies at the break!"

Rita waved him away, and Carlie settled in next to her. "So how long have you two worked together?"

"About three months. He started at Clyo a whole three days before me, so he likes to tease me about being much more experienced." She rolled her eyes. "But he's a fantastic work hubby."

"Work hubby? Are you two...?"

"Oh, no, not that way." She laughed. "I'm his work wife, he's my work husband. My boyfriend hates that we call each other that, but I think it's hysterical. I haven't told him that Paul's gay, which makes it even more perfect."

"Why don't you tell him? Seems like it would smooth things over."

"Well, honestly, if Shawn—that's my boyfriend—if Shawn can't handle my being good friends with a guy, then he's not worth keeping. I'm waiting to see. You know, can he handle me being independent and having male friends?"

"Go you, Miss Thing. I like your attitude," Carlie said. "I wish I had a little more of your spunk."

Rita's eyes grew huge. "You do? I mean, you're like... famous. And you want to be like me? Oh, my gosh."

Carlie laughed. "You realize I'm only a couple years older than you, right? And I'm not famous. That's my dad."

"Oh, but you are! I've read some of your articles. You're internet famous," she confirmed.

"Internet famous? That's a thing?"

"Oh, yes. It's most certainly a thing."

They continued chatting while the speaker set up.

"Hi, everyone. I'm here to get drippy with you," he announced.

Oh, lord. A cutesy presentation. Shoot me now.

A giggle erupted from Rita. "Oh, this is going to be good!"

Everyone was entitled to their own opinion. Carlie tilted her head and turned back to the speaker. As he began to talk about the latest in personalized email automation, she realized this was much more entry-level than she had expected.

"Rita, I'm going to slip out. Have to make a call. Catch me up later?"

She nodded, barely acknowledging Carlie as she scribbled down his lecture, evidently trying to capture every uttered word. Smiling at Rita's enthusiasm, she slipped out the back of the room.

15

*C*arlie walked around the conference lobby and leaned against one of the wide columns in the room as she checked her texts. She returned love and greetings from Chicago to her mom and Rachael and sent a text to Kim, whom she had yet to hear back from regarding Owen. Would he get back to her today? Maybe it would be best if he didn't. Did it make her a bad friend to hope he jumped ship and went far, far away?

"Look at you, up on two feet and everything."

She glanced up at Kurt. "And I can say I owe it all to you," she teased.

"How'd it go?"

Frowning, Carlie tried to figure out how much to say. She didn't want to hurt his feelings or make things awkward. The kinder, more nurturing Kurt was someone she'd love to be friends with.

"Okay, I guess. He apologized, and we agreed to start fresh. See how it goes, you know?"

"You're giving that..." He stopped himself. "Him. You're giving him another chance?"

"I don't know. I just agreed to start fresh. I can't even say what that means yet." She shrugged, trying to be nonchalant.

"Playing hooky?" asked a throaty voice.

They glanced over and saw Lane watching, her arms crossed and hip jutted out.

"Hi, Lara," greeted Kurt.

"It's Lane." She glowered.

"Oh, I do apologize."

She shook out her mane of red hair and pouted. "What are you two doing out here? Aren't you enjoying the breakout sessions?"

"Oh, they're great," Carlie said, waving her phone toward the woman. "Work stuff."

"My session was dull," Kurt replied. "Had to escape before I started snoring."

Lane leaned against his arm. "Why don't you join me for a drink and tell me what you'd like to see instead," she purred. "I'm always open to new ways of doing things. I can be quite flexible."

Gag. Seriously?

"Thanks for the offer, but I'm waiting to talk to Carlie's colleague. Working on a new project."

Carlie shot a look at Kurt, then mentally shrugged and handed over her phone. It was the least she owed him for his help earlier. He turned and talked into the device, walking away. Smothering a giggle, she cleared her throat and glanced at Lane, who was glaring at her.

"So, now you two are working together?" Lane skeptically asked.

"What do you think?"

She huffed, then stalked away. Grinning at her back, Carlie turned to see Kurt returning. "I programmed my number in for you, in case you decide to do more day drinking." He smirked as he tossed her the phone.

"Gee, thanks."

"Any plans for lunch?" he asked.

"Not yet."

"Well, come on, then," he said, holding out his hand.

Why not? She placed her hand in his, not sure where they were off to but trusting his decision. "Let's go," she said.

Kurt studied her from across the table. "Feeling all right?"

"Well enough for now." She smiled wanly, glad that the air heavy with the fragrance of sautéed onions and peppers wasn't nauseating. Black-and-white photos lined the walls of the cozy restaurant, capturing the last century of music. Several had scribbled dedications and signatures across them.

Kurt gestured to the walls. "See what I mean? It's history in the making. These photos, this place... You can't replicate this."

Admittedly, she had been skeptical when they approached the building and had to descend to the basement to get in, but now that they were seated and ensconced by R&B legends, Carlie was geeked. "This place is incredible. Is that Eric Clapton?"

Turning to look at the autographed photo, he nodded. "Pretty cool, right? You know, the first time I came here, I was in the midst of purchasing a dying publishing house. Not the best of businesses to invest in, but it gave me some unique opportunities. Thank you," he added to the waiter as their drinks arrived. "Discovering this place is the best thing that came of that deal."

She coughed out a surprised laugh. "You own a publishing house? That seems a bit out of your domain."

He shook his head at her amusement, then turned serious. "When you encounter a good deal that helps others, you take the leap. The previous owner was struggling with health issues, but they were publishing some great works. We came to an agreement that allowed him to take it easy and keep the place running."

"And now?"

"He's doing much better, and the business is thriving. We transitioned to more digital operations, which was an uphill battle with some of the veteran staff, but the outcome is hard to argue. They do well, and I check in from time to time."

Huh. She found herself at a loss of how to reply. She gazed at his profile. Each time she thought she had him figured out, he surprised her again.

"Do you like Italian beef? It's pretty spectacular here. Hot and wet is the way to go. Though I'm also a bit partial to their cheesesteak."

Looking back down to the menu, she tried to decipher if he was teasing her about liking it hot and wet. But no, there it was in black and white. "I'm intrigued. Italian beef it is."

"That's my girl," he praised, green eyes sparkling.

They placed their orders and settled into shop talk. "How did you get into all these business acquisitions?"

He considered the question and stirred his sweet tea. "Some might say I fell into it. My first business was a lucky fluke—right place at the right time with the right connections. It took about a year to pick up steam and not long after, I took a calculated risk for my first foray into the financial markets, which gave me the capital to begin Hunter Industries."

"Your first was Legend Communications, right?"

"Yes," he said, surprised. "I'm impressed you know that."

"I may or may not have looked you up after you sent me the picture."

"Ah. Learn anything interesting?"

Carlie recalled Kim's commentary about him. "You were on the cover of *Time*. And you've been linked to the World Health Organization's Opal Jean." Opal was one of those women other women wanted to be like, with her effortless supermodel looks and sky-high IQ; she spent her life caring for global refugees and advocating for youth causes.

He laughed. "And you freaked out when I sent you a picture."

Cheeks heating, she threw back, "You have to admit, it was a little forward, right?"

"You don't get anywhere in this world without being forward, Carlie."

She weighed his words and considered how different he was proving to be from her first impression. His dark blonde tresses slid down, shielding his eyes from view, but she could feel he was watching her. He unconsciously lifted a hand to slide his hair back, and she was rewarded with the glow of his crystalline green eyes, a few shades lighter than emerald, like late spring grass. What was happening? When did his looks cease being those of a playboy heartthrob and more of a regular man, albeit a flirtatious, insanely cute, green-eyed, devilish man?

Stop it, Carlie. This was just lunch and talking about careers. It didn't mean anything.

But maybe it did. Was she so wrong about him?

Their food arrived, and she was delighted to discover the sloppy goodness of the Chicago Italian beef. After demolishing the first half, she stared with heart eyes at the remaining half of the sandwich.

Kurt watched with amusement, eyes widening as she licked the juice off her thumb. She laughed inwardly, wondering if she should play it up. Then she decided against it as her thoughts returned to Alex. God. What should she do now? She smothered her thoughts, but Kurt noticed her change in demeanor.

"You good?"

She made a conscious effort to brighten up. "Oh, yeah. Just figured I ought not to make myself sick by devouring the rest of this."

"I'd say leave a little room for dessert. Theirs is pretty epic." He pushed his own plate away and signaled for the waitress.

They splurged and shared a slice of cheesecake after the sandwiches, and Kurt entertained her with stories from some of his failed ventures. "You owned a flower shop?" She laughed and tried to picture Kurt with gardening gloves and pruning shears, putting together a perfect arrangement stem by stem. A big floppy hat covering his golden head.

He winked. "I guess I don't have the greenest of thumbs." He handed his credit card to the waitress, and she walked away.

"You don't have to buy my lunch," she protested.

"Sure I do. Now, I can say I bought you your first real Chicago meal."

She thought about the lunch with Alex but remained silent on the topic. No harm in letting Kurt believe otherwise.

"Thank you." She smiled.

They climbed the stairs out of the restaurant and turned back toward the hotel. "I owe you an apology," Carlie said, tilting her head to look up at him as they strolled side by side.

"What do you mean?"

"I don't think I was fair to you when we first met. I'm pretty good at reading people, and I definitely misjudged your character. It wasn't very nice of me, and I'm sorry."

He didn't respond right away. Instead, he looked up at the buildings around them, as if admiring the architecture. "See these buildings? These were built by men who risked their lives to raise the city. That hot dog vendor over there? He's willing to stand in the stormiest of weather to make a living. Me? I've made a career of being a flirt and using my connections to get to the next level, always watching for the next opportunity. I don't think you misjudged me," Kurt said, looking back at her. "You've just decided that's not all I am."

Lifting a hand to his face, she stared searchingly into his eyes. "I think you underestimate yourself." She raised up on her toes to press a light kiss to his cheek.

He covered her hand with his own and leaned into the light kiss. He turned his face and captured her lips, scrambling her thoughts as his tongue swirled across hers before he withdrew just as quickly. Kurt stepped back and removed her hand from his face, keeping it wrapped in his own. He cleared his throat and started walking. "We should probably get back."

Outwardly she knew she appeared calm, but internally she was awhirl. He kissed her. Did she start it? No, she was just going to kiss his cheek. But he kissed her. And she enjoyed it. What did that mean? She couldn't analyze this now, not with him still holding her hand. *Think of something else, Carlie. Anything else!*

"When do you give your talk?" she asked, breaking the lingering silence.

"Tomorrow after lunch. The worst time. Everyone will be in their post-lunch digestive comas, wishing the day were over already. You?"

"Thursday morning," she replied as her phone vibrated. A text from Kim lit up the screen: *He said he lost his phone. Buy it?* She rolled her eyes and slid the phone back into her pocket. Owen was trying to make amends with Kim. Of course.

"Everything okay?"

"Yes, just relationship drama," she groaned.

"Yours?" he asked.

She found herself opening up to him, giving more of an honest answer than she would normally have done. "No, my best friend. She's in a perpetual on-and-off cycle with this guy."

"And you don't approve?"

"Oh, he's nice enough, and they're both otherwise unattached..."

"But...?" Kurt prodded when she trailed off.

"But they need to figure this out for themselves. Kim is very assertive and aggressive in all areas of her life, but she either doesn't think she deserves more or is deluding herself about Owen. Either way, I am so tired of their back-and-forth drama."

"Maybe the drama is what defines their relationship."

"I don't know. But she's always there for me, and she deserves better."

He stopped walking and looked down at her. "I think we eventually find the right person, but we have to be willing to make the difficult choices."

She stared at him, sure that she was reading far too

much into this conversation. Shaking her head, she decided to take it at simple face value. "Well, I can't make the choices for her, so I just have to support her."

He started walking again. "Sometimes being there, offering support, is the best thing you can do until she makes up her mind."

Carlie thought back to this morning. "Perhaps," she murmured as they entered the hotel.

16

*S*lipping back to her room before the afternoon sessions, Carlie figured she owed Kim a call. And she could honestly use a few minutes to sort out her own head.

Call? she texted Kim.

Gimme 5, she replied.

Opening Instagram, Carlie saw a new photo of Rachael and one of her friends eating lunch together at a fondue place. The caption read, "You can't come here without getting the chocolate. Life is too short XOXO." She smiled at her sister's philosophy. And it didn't hurt that Rachael could eat whatever she liked and remain a perfect size six. Or four, she amended. Tapping the heart to like the photo, Carlie closed the app before eyeing her own figure in the mirror. "Strong hourglass," Marie had told her once. She thought she was a bit too full of minutes to call it an hour, and definitely too tall. Maybe she was an hour and fifteen. And with her love of food, she was never going to be a supermodel, ha! It was a good thing she had gotten her dad's height and that she enjoyed running. Otherwise, she'd be closer to an hour and a half.

The phone's chirping mercifully interrupted her personal critique session. She answered automatically.

"I missed you at lunch today. Have something better to do?"

Alex.

"Oh, you know. After my morning, I wasn't in the mood to hang out with the masses." God, she was so screwed if they started comparing notes.

"Coming to my session this afternoon?" he asked.

"Wouldn't miss it," she said, perhaps a bit too brightly.

The call waiting signaled. "Home is calling on the other line. See you down there in a bit, Alex."

"I'll be looking for you. See you soon. Dinner tonight?"

"Maybe. Have to run. See you in a few," she added before switching over to Kim.

"What up, lady?" Kim's voice burst out from the phone. She was clearly in a much better mood than last night.

"You know—trying to figure out if the world as I know it is a complete mirage. But otherwise good," she said. "You work things out with Owen?"

"Oh, Carlie. He did lose his phone. He stopped by my office this afternoon with his new phone and to grovel at my feet." She sighed happily.

"I'm going to trust you know what you're doing," Carlie replied, not wanting to agree or disagree with her comment.

"How are things going with Mr. Writer?"

"Well," she drawled. "He's definitely interesting, but now I'm not so sure about things." She filled her in on the morning's drama and how they had decided to start fresh.

"Hmm... I don't know about this, Car. He sounds like a wolf in sheep's clothing."

"He did apologize," she added. "And while it wasn't groveling at my feet with his new phone, ahem, I believe he really hates that he hurt me with his writing."

Silence filled the line.

"Touché," Kim replied. "Too bad your other option took off for greener pastures."

"About that... turns out they're just friends. And he's not quite the same person I thought he was."

"The plot thickens. Inquiring minds want to know—what are you going to do, CarCar?"

"Right now? I'm going to get washed up and head back down to the conference. After that, I have no freaking clue."

"Which one do you like? I mean, I'm wondering if I should be, like, Team Edward or Team Jacob," she teased.

"Isn't that the question *du jour*," Carlie responded. "Talk soon, Kim. Love you, girl."

"You too, babe. Good luck!"

"Thanks."

She ended the call and finished getting ready for the next set of sessions. *Deep breath, Car. Just play it as it comes.*

"...it's his third *New York Times* bestseller and winner of the National Fresh Perspectives Award. Please join me in welcoming Alex Williams," bubbled Melanie at the microphone.

Alex walked to the podium to a round of enthusiastic applause.

"It should be illegal to be that handsome," breathed Rita.

"I'll second that," agreed Paul.

"He is incredibly attractive, isn't he?" Carlie said.

A large screen behind the podium filled with a Power-Point slide titled "Marketing: Facts and Fiction." Though Alex had yet to begin talking, Rita had her notebook out and pen in hand to continue her dictation services. A few rows behind Carlie, Kurt sat and watched Alex closely, Lane next to him. Guess he hadn't been able to shake her this time. Car searched his features, realizing he was every bit as handsome as Alex, but in a more casual, California way. He caught her looking at him and winked playfully at her. She gave a little wave then turned back to watch Alex.

"Thank you for having me," Alex began at the mic. He launched into a summary of current marketing practices and examined each for their role in expanding the gap between traditional values, as well as their impact on socioeconomic dynamics. "I'm not suggesting we should be living a *Leave It to Beaver* lifestyle, but the continued need to capture attention and market share by leveraging excessive use of sex, violence, and drugs is deadening our natural urge to find ways to overcome these societal dangers. We now see teenagers and young adults flocking to lifestyles that put their very existence in jeopardy."

She listened to his well-researched and passionate plea for a common-sense base of morality to guide their work. Surprisingly, Carlie agreed with much of his presentation, but she was still troubled that he likened what she and her family did to this degradation of moral boundaries.

"We'll now take some questions. Please wait until Lane or I hand you a microphone, so we can all hear your brilliant questions," announced Melanie.

Lane and Melanie walked up and down the aisles as they facilitated the question-and-answer session. Carlie had begun to tune out when she heard a familiar voice. "You often use a personal moral compass as a way to trivialize the work of many in this room," said Kurt.

Shots fired?

Carlie swiveled in her seat to better see his now-impassive face. Yet his burning green eyes hinted at the direction he was moving.

"I've read some of your books," he continued. "And while I appreciate the sentiment, I wonder if you've considered how your words impact those who have spent entire careers devoted to the craft. How do you justify linking questionable relationships for your own financial gain?"

Deafening silence flooded the room.

"Thank you, Mr. Hunter. I understand we have much in common in that respect." Alex smiled from the podium. The smile quite possibly hid a snarl. "However, I am not in the business of buying others' work for my own gain, but rather analyzing how current activities are relegating personal beliefs and values to sideline considerations. I am fortunate to make a living from my research and writing. I believe the educated reader is quite capable of seeing the rationale behind such correlations and see for themselves how strongly one affects the other."

Confused, Carlie looked back and forth between these two wolves. Was that an actual question? And a real reply? She'd need to replay that a few times to get something besides the palpable animosity between the two.

Melanie quickly handed her microphone to the next attendee to ask their question and Kurt returned to his seat, catching her eye as he did so. Carlie raised her brow in question. He shook his head and sat.

"Wonder what that was all about," whispered Rita, gesturing back at Kurt, now making his way out of the room.

"I don't know," she mumbled.

Carlie turned back to the front and watched as Alex deftly handled the remaining questions, having smoothly moved on from the confrontation.

17

"What did you think?" asked Alex, bounding down the aisle to greet her. He sat in Rita's empty chair and draped his arm across the back of Carlie's seat.

"I think you are very passionate about your work, and you are a great speaker," she replied before glancing down at her hands clasped in her lap.

He tipped her chin up so their eyes met. "Why do I feel like you just sidestepped my question?"

She shrugged.

Alex moved on. "Which breakout session are you off to next?"

"I don't know. This group of sessions doesn't hold much for me."

"Want to take a walk?"

His eyes were warm and his smile genuine. Seemed like a good opportunity to figure out if he was serious about a fresh start.

"Sure. Let me go change my shoes."

Alex politely waited in the hall while she popped into her room.

"Ready." She smiled. "Where to?"

They stepped out into the warming afternoon. The rain and clouds were on a temporary hiatus, allowing the sun to shine through. Alex led her away from the hotel. They enjoyed the wash of sunlight for a while before he mentioned the elephant in the room. "What's going on with you and Kurt?"

She stumbled briefly before regaining her feet. Keeping her eyes focused straight ahead, she considered how to respond. "I don't know," she finally answered.

"What do you mean, 'I don't know'?"

"I mean, I don't know," Carlie replied, exasperated. "I've known both of you for all of three days. I don't know what you expect me to say right now."

They continued walking, and she struggled to think of something, anything else to talk about. Three days ago, her biggest issues were trying to survive wedding planning with Rachael and putting Brent and Gina out of her mind. Zero love interests in her life. But she had known exactly who she was and where she was going.

Now? She was a hot mess.

"Fair enough," he said. "Me and you, though... This is something good."

He turned another corner, and they approached Lake Michigan. A small stretch of beach lay across the way on the other side of the road. They stopped at the crosswalk and joined the trickle of pedestrians crossing over to the sandy shore, slowly filling as others took advantage of the sunshine. "This is nice." She inhaled, savoring the fresh air blowing in from the water. "I've been wanting to get out here."

Alex guided her to a small bench where they could watch the waves slide up and down the shore. He tugged her closer, and she leaned against him, his arm wrapping around her. He smelled divine, and it all just felt so...right. She felt safe. Carlie breathed deeply and watched the seagulls circle the shore, the squawking mass hoping the humans brought seeds or bread. Her hair and her emotions stirred as he exhaled and pressed a kiss to the side of her head, and she burrowed closer, soaking in his warmth to banish the light chill from the blowing wind.

Her thoughts turned to Kurt, and she stiffened a little. Where had he gone?

"You okay?" Alex murmured against her temple.

Carlie returned to the present and glanced into his blue eyes, so focused on her. "I'm fine."

His lips twisted, but he pressed on. "What are your plans after this week?"

"Back to Cincinnati. Have to get back to the office on Monday. You?"

"Minneapolis for a few book stops and speaking engagements. Back to reality, I guess. I don't often get the luxury of spending a whole week at one conference."

They sat in silence, watching the people, birds, and water conduct a timeless dance, swaying back and forth with the tide. Carlie considered what his life must be like, hotel after hotel, city after city. It seemed lonely.

"Do you always tour like this?"

"Not always. Typically only when a new book drops— maybe a month or two each year. Then there's the campus tours, which can be unpredictable. Beyond those it's more private speaking engagements or back to my place to work on the next book, and the cycle continues. Not much of a life, right?"

"Do you like it?"

When he didn't respond right away, she turned back to see his expression. Stoic, he watched the water another moment longer before answering. "I like writing, making a difference. And I suppose I used to love the traveling, the places, the people. Now it definitely feels like work. Trying to remember which city I'm in, wondering if anyone will show up to my next gig. It's exhausting. But I'm lucky. Many writers don't get to do all this." He gestured around them. "At least, that's what I tell myself."

From under his arm, she considered the weariness lining his face. Her heart clenched at his forlorn expression. "I'm glad I met you, Alex." She nudged his side, trying to cheer him up. And she was. He was soulful and had deep convictions. He believed in what he did.

He looked down, his eyes dropping to her mouth. He inched down and kissed her. "I am, too."

Turning her face up to his, she returned the kiss, sensing his hesitation, his nerves. The unconcealed insecurity affected her, melting away her questions, her remaining reservations.

Butterflies stirred in her stomach, flitting like mad as his blue eyes heated with desire. A light rain began to fall, and he stood, pulling her to her feet.

Alex hailed a taxi and held the door open for her. She knew what would happen if she got in the taxi. He waited patiently, letting her decide. She took a deep breath and entered ahead of him while he communicated with the driver. When he dropped into the seat, he pulled her against his side, watching her. The desire in his eyes had not faded, and she suspected hers looked the same. How was she so attracted to him? She barely knew him.

At the hotel, she allowed him to sweep her along. A crowd of people entered the elevator with them. He hit the button for their floor and leaned against the rear corner of the elevator, tugging her hand to position her in front of him. Her back to him, she swallowed a surprised gasp as his hand snaked about her waist, plastering her against him so she could feel every inch of his desire building. Drawing circles and seductive patterns across her abdomen, he possessively gripped her hip with his other hand and dipped his head to nuzzle behind her ear. Lost in sensation, she fell into him, allowing him to sample her neck as his hands continued their mesmerizing study of her curves. She bit her lip to keep from sighing aloud, though no one seemed to be paying attention to the pair in the corner.

The elevator stopped several times on the way up, until it was just the two of them. "Thank God," he murmured, as he grasped her shoulders to spin her about.

Her mind flitted back to her dream, the passionate embrace they'd shared in her mind. Smiling, she lifted her chin as he trapped her against the elevator wall. His teeth grazed along her chin before his lips sought hers, which he claimed with a thorough kiss. The elevator swished open, and Alex drew her out, bypassing her room as he led her straight to his. He slid his card into the slot, and the light turned green. He ripped open the door and tossed the key card on the desk before turning back to her.

Alex paused, searching her face. She knew this was madness, but she wanted it. It had been nearly ten months since she'd been intimate with a man, and she needed this. With him. She nodded and a relieved smile fleetingly lit his face. His hands worked the hair tie out of her knot, and her hair fell in long golden caramel waves around her shoulders. He picked up a lock and twirled it around his fingers, inhaling the fragrance before releasing it and sliding his hands down her arms. "Say you want this," he whispered hoarsely against her hair.

Instead of replying, she pulled his head down to hers, brushing his warm lips with hers as she wrapped her arms around his neck. He caged his arms around her and kissed her with an intense passion, his tongue exploring as he increased the pressure against her back. Unable to resist, she squirmed against him, wiggling closer and feeling his body tighten in response.

He lifted her into the air, surprising a giggle from her, and unceremoniously dropped her on the bed with a smirk. "Alex!" she squealed, before crooking her finger and encouraging him to follow. Settling on his heels beside her, he tugged her shirt from her waistband, sliding the light sweater up and over her chest and head. He held his breath as the material rode upward, revealing her satin bra and curves swelling up over the cups.

"God, Carlie. You're fucking perfect," he swore, before tossing her shirt aside and pressing hot kisses to the tops of her breasts.

She pulled at his shirt, trying to focus on the buttons until the shirt spread open, revealing his broad, muscular chest sprinkled with a dusting of black hair. He pulled back and dropped his shirt onto the ground before reaching around to unhook her bra. The satin flew across the floor, and his satisfied smile elicited a matching one from her. Sitting back and stretching his legs out, he tumbled her onto his lap so she straddled him. Their mouths fused together, and they each explored the wealth of deliciously exposed skin. Carlie traced her hands over the long, muscular lines of his back, fingers dancing and teasing out his responding twitches, before bringing them up to trail through his cropped black hair.

His hands massaged up and down her back, cradling her head in one hand and letting the other explore her body. The warm palm came to rest on her breast, cupping the weight of it and teasing her nipple, working it to a nearly painful peak. He relinquished her mouth, shifting her higher in his lap as his mouth replaced his hand. His tongue swirled around the tight bud, and his hands grasped her hips, holding her in place while he worked his tongue around in heavenly wicked ways, finally closing his lips around her nipple and biting down before suckling deeply. She moaned as the tension grew and a thread of pleasure raced between her nipple and core. Her shudder evidently amused him as he grinned and moved his attention to her other breast. She arched toward him, circling her hips over his while he worked his magic with his mouth. His body was firm and tight, straining to reach further, bring them closer.

"Fuck, I need you," he breathed before capturing her mouth, removing all thoughts of the world. Nothing existed beyond this room, this bed.

Keeping her wrapped around his waist, he rolled over, pressing her into the soft mattress. The firm weight of him pushed against her, and she kicked her shoes off behind his back, a pair of clunking thuds the only noise as they hit the floor. His mouth trailed a path down her stomach while he unbuttoned her pants, teasing them lower as he chased the receding fabric with wet open-mouthed kisses. Satisfied at last when the final article of her clothing hit the floor, he unbuttoned his own pants and slid off the bed to remove them. His enlarged member sprang to attention the moment he released it. Alex turned to the desk, lifted a bag from the floor, rummaged, and returned with a strip of condoms. Watching with interest, she rose to her knees to assist him.

Carlie tore a package open, pulling out the rubbery disk. He jerked and throbbed as she grasped him, the rest of his body frozen as she ran her fingers up and down the velvety skin. She heard his swift intake of breath and smiled. With painstaking slowness, she rolled the sheath down his considerable length before sliding her hands back up his chest and tugging him back down onto the bed with her. "I want you," she whispered.

He groaned as he ran his hands over her body, leaving no spot untouched, unclaimed. He devoured her ear, her neck, her chest and inched down the bed, pressing kisses to her hip bones, then grazing her thatch of curls. She grabbed at his shoulders. "Alex, kiss me."

He readily obliged and returned upward to reclaim her flushed lips. While their kiss erupted, his roving hand ran along the inside of her thigh until it encountered the moist junction. She gasped as he ran a finger back and forth along the outer folds, before slipping into the slick silk beneath. He circled his thumb around the sensitive nub at the top while the rest of his hand teased and caressed, one long finger pressing into her passage. She flexed and moved her hips in time to his movements while his thumb continued to issue waves of pleasure. Back and forth, in and out, circling and teasing.

Carlie gasped as the sensations built. "You like that," he said, grinning against her cheek. He added a second finger, and she moaned at the new fullness. Needing to touch him, she reached down and grazed his sides before slipping between them to caress his hard length. She wrapped a hand around him and slowly moved it up and down, the encased skin becoming steely.

"You're sure?" he panted, his darkened blue eyes betraying his unraveling control.

"Yes," she breathed, wrapping her arms around his neck. He used his knees to spread her legs farther apart, positioning his thick head at her entrance. He paused then watched her face as he eased his hips forward, their bodies meeting where they both wanted the other to be. Carlie gasped at the expected intrusion, and he stopped briefly, allowing her to adjust before pushing in further.

"More," she sighed. "Yes."

Alex smiled, his eyes an indigo tempest as he receded then filled her again slowly, sliding back then plunging home, her body rising to meet him. Eyes locked on one another, they started to move, gently at first, then increasing as the urgency built. She grasped his hips, matching his movements and tilting her pelvis so she could rub her tingling clit against him, grinding relentlessly. His mouth feasting on her neck and breasts, she closed her eyes and focused on the sensations, the friction, the heat building. Carlie gasped as he shifted, his pace faster and thrusts harder. He sealed his mouth over hers, drinking her in. The tightness at her core verged on pain, unbearable. Her skin was alive with burning sensitivity, heat.

"Christ, I don't have much longer," he said against her ear. "I'm almost there." Biting his neck, she urged him on.

He drove deeper into her, each thrust moving them higher up the bed, the damp sheets unmoored from the mattress. Her abs tightened, and she matched him, stirred by the coarseness of his hair rasping across her breasts, her clit. The roaring built in her ears, her eyes lost focus, and the edge neared. Nothing else mattered or existed in her world as she shattered around him. An explosion of color and light filled her mind, leaving her gasping as she rolled along the waves of ecstasy.

"I'm... I... I can't stop," he panted. He groaned her name as he gave a last forceful push and buried himself, holding her to him in a bruising grip. His pulsing, throbbing release triggered more waves to spread through her. "Holy shit," he gasped, collapsing onto her.

---

18

*S*tretched next to each other on their backs, they unhurriedly returned to life, their breath slowing to normal and bodies cooling. Alex trailed a hand over her arm, noting the raised gooseflesh, and pulled the discarded sheet up to cover her.

"That was...incredible," he said, his hand caressing her abdomen under the blanket.

"Mmhmm," she agreed, sated and relaxed in his arms.

Carlie rolled onto her side, looking down at his face. With his eyes closed, she traced her finger along the ridge of his forehead, the straight edge of his nose, the fullness of his lips, the stubble on his chin.

"You'll put me to sleep doing that," he murmured with a smile, his eyes still closed.

She leaned up to kiss his jaw, then scooted to the edge of the bed.

"Where are you going?" he asked, slitting open one eye.

"I need to get dressed," she said, looking around the room to take stock of where her belongings ended up. Picking up her slacks and underwear, she squealed in surprise when he grabbed her from behind and swept her beneath him on the bed.

"And why is that?" he asked, planting kisses beneath her ear, trailing more along her collarbone.

"Alex!" she squeaked as he began to tickle her sides, his mouth moving lower to kiss the pale, soft skin between her breasts.

He looked up from his work, a devilish glint to his eyes. "And if I decide to keep you here?"

She sighed and lay back on the pillows as he pampered her with his mouth and hands.

"Alex?"

"Hmmm?"

"What are we doing? Can this even work out?"

He paused his exploration. "What do you mean?"

She hesitated, not wanting to ruin the moment but unable to stop herself. "I mean, we both go our separate ways after this week. You'll be off to Minnesota, and I'll head back to Ohio. Your schedule is unpredictable, and my work is too demanding."

He scrubbed his hands down his face, considering her words. "Why focus on that now, Carlie? Let's enjoy the time we have together and worry about tomorrow, tomorrow. I am perfectly content at the moment. Better than content, actually."

Frowning, she sat up again and resumed pulling her clothes together. He didn't stop her this time. She tracked down the last of her clothes and walked to the restroom to wash up and dress. When she came out, he was standing by the bed in a loose pair of sweatpants, pulling the duvet up from the floor. She watched him, unsure of what to do next. That was the problem, she considered. She had too much running around her head.

"I need to go back to my room for a little bit, catch up on some work," she said.

He turned to her, wary. "You okay?"

"Yeah, I just need a few minutes to process everything. This has all happened so fast. I need to breathe."

He crossed the room and wrapped her in his arms before pressing a lingering kiss to her lips. "Dinner tonight?"

She smiled. "Meet me at the bar around seven?"

"Sounds like a date," he replied.

Collecting her handbag, Alex beat her to the door by a breath. He stood at the doorjamb and watched her return to her room.

She sent an exaggerated wink before slipping into her room. His responding chuckle echoed as he closed his door.

Leaning back against her door, Carlie sighed and slid to the floor. *Holy moly. That was amazing. But what in the hell am I doing?*

She needed to meditate to calm her mounting anxiety, but the bathroom beckoned first. A long, hot shower was the prescription for any ailment. Maybe it didn't offer a full cure, but it helped with the symptoms. Wrapping her hair in a towel and climbing onto the bed with a fresh, cold bottle of water, she sat and embraced the silence.

Her computer and phone waited, the television asked to be turned on, but she craved the unplugged silence. Breathing deeply, she crossed her legs and closed her eyes.

Clear your mind. Clear your thoughts. Clear your anxiety.

She batted away the many questions that tried to infiltrate her peace; this was her time. Her recharge. Inhale. Exhale. Focus.

I am whole. I am present. I am grounded.

Eventually she began to lighten, calm. Too much stimulation, too many distractions, too much...everything. Others didn't often understand this about her. Brent never understood. As a solid introvert, Carlie required "me time." She needed to fill her own cup. She needed her space, isolation. These were the moments when she allowed herself the freedom to drift so she could defragment and pull herself back together. It was one of the many techniques her various doctors had recommended over the years that actually worked. As long as she could meditate and work out, she could avoid panic attacks.

Eyes opened, she assessed her current disparate thoughts.

First off, Alex. He was incredible. She craved him. No other man had ever affected her this way. Lord knew Brent had never done so. At least not in a good way. But she couldn't see a future with Alex. He was constantly on the move. It felt like a tease, and it was frustrating that he didn't have more of a connection to her world. Dare she go with the flow? She needed to steel herself so she wouldn't get hurt. But it was probably too late for that.

Kurt. She should talk to him, find out what had triggered his outburst at Alex's session. While she admired his desire to break things into the open, she worried he was doing so without considering how it could hurt future opportunities. Under all that machismo, there were glimpses of a man who was caring and empathetic, funny and selfless. She wasn't naïve; she knew he wanted more, and she was attracted to him (that kiss!), but he was most definitely not her type. Especially given how things were going with Alex, there couldn't be a future there either. She had made her decision.

Kim. And Owen. Back together. How many more times could she watch them go down this chaotic path? Carlie loved her dearly, but this mess could not be what Kim wanted, could it? Should she continue to sit by and watch her best friend whip around in this bumper car? Or was Kurt right—was the drama part of their identity?

Rachael. Her sister knew how to push Carlie's buttons better than anyone without even trying. But Carlie needed to try harder. Rachael was her sister, and this would be, presumably, her one and only wedding. Who cared if she let go of another acclaimed professional for disagreeing with her? It was her day. While patience had never been Carlie's strong suit, she vowed to make more of an effort. She would be there for her.

Work. Alex's comments bothered her more than she let on. She loved her job, piecing together what made people tick and how they could deliver the right content at the right time to the right people. But how could she balance what she was doing with helping others? Bernie could be the key here. Carlie needed to talk to Dad and the Brians about this. What could EHL do to help make a difference? The seed had been planted.

Taking another deep breath, she stretched and stood up. Having a clearer head helped, but it didn't answer the lingering questions and doubt. She shook her head, grabbed her idle computer, and turned on some instrumental piano music before responding to the unending buildup of emails.

Later, satisfied with her progress personally and professionally, she glanced at the clock and was surprised to see it was after six already. Looking at the limited options in her closet, she selected a red wrap dress and black heels, then sighed in defeat as she stared at the tangled mess that was her hair. Where was Marie when she needed her?

19

*W*ashed, dressed, and refreshed, Carlie slipped out the door a little early. The faces in the bar were becoming more familiar after a couple of days together. She eased into a seat at the bar and saw the orange tickets were up tonight. The bartender held up the bottle of vanilla vodka with a questioning look. She smiled and nodded, relieved that no words were necessary. Leaving the drink ticket and tip on the bar, she settled at an empty table off to the side. She checked her phone and saw a missed call from her dad. She sent him a text.

In a crowd, can't talk now. Everything okay?

Yes, honey. You know I hate texting. Call when you can.

He ran a major global marketing technology company and still didn't text. Carlie shook her head and flipped to Twitter, checking her favorite hashtags and conversations to catch up. She hadn't cared much for this platform at first, but now it was where she turned first to find breaking news and catch whiffs of any upcoming trends or trouble. She retweeted a few items she wanted to go back and re-read more closely, then closed the app. It was 7:10, and she was still alone at the table. She smirked, thinking that sounded awfully close to a bad country song.

"Mind if I join you?" piped up a young voice.

"Please do," Carlie returned, watching Melanie take a seat. They chatted briefly and when the silence stretched, Carlie eyed the young blonde thoughtfully. "I hope you don't mind my asking, but what's the deal with you and Lane?"

Melanie's nose wrinkled in disgust. "Just between us, right? She hates me. When we were checking into the hotel, she hinted that she wanted to hook up with Kurt. I go way back with him—just friends, you know, nothing like *that*— so she thought I'd help her with some insider info. I laughed and told her it wasn't going to happen. Lane got all pissy and has been a general bitch ever since."

Carlie nodded in sympathy, recalling Lane's bizarre behavior toward herself previously.

Melanie scanned the room, looking a little uncomfortable. "Speaking of Kurt, you haven't seen him lately, have you?"

"No, not since this afternoon's, uh, presentation. Why?"

She frowned, then met Carlie's eyes. "I heard from the front desk that he checked out."

Oh. "Did he say why he left? Probably something came up...?"

"No. I know he was spending time with you." She blushed. "So, I thought you might know."

"Do you know when he left?"

"It wasn't too long ago. Maybe an hour?"

Carlie drummed her fingers on the table and took another drink, mulling over what could have happened. It couldn't have anything to do with her, right? "Isn't his presentation tomorrow?"

She shrugged and craned her neck, surveying the room again.

Well, then...

"Would you like me to try to get ahold of him? Though I'm not sure that would do much," Carlie offered.

A relieved smile lit her face. "If you could, that would be appreciated." Carlie was baffled by Melanie's confidence, but she picked up her handbag and walked to the lobby. "Watch my drink for me, will you?"

"Will do," she bubbled.

Catching Alex's eye as he entered the lobby, Carlie waved him onward. "I have to make a call, but go on in. Melanie's sitting at the table." He nodded and entered the bar. *Oh crap, please don't let her tell him who I'm calling.* She doubted that would go over well.

Sinking into a plush sofa in the corner, she stared at her phone, biting her thumbnail. What could she even say? *Hey, Kurt! Did you freak out and leave town?* Ugh. She pulled up the number he had programmed into her phone and hit the call button. What if he didn't pick up? What if he did? The call went straight to voicemail. Carlie hung up without leaving a message. Either he was avoiding her, or his phone was off. Plan B. She opened her email and found the message he sent her. She hit reply and sent off a short note to see if he would be here for his presentation tomorrow. That was all she could do on that front.

As long as she was out here, she decided to return Dad's call. Dutiful daughter and all that. "Charles Eller, at your service," he answered. She laughed at his cheesy greeting, fully aware she was far too much like him.

"Hi, Dad," she groaned.

"How is my little Carlie-Q?"

"I'm fine. Just checking out a networking social."

"Meet anyone interesting? Say, Bernard Bartlett?"

"Bernie? Yes! I wanted to talk to you about that. He's such an amazing person, Dad. You wouldn't believe the stories he had to tell. I wish we could have had more time to chat."

"You'll get that opportunity, honey. He invited us to his estate in Atlanta. I've asked my assistant to clear your and your sister's schedules for next weekend so we can all go."

"Great! I hope Rebecca is fine with me leaving again so soon."

"Rebecca is fully capable of running that entire department. If she weren't, she wouldn't be in that position. She'll be fine without you for another few days."

"Days?"

"Yes, we'll leave Wednesday and return Sunday. Of course, if you have other plans...?"

"Nope, that sounds great." And it did. She couldn't remember the last time the Ellers had taken a trip together, just the four of them.

"Perfect. Your sister and Rick will be getting a room, your mother and I another. I thought you might see if Kim wants to join us so you two girls could share a room."

Correction. The five of them. Or six.

"I'll check with her."

"Just let Tammy know," he said, referring to his assistant.

"Will do. Love you, Dad!"

"Love you too, Carlie-Q."

She sat for another moment, checking her email to see if Kurt had replied, but nothing new appeared. She didn't know him all that well, but she was disappointed. Did he leave because he felt embarrassed? That didn't seem like him. Though maybe she was wrong; she had been wrong about him before.

Giving up, she returned to the bar where Melanie and Alex were laughing like teenagers. Sliding into her seat, she looked back and forth until they clued her in. "He was telling me about his book signing in Syracuse while he had a cold. Did a reading and question and answer session while under the influence!" Melanie explained.

"Cold medicine," he added. "Let's say I'm not terribly proud of that day, and I also maybe don't recall exactly what I said, so..." He trailed off into more laughter.

An irrational small knot of worry started to form in her stomach, and Carlie was having trouble joining in the laughter. "I'm going to get another drink. Need anything?"

"We're good. Want me to get it for you?"

"No, I've got it." She waved him back into his seat. "Be right back."

Tripping over a chair leg on her way, she caught herself on the back of a barstool. Shit. She rubbed her ankle and hopped up onto the barstool, hoping no one saw that.

The bartender hurried over. "You okay?"

So much for not being seen. "Perfect," she grumbled.

"Surprised to see him back down here so soon," he said, gesturing to her table.

"Oh?"

"Yeah, he was down here with your other friend a little while ago. They really got into it."

Huh. Interesting. "Was it the other guy we were sitting with the other night?"

"Blonde fella? Pretty boy? Yeah, that was him. They seemed friendly enough that night, but not so much today. Another vanilla and diet?"

"Yes, please," she mumbled, processing this new info.

Kurt and Alex had been down here? Fighting? She

glanced back to Alex, who was still laughing with Melanie. What on earth?

She thanked him and returned to the table, watching Alex more carefully. Melanie leaned over and said, "Any luck?"

Carlie shook her head no and slumped back in her seat. *Why can't anything just be simple?*

Melanie saw another friend enter the bar and excused herself.

"Thank God," Alex groaned when she was across the room. "She's driving me crazy."

He reached over and tugged the arm of her chair, sliding it closer to him. She tried not to think about the bartender's comments and just enjoy the moment. He leaned over to press a kiss to her lips, and she wanted to sink into it. She really tried. But it wasn't working.

"Carlie?"

"Hmm?"

"You're being quiet."

"Yeah, lost in thought I guess."

He watched her for a minute, then leaned closer. "You look amazing," he breathed into her ear. "I really enjoyed our time together today. That's not what's bothering you, is it?"

"No, that's not it. I'm just...thinking."

"Care to share?"

"I heard something strange." She leaned forward to turn toward him, wanting to see his expression. "Were you in here a little while ago with Kurt?"

He looked away and picked up his drink, not answering.

Carlie waited, willing him to answer, to say it wasn't him. She wanted the bartender to be wrong.

After a long drink, he leaned back in his seat and exhaled. "I was."

"And...?"

"And what? I came down here to grab a drink and Kurt happened to be here too. We had some words, and he left."

"That's all?"

"That's all."

She glanced down at her phone, refreshing her inbox. Still nothing.

"What did you two talk about?"

"Christ, Carlie. What is this, twenty questions?"

Defensive much? She leaned back, wondering at this side of him. It was eerily reminiscent of some of the arguments she'd had with Brent before she found out he'd been cheating on her. She sipped her drink and tried to ignore the growing knot in her stomach.

20

*A*lex flagged down one of the waiters and ordered a few appetizers for them to share for dinner. She continued to watch for clues as to what happened, but he never even alluded to it. And really, why did she care? She could imagine what they had argued over; it wasn't a big shock after what happened during Alex's presentation. But still, it was strange that he refused to talk about it.

They dined on spring rolls and calamari, chatting with the various conference attendees who rotated through the lounge. He amused her with stories from his travels, talking about the weird gifts he received from hosts and fans and the religious fanatics who often appeared to thank him or curse him. "People see what they want to see when they read my books. Or they read the summaries and fail to understand the full scope," he said, dipping his spring roll in the tangy sauce.

Was he trying to send a message, buried between the lines? Or was she way overthinking this? Carlie pushed her drink away and dropped her napkin on the plate. "I hate to do this, Alex, but I am not feeling well. Would you mind if we call it an evening?"

Her stomach was legitimately starting to churn. He regarded her with concern. "Let me get the check. I'll walk you up."

"Thanks," she mumbled and rushed into the lobby, hoping the quiet would help.

After an interminable wait, he arrived to walk her to the elevators, at last. She wiped her forearm along her forehead, noting the clamminess and cool skin, the nausea ratcheting up. Ugh. Just what she needed. Alex massaged her shoulders then followed her into the lift. Closing her eyes, her body swayed against the wall. "Whoa, you're really not feeling well, are you?"

She shook her head, then regretted it, keeping her eyes closed until they hit their floor. Carlie trudged to the door and thrust her bag into Alex's hands. He wordlessly located the room's keycard and let her in. She kicked off her shoes and stumbled to the bed, crashing hard. Alex deposited a fresh bottle of water on the nightstand next to her. "Can I get you anything?" he asked, concerned.

"No, I just need to sleep this off, whatever it is."

He leaned over and kissed her cool forehead, then pulled a blanket up over her. "Want me to stay?"

Want to see me throw up? Hells to the no.

"Thank you for asking, but no. You should go back down —you were having fun. Go enjoy the night."

He frowned but nodded reluctantly. "Call or text if you need anything at all. I mean it, Carlie."

"I will. Thank you."

"Good night, Lois Lane," he teased, earning a weak smile.

"Good night, Superman."

He closed the door, and she sat up, debating if she was going to need to haul ass to the restroom. The urgency passed, and she lay back again, considering the evening and piecing together what could have happened.

She dragged herself over and checked her phone. Still nothing from Kurt.

Groaning, she pulled off her dress and scrambled into an oversized T-shirt. Defeated, she crawled into bed, exhausted.

IT'S DARK OUTSIDE, and I'm scared. All alone. The echo of distant footsteps is somewhere behind me, but the darkness is pervasive; I can't see anything.

Reaching my arms straight out at my sides, I hesitantly turn in a circle, fingers grasping—both hoping for and fearing what I might encounter. There's nothing there. I take a tentative step forward and my bare foot touches dry pavement. I inch forward another step, and another, and continue testing, gingerly toeing forward into the unrelenting blackness with each foot before moving.

I don't know where I'm going, or who is following me, but I must hurry. I'm going too slowly. I'm not going to make it in time.

The echoing footsteps sound louder, closer, and my panic is starting to rise. I must find somewhere safe and meditate. I need to breathe. But I need to go faster.

Light. I need light. I reach for my phone, but I'm only wearing my nightshirt. Why didn't I put on pants? Where is my phone?

Without a light, I am forced to keep moving at a snail's pace. My hands stretch out again, testing the space around me, but there's nothing, just vast emptiness.

Yet something is out there. A breeze blows across my right side and I freeze, a whimper escaping my lips. The anxiety cranks up, and I wait. Wait for something to come, to attack. Nothing.

Listening for the footsteps, I estimate how much longer I have. The repetitive thud of heavy limbs eating up the pavement continues to get incrementally closer.

I drop to my hands and knees. I'll be able to move more quickly this way. Scuttling forward, tears begin to dampen my face. Any moment. Any moment and they'll catch me. I'll be caught and never found again. I'll be lost.

My tears dry, and I continue the endless journey. At long last, light peeks over the horizon. As more land becomes visible, I stand and move faster. Blood trickles from countless lacerations on my hands and bare knees, but I keep moving. I have to keep moving.

Closer, the footsteps get louder. Each step is a stab in my gut. I begin running. If I can reach the edge, get to the horizon, I'll be safe. I have to get there.

An unseen crack in the pavement, an otherwise innocuous fissure, catches my foot and I tumble, sprawling flat onto my stomach. I close my eyes. This is not real. This is a dream. But still the echoing gets closer. They, too, are running now. In a panic, I scramble, trying to regain my feet, but I keep falling, the ground beneath me crumbling.

The breathing of my pursuer is now noticeable. They have come too close. I must go. I must get up. I must wake up!

CARLIE JERKED up in her bed, tears streaking down her face. Trembling, she tore the blanket from her struggling limbs and fled to the restroom. The remains of her sparse dinner were no more. After a shuddering breath, she chanced a look at her hands and knees, surprised to find no scratches or blood. Sinking to the cold tile floor, she wiped the tears from her cheeks and leaned back against the tub, forcing herself to breathe. In and out. In and out. Deep breath.

Time returned to normal, and her pulse slowed. Unfolding herself from the bathroom floor, she sat on the toilet lid, staring at her reflection in the mirror.

What is happening to me?

21

*S*omehow, Carlie navigated back to the huge bed and settled into a deep, blessedly dreamless sleep. She awoke hours later, groggy and confused, throat sore, but no longer nauseated. After stretching and waking up fully, she searched for the remote and flipped on a network morning show, scowling at their imitation cheerfulness.

The date and time scrolled across the bottom of the screen, and her thoughts turned to Kurt. Had he returned? Where was he? Would he be here today?

Rubbing her face, she rolled across the bed and searched for her phone on the nightstand. Battery was dead. Fantastic. After plugging it in to let it charge, she immersed herself in a near-scalding shower, washing away the remnants of that horrid night and dream. Pulling on her flannel pants and tank top, Carlie curled up on the bed to see her phone was starting to come back to life. Giving it a few minutes to boot up, she checked her laptop. New emails, of course... But nothing from Kurt. Damn. Why was this eating at her so much? *Don't stress about the things you can't control, Car. Focus on what you can control.*

Her phone resurfaced from the void. She scrolled through some missed texts from Alex. He was worried.

Good thing you didn't stay, she typed, adding the sick-person emoji.

Feeling better? Can I get you some coffee? Breakfast?

She shuddered at the thought of coffee or food just yet. *No thanks, I'm going to quarantine myself here for a while longer and just relax.*

Feel better. I'll stop by during the morning break. Text if I can bring you anything at all.

That was sweet. He really was a good guy. She had been ridiculous last night. Maybe it was guilt over sleeping with someone she didn't know well. Yet. That was going to change, though. Alex was definitely worth getting to know better. She kept her phone on the charger and rolled onto her back, burrowing deeper into bed.

Wednesday. After yesterday's roller coaster, she was ready for a quiet day.

Please be good to me, Wednesday.

As if on cue, her phone rang. She stared at it for a long moment, not sure if she even wanted to know who Wednesday sent calling. *Coward,* she berated herself and glanced at the device, eyes widening at the name on the screen.

"Kurt?" she answered breathlessly.

"Miss me yet?"

"Where are you? Melanie's worried about you."

"Melanie is?"

"Well, we all are. Where are you?" Carlie asked again.

"I had some business matters that couldn't wait. I wasn't sure how long it would take, so I checked out."

"That's it?"

After a hesitation, he replied, "That's it."

"And you still didn't answer me... Where are you?"

"Right now?"

She groaned aloud. "No, last week. Of course, right now, you moron."

"Well, right now I'm about to lose my signal. Call you back."

Jerk. She smirked as she contemplated not answering when he called back. But she needed to answer. She had promised Melanie she'd try to find out if he was going to speak today.

She did feel much lighter, though, one weight lifted. A knock sounded at the door, and she smiled, thinking Alex must not have waited until the break. Opening the door, Carlie was startled to see clear green eyes, messy blonde hair, and a self-confident grin.

"Oh!"

"And good morning to you too," he said, bending in a dramatic bow with a flourish. "May I come in?"

She nodded in confusion and let him in. He surveyed the room. "What happened in here?"

"Ate something that didn't agree with me." She shrugged, trying to disguise her embarrassment. "Barely made it to bed."

He meandered about, picking up her discarded shoes and clothes. Carlie smiled at his actions, wondering if he was a natural neat freak.

"One of these days you're going to give yourself a concussion tripping over these things," he said, holding up one of her black heels. "And don't smile like that, I'm serious."

She tried not to smile but failed miserably. Sinking back down on the bed, Carlie rubbed her temples, still not feeling one hundred percent. Kurt stopped and noted her pallor, concern crossing his face. "How are you now?"

"I've been better. But I'm not going to throw up on you, if that's what you're worried about."

Placing his palm to her forehead, he smiled. "No fever."

"Thank you, doctor," she teased. "Like I said, it was something I ate. I'm feeling better already."

He continued to prowl around the room—was he checking for more hazards? He finally ceased and watched her, a vertical line burrowed between his brows.

After another minute of this, she couldn't take it any longer. "What are you doing? You're weirding me out."

He shook his head and took a deep breath. "I need to ask you something. And I need you to be honest," he said, sitting next to her on the edge of the bed, taking hold of her hand.

It sounded serious. A chill wound its way down her spine, but she gestured for him to continue.

"Did you sleep with him?" he asked.

She gaped at him, withdrawing her hand from his grasp. Surely, she did not hear that correctly. "What?"

"Did you. Have sex. With him?"

Aghast, she wondered if he'd lost his mind. *Wednesday, you're a bitch,* ran through her head. Her fury rose, and she scrambled away from him. What business was it of his?! Who did he think he was?

Undeterred by her visible anger, Kurt continued. "In his room. Did you fuck him?"

She recoiled at his words. "That is *none* of your business!"

He batted her words away. "Apparently it is. I need to know if he was bluffing, Carlie. He told me he has it on video. Tell me the truth. Was he lying?"

Video?

Oh. My. God.

She stared at him, her red haze of anger fading to a pinpoint of blackness as she passed out.

22

Wrapped securely in fluffy blankets, Carlie came to, blissful for a few moments before her memory crashed into place. Closing her eyes again in disbelief, she heard Kurt talking on his phone.

"Keep it quiet. I want an update in one hour, whatever you've got." He cut off the call and leaned forward, his hair falling over his eyes.

"How long have I been out?" she mumbled from her cocoon.

"About ten minutes."

"Oh."

Time was strange. Eleven, maybe twelve minutes ago, her world was confusing but manageable. Now, everything was definitely not okay.

She thought back to Alex's room, recalled how he shifted his bag around before they... That bastard! He had set her up. "What am I going to do?" she whispered, the disbelief and anger giving way to a bleak outlook.

"For now? Nothing. You're going to go on as though

nothing has changed. Alex assumes that I'm gone and you don't know about the video. Let him continue to think that."

"Why? Why would he do this?"

He blew out his breath and looked out the window before returning to her.

"That publishing company I told you about? The one I invested in? It's the publisher for Williams' books. His sales have been declining, and his agent was informed we're terminating the contract."

Carlie absorbed this. "You're Alex's publisher? You know each other?"

"I knew of him, but we had never met. I didn't know who he was when we were first introduced."

"But why all this? Why me?"

He shook his head. "Maybe he saw something. Maybe he thought you and I were... Shit. Maybe it's because you're an Eller. I don't know."

Oh, God. Oh, God. Oh, God. A freaking sex tape? She imagined her mom's reaction. Her dad. Their business. An angry tear ran down her cheek, and she dashed it away. "So, his whole 'American values' talk is complete bullshit? He's going to use me to get ahead?"

"Try to. He's trying to, Carlie. He has not succeeded, and I want to make sure he doesn't. I've already got people working on this. We'll find out what he's doing."

Her nose scrunched up as she attacked the mental jigsaw puzzle. "Why is he going after you with a tape of me? It doesn't make sense..." Voice trailing off, she glanced at him again. "And why are you helping me? You could ignore him and just walk away. This doesn't have to affect you."

He looked uncomfortable enough that she replayed her words. "You *did* walk away." She nodded slowly, fitting together the corner pieces. "But you came back," she said wonderingly. "Why?"

Hands in his pockets, he turned to the window again. "I tried to leave it behind, wash my hands of it and maybe feed a tip to the cops. I didn't want to get involved, and you had made your choice—made your bed, so to speak." She winced at the turn of phrase. "But I'm already involved. And when I got your email, I knew I had to come back. Damn it, I like you, Carlie. You're a good person, and I'm not going to let that asshat use you like this."

"I'm so sorry," she whispered. "I didn't know. I wish I could change what happened." More tears escaped. She let them fall.

A knock sounded at the door.

"Oh God," she whispered in a panic. "It's him. He told me he'd come check on me at the break. What do I do?"

Kurt stood and slipped into the restroom. "Play it cool and get him to leave. Remember, you know nothing about this."

Easier said than done.

Deep breath. In and out. In and out.

He knocked again, louder. "Carlie? You awake in there?"

She could pretend to be asleep. She could simply not answer.

But he'd come back.

Carlie glanced at her blotchy, pasty face in the mirror. She was supposed to be sick, so... Guess she had that going for her.

"Coming," she called hoarsely and grasped the door-knob, opening to face the number-one shithead in her life. *Good for you, Gina and Brent—you've officially been demoted to Things Two and Three.*

He took in her appearance, eyeing her flannel pants,

wrinkled tank top, and red, puffy eyes. "Still not feeling well?" He wrapped his arms around her and kissed the top of her head. Carlie recalled how sweet the gesture was when Rick did that to Rachael. Alex made it feel grimy, foul.

She turned away to hide her grimace. "No. I'm feeling pretty wretched." Totally honest here.

"Can I get you anything, do anything for you? To you?" He followed, squeezing her shoulders possessively before massaging and kissing the sensitive spot where her neck and shoulder met.

She swallowed her disgust and forced a weary smile over her shoulder to him. It took a solid effort to not flinch or throw his hands off her.

"Thank you for the offer, but I'm beat. I'm going to stay in, order some room service, and relax. Can you send my apologies to Melanie? And Lane, I suppose."

"Of course," he said, sitting on the bed and pulling her to stand between his legs. "Looks like you're not going to miss too much today. Your buddy Kurt was a no-show."

She felt her anger rising and needed him to leave. Now. Five minutes ago. *Deep breath, Car.*

"Really?" She struggled to keep her voice even. "Maybe he was embarrassed about his behavior during your presentation yesterday."

"Mmhmm..." Alex leaned forward and nuzzled her stomach. Carlie fought the very visceral need to slap him, shove his head away. He ran his hands up and down her back, before squeezing her backside and pulling her closer. His head dropped lower, and he licked the exposed skin above her waistband, his thumbs slipping beneath her pants to caress her lower back.

She caught Kurt glaring around the corner of the bathroom doorframe, his face dark with anger. Carlie returned his glare, coughed, and pulled back. "I'm sorry, Alex. But I'm not feeling well. Seriously."

He sighed and captured her hands. "Come with me this weekend. To Minneapolis. Say yes."

If she could erase the last hour from her mind, she would have been thrilled by this. But instead, she seethed beneath the surface. "I'll think about it." *When hell freezes over, you sleazy bastard.*

"Do more than think about it. Say yes, Carlie."

"I have so much work waiting for me, Alex. And this is all happening so fast. I need some time to think."

He leaned in and kissed her, his hands framing her face. "Then think. And tell me yes later."

Why? she screamed inside her head. *Why did you have to ruin everything?!*

She walked him to the door. "Enjoy the rest of the day, Alex. I'm going to crash, sleep around the clock. I'm sure I'll feel better in the morning."

He left with a final light kiss, then returned down the hallway to the elevator. She watched him get on and waved before closing the door. Carlie leaned back against the door and slammed her head against it. Once. Twice. A third time. First Brent. Now Alex. She was a damn magnet for wackadoodles. She slammed her head a fourth time.

"If you like, I can toss your shoes around the room again so you have better odds of injuring yourself," Kurt said, rejoining her.

"Ha, ha, ha." She slow clapped. "Such a comedian, aren't you?"

"More like a carnival clown. Laughing on the outside, crying on the inside. That type of thing," he said absently, walking over to the desk to grab the room service menu.

"Do you even hear the crap you say?" she wondered aloud.

"It just comes to me." He smirked and tossed the menu in her direction. "Pick something out. You need to get some food into your system."

23

*P*icking at steamed rice and grilled chicken, she watched Kurt check his phone incessantly. "Expecting a call?"

"Hoping for one. While you were, uh, catnapping earlier, I called my security engineer. He's doing some digging around."

"A security engineer? Of course. We all have one of those on speed dial. What are you looking for?"

He rolled his eyes. "Several things. Starting with the hotel's IT network. And Alex's agency, investments, contracts, connections—among other things."

Oh. Carlie continued eating in silence, wondering how this was going to help. She still couldn't believe she had fallen for such an egomaniac. She had thought she could trust him. How could she ever trust her instincts again? She had been so worried about who might have seen them on the street, and now her interlude with Alex might be seen by the entire freaking world. Her dad! Ugh. Tossing the fork down, she got up and paced, shaking her hands out at her sides. "I can't do this, Kurt. I can't play ignorant. I have to do something, show him that he can't use me like this."

She pulled out her phone, and Kurt raised an eyebrow. "Who are you calling?"

"My mother."

He blinked. "You're calling *your mom*? About this?"

"Yes."

Kurt looked appropriately confused.

"My mom isn't your typical Susie Homemaker," she said as she texted her mom to see if she was available for a phone call. "She's... different."

Carlie continued pacing as she waited for her response. *Come on, Mom. Check your damn phone.*

"Different, as in she's cool with you telling her over the phone you made a sex tape?"

She glared at him. "No. Different as in she'll know how best to nail this asshole to the wall. EHL Global isn't where it is today just because Dad and the Brians had innovative ideas and made some good deals. Mom is like a legal ninja. She anticipates things before they even happen. She lives and breathes strategy. Shit, she probably has a plan for this type of scenario."

Her phone vibrated. *Mary said to call her direct line in 20 minutes. LG*

Larry. She could not imagine his reaction at being told to text her. Larry Grant had worked for her mother since Carlie was ten or eleven. He was a great lawyer and a good assistant but had the personality of a brick. An old, set-upon brick. She was tempted to text him back with some cute, annoying emojis or GIFs but instead set the timer on her phone. When Mom said twenty minutes, she meant twenty minutes.

Standing at the window, she glanced through the skyscrapers of Chicago and spied the dark shadows over the lake. Yesterday she was sitting out there with Alex, content and watching the people and birds at play. Today, it seemed as though the weather matched her feelings, turbulent clouds heavy with unshed rain and thunder. It was just a matter of time until the storm broke. Kurt's reflection merged with hers as he joined her at the windowpane.

"What are you going to tell her?"

She met his eyes in the window. "The truth."

"Carlie, this isn't exactly the kind of thing you should spring on her at the office. Over the phone."

Dropping into the chair, she closed her eyes. "If you have my mother, then that's exactly how you share all of life's big moments." She waved her hand airily to shoo away the conversation.

They passed several minutes in silence before Kurt's phone vibrated. "Excuse me," he murmured, taking the phone into the restroom.

She fidgeted in the chair, twirling a piece of hair around her finger as she had when she was a young girl waiting for her mom to pick up the phone, excited to tell her she'd lost her first tooth. Catching herself, she dropped the lock of hair and sat up, plucking a piece of chicken off the white room service plate with the flecks of gold throughout. She idly thought it was odd that their plates matched the lobby floors. The timer went off, and she called her mom's office number, taking a deep breath as she listened to it ring.

"Hi, honey," her mom breezed over the line. Carlie imagined her kicking her heels under her massive desk and swapping them with her walking shoes. "What's going on?"

"Hi, Mom," she started, trying to visualize her way

through this conversation. *When in doubt, get straight to the point*, she heard in her mother's voice. Swallowing hard, she laid it out: "I'm in trouble, Mom. I don't know what to do."

Barely pausing, Mom whipped straight into legal mode. "Are you safe? What's the nature of the problem? Who's involved?"

Carlie smiled, practically hearing her pen at work on her notepad. "I'm safe. I met someone, someone I really liked..." She continued to spill out the pertinent details, blushing as she confessed what happened in his room.

"I see," Mary said, trailing into silence. "Well, this is unexpected, but it's hardly the end of the world, Carlie. Pull yourself together and tell me more about Alex. What do you know about him?"

"Not too much," she admitted, sharing what she could.

"And who is this other man you mentioned?"

"Kurt Hunter," she squeaked out, knowing what was coming.

"As in Hunter Industries?"

"Yes."

Pause.

She tried not to fidget. *Remain calm, Car.*

"And you were rude to him?"

"Um... maybe?"

Silence filled the line.

"Mom?"

"Carlie Lynn Eller. What have I told you about burning bridges that very well could prove to be useful in the future? I don't care how distasteful or forward he was. We are not rude to national or corporate leaders. How many times must I tell you this? I swear, it's like you weren't even listening to..."

She alternated cringing and eyerolling as her mother continued lecturing her, recalling her sister—a younger version of their mother—reaming her out over Kurt earlier. How could her dismissal of Kurt be worse than a role as an unwitting porn star? Only her family. Kurt walked back into the room. "Everything okay?" he asked.

"Who was that? Is that Kurt?"

The woman had freaking bionic hearing.

"Yes, Mom."

"Put him on the phone," she demanded.

She held her phone out to him. "She wants to speak with you."

He reached for the phone, mouthing, *Your mom?* She nodded and waited.

"Mrs. Eller, it's a pleasure to—" And he was cut off. Carlie smirked and watched him get an earful from Mom.

"Yes," he said. "I understand. Is it necessary? Of course, I will... When is that? Oh... Writing it down now... Yes... Thank you, you too, ma'am." Sporting a Cheshire grin, he handed the phone back.

Mystified, she returned to the call. She'd never heard anyone get off that quickly or easily when her mother was in ninja mode. "Mom?"

"I've talked with Mr. Hunter, and we've come to an agreement. You are going to stay there and give your presentation in the morning, then you will come directly home. Give whatever excuse you need, but make it compelling. Larry will meet you at the airport. We'll talk tomorrow night. Have to run, dear, but listen to Mr. Hunter. And be nice!"

Her mother hung up, leaving Carlie to stare down at her phone.

"Interesting woman," he said, green eyes glowing.

"You have no idea. Any news on your end?"

"He's racked up a substantial amount of debt and has listed his New York residence well above market. Not a good sign. His student loan debt is in default, and he's effectively living off his book advances."

"You got all that in the last hour?" she asked, incredulous.

He looked at her askance. "That was just his credit report and Google."

Of course. God, why hadn't she thought to do that earlier? Would she have uncovered something to prevent this mess?

"There's more, but it's complicated, and we couldn't go into it over the phone."

"Kurt, I'm so sorry. I didn't mean for this to happen. And I didn't mean to hurt you."

Muttering incoherently under his breath, he turned and stared at her. "You didn't cause this, Carlie. You were manipulated. This son of a bitch is using you. He's desperate and grasping at straws."

And yet plastic straws were evil, she groaned to herself.

"And don't worry about me." He lowered his voice. "I'm fine."

That made one of them. "I need to get out of here, Kurt. I can't sit in here and wait to see if he comes strolling back to my door."

He nodded toward the bathroom. "Get dressed and let's see what we can do."

With food in her stomach and some perspective from her pragmatic mother, she felt a little less end-of-the-world sick. She pulled on a pair of jeans and a dark blue sweater and dragged a brush through her knotted hair. She glared at herself in the mirror. *Listen up, Car. You are done with this "poor me" crap. You got yourself into this situation, and you are going to work your way out.* Nodding at her personal pep talk, she threw on enough makeup to be presentable-ish and returned to the bedroom.

24

"*E*ver been to Navy Pier?" Kurt asked.

She shook her head. "No, but if it's outside of this hotel, it sounds perfect."

After a blessedly uneventful trip down the elevator and out of the hotel, Kurt escorted her to where a private car and driver waited for them. She raised an eyebrow and glanced at him. Kurt shrugged. "I prefer to stick with regular, everyday options, but given recent events... I thought you might appreciate the privacy."

Carlie thanked the chauffeur and slid into the sleek black car. Her mother would approve. Kurt muttered instructions to the driver, then followed her into the car. "Nice ride," she observed. "Yours?"

"It's a company car."

"Which company?"

"Does it matter?" he asked absently, cracking down the window to take in some fresh air.

Oh. "I suppose not."

They traveled past the strip of beach she had visited with Alex. Was that only yesterday? The traffic inched along, and they sat quietly in the car. She watched Kurt covertly from the corner of her eye. What was he thinking? What had driven him to return? Whatever the reason, she was grateful he was there.

The driver looped around and sat behind a line of school buses. "This is fine here," said Kurt. He hopped out and came around to open her door. He helped her out, and they started walking. The hushed carnival sounds drifting toward them reminded her of summertime visits to the amusement park back home, Kings Island. She caught a whiff of cinnamon sugar in the air, mingling with the diesel from the surrounding vehicles. It was enough to make her want to ask Rach to go ride The Beast roller coaster with her.

The clouds hovered low over the lake and the two ducked into a long, covered building. Restaurants, shops, popcorn, families. It felt so good to be out doing something normal, touristy. They wandered through various shops, finding all things Chicago. Carlie picked up a magnet with a picture of a beef sandwich that read, "Wetter is Always Better in Chicago." Laughing at the ridiculous magnet, she dropped it back into the bin. Kurt scooped it up and brought it to the register. He dangled the small plastic bag on his finger, offering it to her, blonde hair covering one of his eyes. "If it can make you laugh right now, it's worth taking home."

She resisted the urge to push his hair back and instead accepted the gift, tucking it into her purse. They continued onward, locating the roasted almonds. She bought a small cone of the warm goodness, and they found an empty bench to relax on. Snacking on the delicious treat, Carlie watched grandparents stroll by with their young charges. The youngest waved as he toddled by, and Kurt returned the gesture, a bit overenthusiastically, his eyes twinkling at the tyke. "You like kids," she observed.

He nodded, totally at ease. "I'm an only child, but I was always surrounded by cousins and other kids. I love to be around them. Their perpetual honesty and joy over the small things... It's refreshing."

Leaning back on the bench and watching the children plead with their caregivers for treats, Kurt looked different. His green eyes were calm, his posture was...relaxed. That's what it was—he was relaxed, perhaps the most relaxed she'd seen him all week. No pretense, no rush. She puzzled over the change.

Thinking back over the day, she realized he hadn't made one flirtatious comment. He hadn't held her hand. Hadn't hit on her once. Hadn't once teased her or offered to sweep her off her feet.

The answer smacked her in the face. He was no longer interested in her. Not that way.

Feeling a little diminished, Carlie wondered what other damage she had done to herself and her future. Crazy to think that days ago she was still not ready to even consider dating after the nightmarish ending with Brent. Alex managed to make that nightmare look not quite so scary. She brushed away the thoughts of the men and the crumbs from her lap as she stood up. "What now?"

"Now? Now you have to choose. Ferris wheel or merry-go-round?"

At her laughter, he crossed his arms over his chest. "I'm serious. You can't leave here until you do one of the two. Hunter family rules."

"Oh, yes. Of course. Rules. Sounds legit."

"Practically law."

"Which would you suggest?"

"It depends on your acceptable level of risk and adventure. A carousel will keep you on the ground, spin you in circles, but you can choose your own beast to ride. The Centennial Wheel, however, makes you lose your footing. For the extra daring, I might even suggest the gondola seat. The glass bottom is worth the view."

"Glass bottom? I'm in."

Kurt purchased tickets and she watched the sky. The ominous clouds still hovered above the lake, but the rain had yet to show. While she waited for his return, Carlie considered her position. She knew now that choosing Alex had been a mistake. A huge one. She had never dreamed that someone would stoop that low, be that deceitful. Alex had so much potential. And he had ruined it. He had done it. Now she had to deal with the consequences of his betrayal.

On the flip side, she would never have dreamed how surprisingly kind, charming, and sweet Kurt was. Could she make this right? If she were him, what would she think of herself? "Ugh," she grunted. She shook her head in disgust.

Just give me the damned scarlet letter already.

"Change your mind?" he called, weaving through the light crowd toward her.

She smiled into his twinkling green eyes. "No, let's do this."

They lucked out in the timing and walked right on, the four-seater car empty except for the two of them. They took seats across from each other, her eyes growing round as the ground slipped away beneath the enclosed gondola.

"Whoa, this is crazy," she screeched, lifting her feet off the floor as they climbed higher. The people below grew smaller, more insignificant.

"Look across there," he said, pointing to the vista.

The clouds swirled, casting various shifting shadows across the water. The boats left subtle wakes. She looked at the city skyline and the gradual fade and merge into the suburbs.

"I love this view," he said. "It reminds me of how much there is out there. How much more we can do. It's invigorating."

Surprised at his words, she watched him watch the world. It felt like they could see forever from up here. They rose and fell, rose and fell, and rose once more before regaining solid ground.

He sent a text, presumably to the driver, and they started to make their way back down the road.

"Thank you for bringing me here," she said. "I know I messed up, did things I can't undo...but I am so glad you're here with me. I cannot imagine what would happen if you weren't here."

He didn't say anything, but walked a little more closely to her side, taking hold of her hand. Carlie was grateful for his willingness to be her friend right now. She didn't know what she had done to deserve it, but she was grateful.

25

They returned to the hotel, and the car stopped at the entrance. "I have to take care of a few things, but I'll be back soon," Kurt said. She nodded and stepped back into reality. Quickly. The conference soon would be letting out for the day, and Carlie had no desire to run into anyone.

Entering her room, the laptop loomed. She still had her presentation to do in the morning. Groaning, Carlie sat and pulled open the deck of slides, flipping through the order she had essentially memorized by this point.

Her email was overflowing with work and sales pitches. She made quick work of deleting all the sales stuff, then started replying to the interoffice correspondence. She lost herself in the work; time passed and the sun sank below the horizon. Wrapping up, Carlie stood and stretched, trading her jeans for comfy pants and collecting a fresh bottle of water. Eyes closed, she mentally prepared for tomorrow, visualizing the presentation, the people in the room. Alex.

The knock on the door startled her. She glanced at the time, wondering if it was Kurt returning yet. What if it was

Alex? She did not want to face him. Her phone vibrated on the desk, glowing with a simple message: *It's me.*

Heaving a sigh of relief, she opened the door to the man she was coming to depend on, much more than she should.

"Welcome back." She smiled up into his green eyes.

He looked down distractedly, then returned her smile. "Thanks."

"Everything okay?"

"I received a message from Alex. He wants money and a multibook deal in exchange for the video."

Jesus. "What?!"

"And there's no guarantee it's the only copy. I have ten days to respond. If I don't, he'll go after your father."

Carlie sat on the bed and pulled her knees up to her chest, stunned. All the pleasantness from the day evaporated in a matter of moments. She glanced up out of the corner of her eye. What if Kurt was making this up? He wouldn't do that, would he?

"Can I see the message?" she finally asked.

Kurt's brow furrowed. Without hesitating, he unlocked his phone, pulled up the email and tossed her the device. The words danced before her, the sheer audacity and menace making her blood boil.

"He can't do this!"

Kurt sat on the corner of the bed. "I'm doing what I can from my end. But we may need to bring in the police, Carlie."

"If the police get involved, the media will find out. And the scandal would... Damn it! I could handle it if it were just me, but this will affect my whole family, our work, my dad's legacy. The contracts will dry up. This could ruin EHL."

"That's a little dramatic. I don't think this would kill the business."

"You don't understand, Kurt. It's my family. My whole life! And even if you two do settle things between you, what's to prevent him from still contacting my dad?"

"Calm down. Let's slow down and think this through."

Fuming, she pushed off the bed and started pacing. She needed to think, she had to figure this out. *Order, Carlie. Find the path. Find the process. What can you control?*

"Does he know that I know?"

"No. I'm fairly confident that he believes me to be out of town. He has no reason to suspect I'd contact you."

"Okay. I guess that's good enough for now. First, I have to get through tomorrow morning. I need to do this presentation, hit it out of the park, then get the hell out of here without letting on that I know."

"Then?"

"Then, I'm going to figure out a way to get this guy. He's not going to get away with this."

"We. *We'll* figure this out."

She shook her head. "I can't ask you to do this. You have too much at stake."

"Carlie, in case you missed it, it's *me* he's trying to extort."

"Using a video of *me*!"

He took a deep breath. "Suffice it to say, we're in this together."

"But you don't have to. Tell him you don't care. He'll have to move on."

"No." His mouth tightened with anger.

Surprised by his vehement reply, she paused, then nodded. "Well...all right then," she huffed, continuing her route around the room. "Did you book a room?" she asked, realizing it was getting late.

"No, I was hoping I could stay here. If that's okay with you."

"Oh. Yes, of course. That's fine." *Please don't let me be blushing as much as I think I am!*

"Thanks. I'll call down for a rollaway."

She hummed and went back to stalking about the confines, trying not to think about him sharing her room. *Good lord, Carlie. You slept with Alex yesterday and look where that got you. You are* not *going to fantasize about Kurt. Get a grip!*

Deciding to do something productive, she messaged her sister and Kim, asking them to meet at her place tomorrow night. She was going to need their advice. Rachael had gone through a roller coaster of emotional shit with Rick. She would know how to make this better. Carlie glanced back at Kurt, who looked to be on hold with the front desk, and wondered if he was planning to come to Cincinnati.

One thing at a time, Carlie–Q, she heard in her dad's voice. *Multitasking is the fastest way to a disaster.*

Sleeping with Alex was a pretty fast way to disaster, too.

She still couldn't believe he had recorded them. How could she have misjudged him so severely? Where had the camera been—in his bag? She replayed their encounter and cringed, wondering what it would look like to someone watching. Some people were into that kind of thing, but yeesh. Imagine if you *knew* someone was watching. Her skin crawled with the thoughts that followed. Her phone vibrated.

You're coming back early?

Kim. Leave it to her to remember her schedule.

Yes.

Everything good?

She rolled her eyes and groaned. Things were so far from good that she would need a passport to find good again. But how much to say now? No sense in stressing her bestie out about it for the next twenty-four hours.

Some drama. I'll fill you in tomorrow.

Hopefully that drama includes you and a handsome man!

She laughed out loud, though it had more than a touch of a manic tint. *You could say that. Talk tomorrow. Night, girl.*

Night, Car!

Kurt sent her a questioning glance. She shrugged and went to wash up.

When she came back out, Kurt was staring at the phone in frustration. He brushed back his dark blonde hair and turned those green, green eyes toward her. That was quickly becoming her favorite color. *Damn it, Car! Stop!*

"No rollaway," he muttered.

"What?"

"The front desk said there aren't any rollaways available. I can sleep on the floor. Or if it makes you more comfortable, I can try another hotel nearby."

"No, that's ridiculous. We're two grown adults. We can share the bed. It's not like anything is going to happen."

"Right," he mumbled, passing her for the washroom. "Why didn't I bring a damn bag with me?" he muttered to himself as the door closed.

Carlie glanced at the bed and tried to tame the butterflies fluttering madly in her stomach. They were really not helping. Snagging her laptop and phone, she plugged them in and considered her escape plan. It would need to be immediately after speaking. She hauled out her empty suitcase and threw all her extra shoes and clothes in, making a mental list of what she'd need to leave out. Suit and pumps, the lanyard, and...

Her mind went blank as Kurt emerged from the bathroom in just his boxers, his clothing neatly folded in his arms. Good heavens. "Is this okay? I'm going to have to wear these again tomorrow, so I'd rather not sleep in them." He held his clothes before him, looking a little uncomfortable, but kept his head high.

"It's fine," she answered, her voice a squeak.

She turned back to packing and tried to ignore him. Carlie heard him open the mini fridge and assumed he was examining the recently restocked contents. "Your choice," he offered.

Raising her eyebrows, she turned and made eye contact. "My choice?"

"Can I get you a drink?"

"Sure. Anything but the wine." She made a face. "I had enough of that already."

He plucked out two cans, holding one out to her. Beer? Why not.

He cracked open his drink and sat in the desk chair. Carlie tried not to stare, but...really. It was just not fair for a man to be that handsome...and that undressed...and to be sitting like that in her room. *Carlie, you're staring. Stop it!*

She took a drink of the cold beer and wandered into the restroom. "How do I have so much crap everywhere when I've only been here four days?" she muttered, tossing toiletries into the open bag.

"Good question. Though I believe it's called being a female," he joked, leaning against the door frame.

"Nonsense," she retorted, trying not to show her surprise at his following her. "I'll have you know that I skipped the 'high-maintenance woman' class. I also don't do all the fancy hair, clothes, jewelry, cooking. So, that's not it."

"Could be you're just messy," he teased. "What are you doing?"

"What does it look like?"

He watched her shove most of her toiletries in a bag and took a long draught of his beer. "Checking out tonight?"

"No, just trying to stay busy," she said, slipping past him and trying not to notice his delectably firm chest as she returned to the bedroom.

"Uh-huh. That's enough, busy bee. You're never going to relax, let alone sleep, as long as you're flitting around here. Sit." He pointed at the bed.

"Bees don't flit; they buzz," she grumbled, following his command.

"Now, drink your beer and chill. You're making me nervous with all this cleaning. I'm more accustomed to you throwing shoes around and creating death traps."

She smiled reluctantly and sipped her beer. "Better?"

"Better."

Her phone vibrated on the desk, and she picked it up, cringing as she read it.

Missing you already. Feel better.

"What's wrong?"

"Alex."

"Hmm."

He settled onto the bed by the other nightstand, and they looked at each other.

"This is weird," he said.

"Very," she agreed. She was amused to see he was blushing too.

He flipped on the television to a late-night show, and they drank their beers, both trying not to notice the other. She eventually relaxed and nodded off. The can was plucked from her hand, and she curled onto her side, finding relief in the escape.

$\mathcal{T}$he front door stands open, and I gaze at it longingly. Can I enter? We haven't lived there in years. It looks like no one is home, and I very much want to go inside. Surveying the area, I see no one watching, so I inch up the stairs leading to the front door.

"Hello?" I call, wondering if anyone can hear me. My voice echoes in the open space. No one answers.

Just as well. They're probably all at work.

I reach the threshold and pause. They'll know. They'll know if I enter. But I can't stop myself from walking into the familiar warmth. I expect to see our old slate-blue furniture, light oak tables, and household knickknacks, but they aren't there. Cool-gray leather couches line the walls and shiny black end tables stand empty. They look so out of place. Who lives here now?

Continuing on, I pass another unfamiliar room. This was where Rachael and I would play with our dolls, fight over game pieces, and later go head-to-head on overpriced video games. But there's nothing familiar in here either. Someone's formal sitting room. A vacuum has left long, starkly straight lines on the carpet.

The kitchen. The light shines ahead, and I desperately want

to see my dad cooking some kind of treat or special dinner for us. He always made that golden apple crisp when I was little, served with just the right amount of ice cream to melt together. Stepping into the kitchen, I'm relieved to see it, at least, has not changed. But there is no one here. Staring at the empty table, I am overcome with sadness, heartbroken to know that I've missed them.

I try not to cry as I turn and go up the stairs to find my room. My solace. My footsteps echo strangely on the wooden stairs, and I look down to see I'm wearing my old black soccer cleats with the white swooping logo on the side. Mom won't like that I'm wearing these in the house, but I don't want to go back downstairs. I continue upward, nervous at what other changes I might discover. Will they be changed like the living room, or will they be familiar?

The first room I pass is Rachael's. It was always so neat and organized. Her bed is perfectly made and not a speck of dust mars the richness of the wooden furniture. Her golf shoes sit in the corner, atop a small platform she set up so the shoes wouldn't get the floor dirty. I stop and smile at the picture of the five of us resting on her nightstand, the fam and Kim, always another sister to us. It's one of my favorite pictures of all time.

Next is the guest room, though I don't remember many guests actually using it. It was a junk drawer of a room, curiosities and odd bits we couldn't throw away. And under no circumstances were we allowed to go in there before Christmas. "Off limits," I hear my mother's voice echo through time.

The order is wrong. My room should be next, but it's the master bedroom visible in the following doorway. The bed is covered with a different blanket. It looks a little shabby. I'm surprised they don't replace it. A small cat paces out of their room, winding around my ankles before leaving the way I came. I gasp with pleasure at Pixie, another echo from previous times, and *recall the hours my cat and I spent snuggling. Relief strikes me. I'm not completely alone in the house.*

Now, to the last door. It should have been my parents'. I know it's mine. The door stands ajar, and no sounds come from within. I need this to be the same. I take a deep breath, nervous and hopeful, wanting to crawl into my old bed and rest for a little while. I'm so tired.

When I push the door open, a bright, glaring light flares to life, blinding me. I stumble forward, wondering where it came from and how to turn it off. I reach from memory, expecting my bedframe. My hands grope and grope, passing through the empty air. There's nothing there. Panic rising, I blink my eyes rapidly, desperate to regain my sight and decipher my surroundings. Where is my bed? My chair? My dresser? I land on my knees and crawl across the wooden floor. Where is my rug?

My vision clears, and I see my room has been emptied. All my things are gone. My pictures, my books, my trophies. My ballet slippers. My diaries. All gone. The closet gapes with empty shelves. The walls are barren of the posters and childish memorabilia that made it mine. I sink down in the corner of the room and stare. The loss, the sadness, overwhelms me. My heart can't take it. I choke on my tears, fighting the vast emptiness that smothers me.

"SHH! Shh, Carlie, it's okay. You're safe," he whispered against her ear.

She was sobbing; she couldn't stop. The lingering desolation of the dream merged with her nightmarish reality, and she was broken. She shook and wept, the sense of loss so acute, all consuming.

Kurt shifted in the bed to cradle her like a child, and she curled into him, heaving as she tried to stop crying. He ran his hand over her hair, again and again, consoling, soothing. Her sobbing ebbed, and she lay there gasping, letting him hold her as the last of her tears dried. She struggled to control her erratic breathing as she tore at the lingering threads, working to untangle the dream from her waking life.

"It was so real. S-so sad. It was gone, everything," Carlie whispered, shuddering in her misery.

"Shhhh. You're safe. I have you now. Nothing's going to hurt you," he murmured, stroking her hair. She shivered again. "I've got you," he said more firmly. Kurt gripped her tighter, and she sighed, her shaking subsiding. He rocked her, still smoothing her hair and whispering soothing words.

Several minutes passed by, and he eased his grip, shifting so that she was once again lying next to him and they were facing each other on their sides. He kept an arm wrapped around her, lending her comfort and safety, and she collapsed into it, pressing her tear-stained cheek to his smooth, warm chest.

"Better now?" he asked against her hair.

"Sorry to wake you," she whispered, embarrassed at how childish and needy she must seem.

"Do you want to talk about it? Are you okay?"

"No. Yes." She shook her head under his chin. "I'm fine, but I can't talk about it now."

"Do you have nightmares often?"

"Sometimes." She shrugged, not wanting to think about it. Not wanting to think about anything other than the surprising comfort she found in his arms.

Carlie tilted her head back, stunned at how close he was, stirred by the understanding and compassion in his eyes.

Their gazes locked, and she found herself drowning in

his now dark, jade-green eyes, soaking up the strength and security he offered. His gaze caressed her lips, and she caught her breath, watching him, waiting. She knew she couldn't be the one to make this move. Not after what she'd done with Alex. Not after what Alex had done to her. And to Kurt.

His head dipped, mouth lowering closer, his breath warming her lips. He paused and pressed his eyes closed. He changed course and placed a light kiss on her forehead before releasing her and rolling onto his back. "Sorry," he mumbled.

Without comment, she rolled away from him, speculating about what he was thinking. After another moment, she vowed to not think. To try to forget. Carlie focused on her breathing and listened for his, wondering if he had gone back to sleep. She was too afraid to turn and look. If he wasn't sleeping... If he caught her looking?

For the millionth time in the last few days, she wondered again what was happening. She had thought she knew what she wanted. Alex seemed so perfect. How could she have been so wrong? She bit her lip and replayed their time together, trying to recall if there was anything he said or did that raised any red flags. He was courteous and charming, dazzling and sincere. Or so she had thought. He had blindsided her.

Now, she considered Kurt, this beautiful man who had cheered and comforted her at every turn since they met. He had seemed like such a tease, an upstart. But the more she was around him, the more she knew he wasn't the careless California golden boy. He was kind and caring. He was smart and protective. In a cruel and ridiculous twist of fate, she realized too late that she wanted him. And she was crushed.

By choosing Alex, she had ruined everything.

Kurt didn't want to want her.

She understood why.

But the rejection was there. And it stung.

After what felt like hours, she drifted off hearing Marie's voice saying, *If it's meant to be, it will be.*

27

*S*he awoke to a buzzing. Groggily, she searched for the source and ended up clutching her phone, the screen glowing with one word:

Breakfast?

One word. One word dug its claws in, scratching and drawing blood.

No! Screw that. She was not letting him get to her.

Sorry, Alex. Going over my notes and finalizing my presentation.

Want me to bring you something to eat? Coffee?

All the right words. All the right gestures. But nothing could change what he did. What he was doing. What he could do.

No thanks. See you down there.

All the things she wanted to say to him, the accusations, the rage. But no, she had to keep moving. Groaning, she slammed the phone back down on the nightstand and rubbed her eyes. They felt puffy.

"Oh, man," she said aloud.

The dream and her embarrassing meltdown came flooding back. She looked across the bed and saw that Kurt was still asleep. Long, graceful lashes shadowed his cheeks, and his tousled hair stood up at stupidly adorable angles. His tanned forehead was smooth in his sleep. His nose sloped down, before a gentle swoop up at the end. His full lips were slightly parted, showing a sliver of those camera-ready white teeth. He was beautiful in a way that would make women envious, but his muscled shoulders and chest, squared jaw, and long, strong hands were all man.

But it wasn't going to happen. At least he didn't want to want her, she amended, which all pointed the same way.

Shaking her head, Carlie scooted out of bed to wash up. She returned to find him awake, staring at the crack in the window's curtains.

"Is that the sun?" he asked.

She followed his gaze and pulled open the curtains, momentarily blinding them. "Figures," she huffed at the irony. All week, they had dodged rain and stared at swollen skies, and now that she was leaving, the sun came out in its full glory. *I see what you did there, God. Nice one.*

Carlie skimmed the room service menu, then tossed it at him. "We should eat before we go down. I won't have a chance to eat, and you... Are you coming down? We didn't discuss that."

"No. It's best that he does not find out I'm here. As far as he knows, I'm at my office reviewing his demands. Besides, it would be poor form to show up now after my missed presentation yesterday."

"What are you going to do? And where is your office?"

"My bag should be delivered soon. I need to get cleaned up and do some work, make arrangements. To answer your other question, I have several offices, including a small place in the city here. But my home office is in San Diego. That's where he likely assumes I am. That's where I was heading when you emailed me."

He handed her the menu. "Southwestern omelet, OJ, and coffee please."

Carlie phoned down for breakfast and prepared for the day, packing her remaining toiletries as she finished with each. While tackling her hair, she took advantage of the quiet to comb through her position. Even with all the worry about things with Alex and the mounting anxiety of her presentation, she couldn't stop thinking about Kurt. His goodness was so obvious to her now. How could she have misjudged him so badly, repeatedly? On the flight, she was just trying to get out of talking to him. And here at the hotel, he had become an unwanted hurdle to being with Alex. How many times had she written him off over the week? And still he came back to let her know what was happening, to help her. He had been there each time she had crumbled this week and asked for nothing in return. How could she have been so blind? *Such an idiot, Carlie. Open your damn eyes next time.*

She had screwed up. Big time.

Shaking her head, she zipped up the last bag and forced herself to focus on the next few hours.

It was going to have to be a heck of a performance, from the moment she left the elevator until she got to the car. She could—would—do this. There was no alternative.

She and Kurt walked through the plans for their departures while they ate. He'd leave before her and wait at the airport. She just had to get through the morning.

Play the part. Don't be an idiot. Don't let on that you know.

Seemed simple enough. But her nerves wouldn't calm

down. She sat on the edge of the bed and closed her eyes, focused on breathing. In and out. Focused on what she could control.

A knock sounded at the door. She heard Kurt ease it open and greet a valet who had arrived with his bag. After he closed the door again, silence filled the room. "You don't have to go down there. We could leave now, Carlie."

Eyes still closed, she shook her head, lifting her chin stubbornly. "No. That won't help. I need to do this." She felt him studying her but refused to give into the temptation to look at him. She needed to focus.

"Why? What's so important about this?"

Carlie cracked one eye open to look at him. "You really want to know?"

He crossed his arms over his chest and nodded.

Sighing, she pushed to her feet and walked to the window, looking out at the water in the distance. "My whole life I've been referred to as Charles' daughter. Mary's daughter. Rachael's little sister. Brent's girlfriend. I've always been defined by the people around me. Then I found my passion and discovered that I'm damn good at it, seeing the big picture and finding a strategic path to get from point A to point B." She traced a line across the window.

"Yet when people see me, they still see Charles' daughter. Mary's daughter. Rachael's sister. They see an Eller. They don't see me, Carlie. They don't see how hard I've worked, what I'm capable of. To them I have no value, no meaning," she said, slapping her hand against the pane of glass in frustration.

"So, yes, I want to do this today." She turned away from the window. "I want to present the work I've done on the Pendulum Marketing Matrix. I want to show the case studies and talk about the benefits to not just the company but to the everyday consumer who will find more relevance and use from the digital world they are immersed in from sunup to sundown."

Her voice dropped to a near whisper. "But mostly I want to prove to myself that I have what it takes to make the matrix function and thrive. That I can stand up and convince others that what I do, what I believe in, what I am capable of... that it's worth their time and attention. I need to know that I am doing something worth doing. I am adding value. I am more than my name, my family, my relationships. My work is worth something. *I* am worth something."

She stopped, embarrassed at her outburst. How pathetic she must seem. Kurt stood still, watching her without giving a clue as to his thoughts. Fan-fucking-tastic, now he was convinced that she was a loose, crazy, unstable woman. She stared down at her hands, watching them clench and unclench.

"Carlie," he said quietly. "You are incredible. But you don't see that, do you?"

Bewildered, she continued to stare down at her hands, now still. Maybe he had lost *his* mind.

He walked over and placed his hands on her shoulders. "You have a fire in you to do something. You have conviction, hunger, boldness. You have it, Carlie. And I see you. I see you very clearly," he said, tucking a hand under her chin to make her meet his eyes. "Simply incredible," he repeated, his thumb rubbing gently across her lower lip.

"Kurt, I..." Carlie trailed off, not knowing what to say. Her eyes searched his, looking for some hint of where they stood.

"Shhh... It's okay." He leaned forward and brushed a soft

kiss to her lower lip, where his thumb had been. "Now, go do what you came here to do."

He turned and picked up his bag, closing the washroom door behind him.

She fingered her lower lip thoughtfully, a smile warming her face.

ervously giddy, Carlie stepped out of the elevator and into the conference lobby for the last time. She was terrified but had a secret store of courage, strengthened by a mesmerizing man far above her. Eighteen floors, to be exact.

Reassessing the floor plan, she nodded and propped her luggage in an unobtrusive spot against the wall near the door. Rolling her shoulders, she joined the line for another itty-bitty cup of coffee. A high pile of blonde hair wafted in front of her.

"Good morning, Melanie."

"Good morning to you too!" Her three-thousand-watt smile could light a dark alley. "Oh! I heard back from Kurt. He's home. He didn't tell me what happened, so I assume it was business stuff. So disappointing."

Carlie feigned a frown. "That's too bad. I'm relieved you heard back, though. I was worried something had happened."

Melanie smiled brightly. "No need to worry. He's fine." She chatted about how great the week had gone, even without one of her star speakers. "But I'm *so* looking forward to your talk today, Carlie."

Smiling, she saluted Melanie with the white cup. "Thank you. And please send me any speaker feedback you get. I would love to know what the attendees think." Carlie hesitated before adding, "Unfortunately, I won't be able to stay to hear it for myself. I must return home as soon as my session is over."

"Oh, no! Is everything okay? Are you well? Alex said you were sick yesterday. I hate when I get sick while traveling. It's the absolute worst!"

"No, that's passed. My sister is getting married, and she's had an emergency come up that I must help deal with."

"It can't wait?" she pleaded. Carlie could absolutely see why Kurt considered her a little sister.

"I'm afraid not. But I can tell you this conference has made an impression on me."

She smiled broadly. "I'm so glad to hear that! Thank you!"

"Carlie." His deep voice rumbled at her back.

Melanie glanced over Carlie's shoulder, then gave her an extravagant wink. "I have to move along, but I'll introduce you shortly."

Carlie braced herself and turned, holding her coffee cup between them. God, he was handsome. But now his trident-like stature was oppressive and disquieting.

"I've missed you. Are you feeling better?" he whispered huskily as he steered her behind one of the lobby's columns.

"I don't know what was wrong with me. I was pretty wrecked."

"Come with me for lunch after your presentation." Not quite an ask, though not a demand either.

"Oh, Alex." Carlie smiled wanly. "I'm sorry, but I have to

leave straightaway after I speak. My sister had an emergency come up, and she needs me. You know how it is. Family first."

"That can wait. I need to talk with you. We need some time together. Come with me."

"Alex, I can't. My flight has already been changed. I have to go."

"Change it again."

Trying to contain her frustration, she sipped the coffee and glanced around the room. He stepped closer and plucked the cup from her hands. He set it on a small planter table and grasped her hands. "Stay. We need more time together," he murmured, running his hands up her arms and settling them on her shoulders. Carlie stiffened, recalling Kurt's hands there just a short while ago. She forced herself to relax and smile.

"You do have my number, you know. It's not like we're all that far away. Just a short flight," she consoled.

He slid his hands over her shoulders and down her back, pressing her against the length of him. Carlie closed her eyes. She just needed to get through this. "I want you; I need you. Can't you feel it?"

She tried to ignore his arousal as he leaned down to nuzzle the skin beneath her ear. "You belong with me, Carlie. Go to Ohio if you must, then come to me in Minneapolis."

"And what's going on over here?" The sultry purr of a redhead, who until now had had few redeeming qualities, was a welcome intervention.

"Lane," Carlie acknowledged, trying not to sound relieved. "We were just heading into the ballroom. Has Melanie made her way up front yet?"

She eyed them, suspicion written plainly across her face. "Not yet, but it's time to find your seats."

"Of course," Carlie murmured. Satisfied, Lane stalked away.

As she started to walk after Lane, she was abruptly pulled up short. Alex yanked her back to him and gripped the back of her neck, crushing his mouth over hers. He pushed his way into her mouth, pillaging with a vengeance.

Stunned, she pushed back. "Alex!" Carlie gasped. "I can't do this right now. I have to go present." She stared hard at him, and he smiled lazily.

"We'll continue this after your lecture," he said before turning away, leaving her against the column.

Jesus, Mary, and Joseph. What the hell?

Glancing around, Carlie made a quick detour to the ladies' room to make sure she didn't look as chaotic as she felt. She stood at the counter examining her pale reflection.

"I heard you were sick, poor thing," said a sweet, young voice.

"Yeah, some kind of stomach bug, but I think I'm over it." Carlie smiled at Rita. She watched her finish washing up from the corner of her eye, a plan forming.

"Rita, can I ask a favor without explaining why?"

"It's nothing illegal, is it?"

"No, no, no." Laughing with relief, Carlie went into what she needed.

"That's it? No problem at all." Rita giggled. "Okay, I'm going in. Paul's saving me a seat. I've heard good things about this next speaker." She winked.

"Thank you, Rita."

Alone in the ladies' room, she took a deep breath, counted to ten, then slowly exhaled. *Find your way to the finish line, Car.*

Adding a last dash of powder and swipe of lipstick, she checked her teeth, straightened her shoulders, and exited the washroom, clinging to all the confidence she could muster.

Carlie slipped into the ballroom, sticking to the fringes as she progressed to the reserved speakers' table at the front. Sinking into her seat, she met Melanie's gaze, who gestured toward the stage, her question clear. Carlie nodded and mentally reviewed her opening.

"Good morning," Melanie bubbled into the microphone. "I am so honored to welcome to the podium a fascinating woman who is sure to make waves in the industry with her new platform, the EHL Pendulum Marketing Matrix. She has a bachelor's degree in marketing from the University of Cincinnati and an MBA from Wright State University in Dayton, Ohio. Her work has been featured in *Rewired* and *The New York Tech Report*, and she's regularly quoted in publications domestically and abroad. Please welcome Carlie Eller."

Focus. One step at a time. Starting up the short flight of stairs, her foot slipped on the bottom stair. *Oh, for God's sake!* She conspicuously caught herself on the handrail and paused before continuing to meet Melanie on stage.

"Well. That was fun." Still blushing, Carlie laughed into the mic and waved her hand toward the steps. The audience laughed with her, applauding and catcalling. Taking inspiration from this, she continued, changing her intro without hesitation. "I find that when we can laugh at ourselves, the world is happy to laugh with us. Humans are wired to identify with the actions of others. When we make a connection, when we are primed, we are much more receptive to opportunities, to messaging. More likely to react to a requested call to action. As a digital marketer, this is an important lesson. How many times have we seen terrible, unfortunate ad placement? Spam emails that are clearly not for products you'd ever be interested in? How many times have we seen brands get tossed to the sidelines for making critical errors in their messaging?"

She paused and the crowd paused with her, following every word. It was a heady feeling. Carlie was a conductor, framing the tempo and leading the musicians. They played a shared symphony, a tragic melody lamenting those whose work hammered the wrong target demographics, pouring millions of dollars into wasteland. Together, they expanded into a crescendo of inspiration, finessing the strings of love within the successes of the case studies. Smiling, she took them through the finale, proud of their successful journey. They gobbled up the info, grabbing cell phone photos of the data and contact information that were projected onto the screen behind her. At long last, Carlie retired her baton, handing it off to Melanie, who launched into the question-and-answer session.

Would the customer experience be affected? How did data privacy come into play with this system? Were the tightening regulations abroad able to be accommodated? What cybersecurity features were included? The questions all anticipated, Carlie answered them with ease, wowing them with the foresight to have built in countless permission levels and options. Her eyes fell on Alex, and she worried he would say something, do something brash. But he wouldn't, she reminded herself. He didn't know she knew.

"I think we can all agree this has the potential to redefine how we market in the twenty-first century," Melanie cooed into her microphone, smiling with pleasure. "Thank you, Carlie." She turned to Carlie. "And one might assume you'll be hearing from most of us." Her laughter spread across the room before it evolved into applause.

Carlie blushed, her job at the podium complete. "Thank you," she murmured into the podium's hot mic and walked back to her seat, ready for someone else to claim the spotlight.

"Now, everyone, I'd like to remind you to complete those surveys in the conference app. The app and Wi-Fi information are available at the center of each table, as well as a QR code for a direct download," Melanie rattled off. Carlie was impressed; Melanie was already implementing changes based on the previous days' feedback. The young blonde would do well in this line of work.

"We'll take a fifteen-minute break, then please refer to your program to locate your next breakout session," said Lane from the other side of the room over the din.

Catching Rita's eye, Carlie took a deep breath and nodded. Rita winked at her, took Paul's arm, and made a beeline for Alex, prepared to talk his ear off.

Refusing to look at him, Carlie strode over to her bags and slipped out the door toward the conference lobby and elevator. A small crowd was gathered, and she took advantage of their clustering, hovering among them and the elevator. Carlie glanced at the ballroom door and saw no sign of Alex yet. At long last, the elevator opened and she all but ran into it, watching with relief as the doors softly swished closed.

At the ground floor, she surveyed the people in the entrance lobby and swerved around them, exiting to the sunshine of Chicago. A line of taxis queued in the street, and she bounced into the first one in line.

Sitting in the escape car, Carlie allowed herself to relax. *On my way*, she texted Kurt. The fatigue of relief hit hard, and she sagged against the seat, staring sightlessly at the traffic that enveloped the car.

"Lucky to have good weather today. Da airport shouldn't be too backed up," he said, his Chicago accent thick. "Where ya off to?"

Carlie smiled at his reflection in the mirror. "Cincinnati."

"Eh, I've been dere..." He rattled off about his visit to the Buckeye State, and she tuned him out, wondering how long it would be until she heard from Alex. He was going to be pissed. But what did he think she was going to do? Even if things hadn't gone to hell, she had to return home at some point. His behavior verged on the irrational. Though someone who did what he did might well be playing a few cards short of a full deck.

"...and so, I says to him, it would take a helluva lot more than that ta keep me away," the driver concluded. Carlie had no idea what he'd been saying, so she smiled politely and nodded. It appeared to be the right response since he looked pleased. They continued the ride in silence. "Which airline?"

She told him, and he zigzagged through the clustered terminal traffic as only cab drivers seemed capable of doing, dropping her off at the correct entrance.

"Dere we are, young lady," he said, depositing her bags at her side.

An affectionate smile broke through at this fatherly Chicago cabbie. She very nearly hugged the portly driver. Thanking him, Carlie looked at the airport entrance and buried her bitterness at how things had turned out. This was to have been her moment to shine. And while she was pleased with how the presentation itself had gone, she had never imagined she'd be running home the way she was.

Rolling to the counter, she pulled her bags up onto the scale and handed over her ID. Carlie glanced around, wondering if Kurt was out here, knowing he was probably on the other side of security. Finally, with tickets in hand and bags on their way to Cinci, she strolled to the TSA line and pulled out her phone.

Going through security now.

She messaged her mom to let her know her location and texted her sister and Kim to confirm tonight. That done, she opened her email and scrolled through the unread messages. A few flattering notes from conference attendees, some vendor sales pitches, and emails from folks at work. She could manage those later.

Her phone vibrated. *Meet you on the other side.*

A big goofy grin split her face. She was in trouble if a simple, impersonal text from Kurt was making her smile. *You're such a dork, Car.*

At the next vibration, she was already smiling before she read his next message. But it quickly faded. It was Alex.

What the fuck? You seriously left?

Shit, shit, shit.

"Please put all your belongings in the bin. Shoes off, jacket off, everything out of your pockets," droned the terminally bored security worker. Carlie dropped her phone and belongings into the plastic tub and shuffled forward, stomach clenching as she tried to decide how to respond.

Passing through the scanner, she swerved around a family to collect her items, tugging on her shoes as she typed a reply.

You looked like you were deep in conversation, and I had to leave to make my flight. Carlie thanked the stars above for the effervescent Rita and Paul.

You didn't need to run off. Are you avoiding me?

Absolutely.

I have to go home. And I need time to think.

The waving dots had her pausing to see how Alex would respond. A flurry of texts arrived.

Maybe we did go a little fast. But I don't regret any of it.

I want to see you.

Damn, I already miss you.

When can we meet?

She sat on the bench by security and stared at the phone.

At a distance, she heard Kurt call her name. Carlie waved distractedly, frowning as she drew a blank.

Did you get an invitation to Bartlett's fundraiser? Alex messaged.

Stunned, she messaged back. *Yes.*

Good. I thought he'd invite you too.

Too?

You'll be there? she queried.

If you're there? I wouldn't miss it.

Kurt now stood over her, watching her fingers fly across the phone.

Have to run to catch my flight, but I'll see you next week then. Bye!

She slid the phone into her bag and turned her focus to Kurt. "What are you doing next week?"

$\mathcal{F}$alling into step with Kurt, the uncertainty circled endlessly around Carlie. Where did they stand with each other? That moment in the hotel room —was that his way of saying there was still a possibility? Or was he giving her a needed boost in confidence? Being nice?

"What's next week?" Kurt asked, breaking her thoughts.

She explained the invitation her father had called her about, that they were all going to Atlanta...and that Alex now planned to meet her there.

"Next Friday and Saturday? That's ironic."

"What do you mean?"

"Saturday is my deadline to respond to him."

Of course. A coincidence? Intentional? Too many questions clouded her brain to think clearly.

They continued walking down the concourse, passing the various coffee shops and bars, newspaper stands and convenience shops, and the clusters of passengers hovering a hairsbreadth outside the lines to board their flights.

"Are you coming to Cincinnati with me?"

"I'm on your flight, but I'll be continuing to California. I have some meetings I can't reschedule and then I have to meet with my security team."

That made sense, but the disappointment was real. She nodded, keeping her eyes trained ahead, trying not to show her thoughts. Mom probably had people on this already, too, so she understood.

They arrived at the gate, and she dropped into an empty seat. Kurt paced around the gate before joining her, worry creasing his face.

"Carlie, we need a game plan. I'm not overly concerned about the financial or business aspect of this, but I have to make certain he's not going to hurt you. Or your family. He's desperate. Someone like that, willing to take advantage of you, of this situation, to cross all lines—moral, legal—that's not a sane person."

"I still can't believe this is happening. This can't be real life."

He looked hard at her. "If I hadn't returned, you would still be with him, completely unaware. During my, uh, discussion with him, he made it clear that it had been a competition and he'd won the girl. You chose him. And he was going to milk the situation for all it was worth."

She didn't look away, but she felt ashamed, nonetheless. "I had no idea he was using me. God, I feel so stupid."

"He's not done with you yet."

"Oh, he's done," Carlie growled.

"Not if he's planning to see you next week. And certainly not if he senses he can get more out of you."

Kurt pulled out his phone and swiped through his screens. "I can be in Cincinnati on Thursday."

"That won't work. We're leaving for Atlanta Wednesday. We'll be staying there through Sunday."

Nodding, he looked back at his phone. "I'll try to join you before you leave, but I may have to meet you there."

"Kurt?"

Those clear green eyes held hers.

"Thank you. I..." She held up her hands, grasping at the air as she searched for what she was trying to say, but the words wouldn't form. "I just... thank you," she finished weakly.

He grinned. "You're welcome." He leaned back into his seat and laid his arm across the back of her chair. They didn't touch, but she felt protected.

Their seats were not together on this flight, so they parted ways upon boarding. Carlie buckled into her regular, coach class seat, already sensing the bruises that were about to be inflicted on her knees, and closed her eyes. She was exhausted. Mentally, physically, emotionally. An older woman sat next to her and promptly pulled out a book to read. Small blessings. She was asleep before they taxied to the runway.

"CARLIE," Kurt said, his voice tinged with humor. "Earth to Carlie?"

In a haze, she blinked repeatedly, trying to focus. She smiled groggily and tried to shake herself awake. "I fell asleep."

"I see that. We're here. I have to run to catch my connector, but I wanted to say goodbye." Kurt leaned down and kissed her cheek. "I'll be in touch soon. Contact me if anything else comes up. Anything."

"I will." She watched him leave and realized that she was

one of the last people on the plane. She gathered her things and exited to face her altered reality.

So many passengers brought their luggage in carry-ons that it was always surprising to see a large crowd in the baggage claim area. Carlie stood in the fray, watching the serpentine belt weave cases of every color and texture throughout the busy room. Sometimes it amused her to try to guess which passenger belonged to each bag, especially the eccentrically decorated bags. Today Carlie didn't have the energy or ambition to try to guess. She just wanted to go home. Spotting Mom's assistant waiting by the door, she lifted a hand in greeting. Larry elevated his chin, the most acknowledgement the man ever seemed to offer.

The first of Carlie's two bags almost passed by before she could nudge her fellow passengers out of the way to snag it. This juggling was repeated for the smaller companion. Bags accounted for, she rolled through the melee to find Mr. Joy himself.

"That's it?" he inquired.

At her brief nod, he stalked off toward the parking area. He was not a man of many words. She wondered if he was always that way or if it was just around the Eller family. At least he was dependable and trustworthy, two qualities that kept him in her mother's favor.

"How's Mom?"

He shrugged and kept walking.

Well, then. "And work?"

His eyes rolled heavenward, likely cursing the gods above for sending him a chatty girl to escort. "Fine."

"Where are we going? EHL, my place, or Mom and Dad's?"

His exasperated sigh made her want to laugh, but she kept herself in check.

"I'm dropping you off at your residence. Your parents are expecting you at their house for dinner this evening."

Plural. Dad would be there too. Her stomach knotted. *Please, please, please don't let Dad know about this.* That would be beyond mortifying, and he would be crushed.

Carlie hopped into the passenger seat and buckled up, preparing for a long, quiet car ride. They hit the highway and crossed over the river into Ohio. She'd always found it odd that Cincinnati's international airport was in Kentucky. The blue "Welcome to Ohio" sign on the bridge felt like an old friend, and she smiled as they passed under it. The car continued by the riverfront stadiums and through the city, finally reaching the suburbs.

Grabbing her phone out of the bag, Carlie messaged her mom.

Almost home. Does Dad know?

She didn't expect an answer right away, but her mother surprised her. *Welcome home. He does not know. But he's happy you're coming to dinner. We'll talk after.*

Relieved, Carlie texted Rachael. *Coming to dinner?*

She waited a few minutes to be surprised again; no response. The whole world had gone mad.

Larry pulled up outside her apartment and made no move to help her out. *That's fine.* She pulled her bags out from the backseat and thanked him as she crossed the front of the car. He did wait to make sure she got in before pulling away. Carlie half expected to hear tires squealing as he made his getaway, but he sedately drove off. Probably had a crazy night planned. Polishing his shoes or something equally thrilling. She chuckled and closed the door behind her, locking it firmly.

Home.

When she and Brent had lived together, she would

return from trips to find his dirty dishes in the sink waiting for her. Now, when she got home, it was to a quiet, empty place. Everything where she'd left it. Orderly. Settled. Just as it should be.

Carlie had enjoyed living alone post-Brent. She needed the quiet and solitude.

But now it just felt...lonely.

She missed Kurt. Glancing at the clock, she tried to imagine where his flight might be now. Would it be weird to text him so he saw something when he landed? She fiddled with her phone and decided against it, though her gaze returned to the screen repeatedly, the temptation difficult to resist. With idle hands, restlessness chewed at her resolve, so with a huff, she jumped into Martha Stewart mode and tackled the awaiting chores.

30

*S*econd load of laundry finished, Carlie checked the time again and decided enough was enough. She had to go. It was time to face her mother.

Because of the nice spring weather, she took her time walking to her parents' house. Carlie lived in a large first-floor rental at the mouth of the affluent neighborhood. Mature trees dotted sweeping lawns, and elegant brick-and-wrought-iron-embellished entrances gave way to long, pristine driveways. The leaves were emerging from buds overhead, and the blossoms would soon be in full bloom on the smaller, decorative trees. The color of the new leaves in the fading sunlight were reminiscent of his eyes, dark and full of emotion after her nightmare. Eyes she could happily drown in.

Carlie sighed and checked the time again. Probably landing now.

Her phone vibrated, and a thrill raced up her spine. She glanced at the screen.

Yup, on my way! her sister messaged.

Not the person she was hoping to hear from, but at least it wasn't Alex.

See you in a few. Miss you, Rach!

You missed me? You were only gone a few days, silly!

Stumbling over her feet, she froze and realized it truly had only been six days since she'd gone dress shopping with her sister. It felt as though she'd aged substantially in that time.

Arriving at their parents' home, Carlie detoured to the back patio, giving herself a minute to breathe. It wasn't the home they grew up in, the house from her miserable dream. They had bought this place when she was in high school. A lovely house, but it had never quite held that home-sweet-home vibe she longed for. She plucked at invisible lint on her knee and peeked at her phone again, giving in to her need to reach out to Kurt.

Made it home safely. Hope you did too. About to see my parents. Wish me luck.

No immediate reply. Just as well.

The back door swung open, and her mother looked down at her. Mary glanced over her shoulder at the kitchen, then gracefully came down the steps to sit in the chair next to her younger daughter.

"Hi, honey."

"Mom, I'm so sorry," Carlie started. "I can't explain what happened."

Her mother collected Carlie's hand in both of hers, giving her fingers the embrace Carlie needed. It was a start.

"We are all young and reckless at some point in our lives. I'm glad to see you breaking out of your shell a little bit, but I will admit this took me by surprise. How are you holding up? Are you okay?"

Carlie felt the urge to cry and choked it down. "Yes," she whispered.

"And how did the presentation go?"

She sat up a little straighter. "Good. Really well, Mom. I tuned out everything else and nailed it."

"I'm glad to hear it. I won't ask more about that now—I'm sure your father will want to dig into it. Was he there?"

"Alex? Yes. I snuck out before I had to talk to him too much."

She frowned. "Avoidance does not make a problem go away."

"I know. But I wasn't ready. One thing at a time."

"You sound like your father." She smiled, then tugged at her hand as they both stood up. Her mother wrapped an arm around her side as they entered the house together.

"Is that my Carlie-Q?"

She laughed. "Dad, you know I'm twenty-four years old."

He turned with a knowing smile. "And?"

"And don't you think I'm a little old for that?"

"If I'm not too old to say it, you're not too old to hear it."

"Fair enough." She shrugged as he enveloped her in a warm bear hug.

"I wasn't expecting you back yet. Everything go well in Chicago?"

Carlie snuck a glance at her mom behind him. Mary shook her head.

"The presentation went well, but I was ready to come home. Is Rach here yet?" she asked, changing the subject and ducking under Dad's arm to slip into the living room.

"No, should be any minute now."

Carlie plopped onto the sofa and slid out her phone. No new messages. Dang it.

She texted Kim, *Two hours?*

Affirmative. Bringing wine. Something tells me we may need it.

Thanks, girl. See you soon.

"You girls and your technology," her mother complained. "Don't you ever put your phones away and just focus on the people around you?"

"Mom, really? I was on it for two seconds."

"If people today spent less time with their noses in their phones and more time reading and paying attention, imagine what we could accomplish."

"But Mom," called Rachael, entering the room. "How would we ever get anything done that way? Everything happens through these now," she teased, wiggling her phone at Mom, the two women nearly identical, but with two and a half decades between them. Rachael slid onto the sofa next to Carlie and hit her with her elbow. "Move over, Car!"

"Get your own couch!" She shoved back.

"And they're twelve again," groaned their father.

Dad made a big lasagna for dinner, with her favorite twisty garlic bread and salad. Carlie thought about the salad lady from the hotel and smiled. She would have appreciated the simple iceberg lettuce salad mix. They talked about Carlie's presentation, and Rachael updated them on the animal hospital Rick was currently expanding and her wedding crisis of the moment. Carlie vowed to get back on board to help her sister with everything as soon as she was caught up at work.

"Rachael, why don't you help your father clean up the kitchen. I need to borrow your sister for a little bit," Mom suggested.

Rach raised her pale eyebrows. *Later*, Carlie mouthed. Rachael nodded and wordlessly started clearing dishes from the table.

"Come, let's go for a little walk," her mother beckoned.

They stepped into their shoes, and her mother handed Carlie her father's thick flannel. "It's starting to cool off. I noticed you didn't wear a jacket."

"It was nice out earlier."

Mom watched as Carlie shrugged into the soft shirt. No way could she fit into one of hers. Carlie had been taller than her mother since the sixth grade.

They walked into the dusky evening and she breathed deeply, catching the scent of fresh-cut grass. Carlie loved cities, but there was something revitalizing about being here. She was grateful her parents had never moved the business to one of the major cities always courting them. She couldn't imagine growing up anywhere else.

"Tell me about him," her mother said.

"Kurt?" Carlie asked.

"No, Alex. We'll get back to Kurt."

The deepening twilight made it easier to talk. "Alex is unbelievably gorgeous. And smart. Confident. Very charming. I thought I could really like him."

"What happened?"

"We hit it off, right from the start. He took me out to lunch, and we spent some time together. But then I found out about his books. He wrote some pretty awful stuff about Dad and EHL. I was pissed."

Mom circled her hand, encouraging her to move on.

Carlie blew out her breath. "He apologized. We decided to start fresh. We went for a walk, and it was crazy, Mom. We had this intense connection. One thing led to another, and we ended up back in his room. And then…" She trailed off, her cheeks scorching hot.

"Carlie, I know this is uncomfortable to talk about, but I need you to think carefully about what happened. Did you know there was a camera?"

Her eyes flew wide. "No! Ugh. I would never!"

Completely unperturbed, her mother pressed on. "What do you think happened?"

"All I can think is that when he went to get, a, um"—her face was aflame—"a condom, he must have set something up. But I don't recall there being that much time, that much he could have done. All he did was move one bag. I didn't see any glowing red lights or anything like that. I can't believe this."

"Sweetheart, glowing red lights are just in the movies. Think about your phone—does it glow when you record something?"

God, Carlie felt so stupid. She wouldn't be surprised if a cosmic dunce cap sprouted from her head now.

Her mother hugged her side. "I know what you're thinking, and no, you're not a fool. I am glad you used protection. Imagine if he had gotten you pregnant on top of this. Then we'd be in a real mess. What happened next? How did you discover the video?"

"Kurt disappeared. He was supposed to speak the next day. Melanie, one of the conference hosts and a sister of his friend, sweet girl actually… Anyway, Melanie mentioned that she couldn't get ahold of him and didn't know where he was. She said he had checked out of the hotel, and it wasn't like him. I offered to reach out, but he didn't answer his phone. I ended up sending him an email to see if he planned to return for his presentation." She stopped for a moment, waiting for a passing car to go by.

"I started suspecting something was wrong when the bartender told me he'd seen Alex and Kurt arguing in the bar. Alex blew me off and got pissy when I asked him about it." She frowned, thinking how it should have been obvious then that he was hiding something. She had felt a parallel between him and Brent; they both had the same dodginess. Though in her wildest imaginings, she would never have guessed his true motive, what he had done. What a nightmare.

"That's when I started feeling sick and went back to my room. Alone. The next morning Kurt showed up and told me what was happening. It's insane, Mom. Who does something like that? And why? Why me?!"

Mary didn't say anything, just kept her arm wrapped around her daughter's waist while they walked. When Carlie's breathing calmed again, her mom stopped walking and turned to look up at her. "Carlie, you understand this more than you let on. You are the daughter of one of the most successful businessmen in the country. Frankly, I'm relieved you girls haven't had poachers after you for years. Rachael found Rick, and I hoped you would settle down before something like this happened to you. But listen to me, I am not going to let him get away with this. Larry is compiling a security detail to accompany the family to Atlanta. I also would like you to carry the mace I got you girls for Christmas. Take extra precautions until this is finished."

Carlie nodded, grateful her mother didn't blame her. She didn't think she could take that right now. "I will."

"Now, tell me about Kurt Hunter."

"Kurt is...well, I had no idea who he was." Her mother huffed, but she ignored it. "I didn't like him much at first. He was too flirty, too cocky. But I was wrong. He's compassionate, thoughtful, and patient. When we went out together, he was funny and surprised me with how generous he is in so many ways. Then when he found out about me and Alex... When he left..." She grimaced. "But he came back. He didn't have to, but he came back. I don't think he likes me anymore, not like that, but he is helping me. Us. Then he snuck me out of the hotel and took me to Navy Pier. He's humble. And honest. And he likes children. And..." She stopped, realizing she was gushing.

"And it's pretty obvious, Carlie."

"What?"

"You like him," she said flatly. "When do I meet him?"

Holy hell. Was she that obvious? Leave it to Carlie to fall for the person who was helping her with a situation arising from having sex with someone else. Oh, and that same someone else was trying to blackmail him over her. Fantastic. Icing on the cake.

"Mom, I've known him for like a minute. Besides, he hates me after what I did with Alex. I hurt him."

She shrugged. "Men want what they want. If Kurt Hunter wanted you before, he will again. He needs to get over his wounded pride."

Carlie pondered this as they turned back toward the house. He had given her that small kiss. And he was returning. But that was because he was the one being targeted, right?

"Give it time, Car," Mom said, leaning against her. "Give *him* time."

They entered the house to find Rachael pacing by the front door. "Finally! I was debating coming to get you."

"What's wrong?" she asked, hanging up Dad's flannel. He sat in the front room, watching the scene with amusement.

"I thought we had plans with Kim?" Rachael said.

"Aack. I totally spaced. Mom, Dad, we have to go. Thank you so much for dinner! Love you. Talk to you tomorrow." She traded a quick hug with her parents.

"Bye Mom, Dad!" Rachael hollered as she dragged Carlie out the door to her car.

31

"Subtle much, Rach?" Carlie grumbled as she fastened her seatbelt.

"Why be subtle? I can smell a juicy story from a mile away. I want details! And I suspect I'm not going to get any info until Kim's with us, too?" She glanced at Carlie from the corner of her eye as she accelerated down the road, quickly eating up the short distance to Carlie's place.

"Yup."

Rachael parked the sedan and turned to her. "Seriously, is everything okay, CarCar?"

Looking out the window, Carlie considered her question. "I hope so," she said quietly.

Her sister took the key out of the ignition, and they listened to the growing silence. "Are you pregnant?"

Carlie whipped her head to turn and look at her outrageous sister. "What? No."

Rachael nodded once, then moved on. "You are not getting back together with Brent."

"Hell no! What are you thinking?"

"I've been trying to figure out what's going on. Those

were the first things that came to mind."

Carlie glared mutinously.

"Fine. Let's go in. Where's Kim? Think she'll be here anytime in the next hour? We should have given her an earlier time, then she'd be here by now."

Laughing, she tossed Rachael a bone. "She's stopping for wine."

"Good girl," she replied with a twinkle in her eye.

In Carlie's apartment, Rach started getting out wine glasses and a bag of grapes. "Gross! These have gone bad!"

Carlie rolled her eyes and sat on the couch, pulling out her phone. "I've been out of town for nearly a week. The cheese is still good, and there are crackers in the cupboard." New text from Alex. Should she open it now? Remembering her mom's words, she held her breath and tapped it open.

Conference is dull without you. Miss you.

She exhaled slowly. *Sorry! Just keep thinking of your next gig.*

Which you will be joining me at, right?

Hadn't they had this conversation already?

She typed back, *No, I have to stay here.*

But I'll see you in Atlanta?

I'll be there. And Carlie would be ready to kick some ass.

"Where is she?" Rachael fumed, pacing back and forth.

"Chill, Rach. She's on her way."

Carlie flipped through a magazine on the couch and pretended to read. Her mind was far away, though, picturing green eyes and dark blonde hair. Was her mom right? Would he come back around? He did kiss her that one time, but that hardly even counted as a kiss. And he was coming back, but primarily because his money and company were involved.

And that was bothering her. Kurt had money and influence. Hunter Industries certainly owned plenty of companies, but it wasn't at the same level as EHL. Or not yet, at any rate. Why would Alex target him instead of going straight to Dad? Was it really about the books? It also seemed like a stretch, using a tape of her as bait. Kurt and she had only known each other for a matter of days. How could Alex be sure that Kurt would bite? It just didn't make any sense. Frustrated, she tossed the magazine on the coffee table and walked to the window, looking into the clear night. "She's here," Carlie said.

"About damn time. I don't know how you can stand that, Car. Honestly, if I say I'm going to be somewhere..." She rattled on and Carlie tuned her out, having heard this rant dozens of times. Punctuality was a big thing for Rachael. The apple didn't fall far from the mom-tree on that one. "It's the principle of the thing, a sign of respect," Rachael continued.

Carlie humored her sister with a nod and opened the door, watching Kim dance up the walk and cha-cha with her loaded wine bags. Everyone needed a friend like her.

"Hey, babe! Welcome home!" She planted a smooch on Carlie's cheek and sailed into the apartment. "How's the planning going, Alice?"

Rach, predictably annoyed at the Alice in Wonderland reference, pointedly looked at her phone before responding. "Fine. Good of you to show up."

"Oh, stop it, you two," Carlie grumbled. "What kind of nectar did you bring?"

"Pinot and Riesling. Also grabbed a bottle of red—wasn't sure what level of crisis we were facing."

"Crisis? What's going on, Carlie?" Rachael asked.

Carlie pointed to the red and sat while they spread the wine and snacks. The threesome settled around the coffee table and she wove her tale, skipping over very little. Aside from a few interruptions and wicked laughter from Kim, they listened intently. They cracked open a second bottle of wine and Carlie paused, embarrassed to say what had happened when Kurt returned. She took a deep breath.

"He called me the next morning; I was so relieved to hear from him. Melanie's conversation had me a little concerned, and I never got the sense that he was a cut-and-run kind of guy, know what I mean?"

They nodded in unison.

"Turns out he was calling me from the hotel and appeared at my door moments later. I'm sure I looked like hell, I had been in and out of the bathroom all night. Gag. But he came in and sat me down, and...and asked if I had slept with Alex."

"He what? Why is that any business of his?" Rachael shouted.

Carlie took a deep breath and turned sad eyes toward her older sister. "Turns out it is his business. He and Alex had a bit of a fight in the bar. About me. Alex told Kurt he had a tape of us. From his room." She groaned and fell back against her chair, spilling a bit of wine on her shirt. At least they had moved on to the white wine.

Stunned silence greeted her.

"Whoa," Kim said, shocked.

"Right?"

"Son of a bitch!" spat Rachael, fury staining her cheeks.

"Why would he tell Kurt?" asked Kim, trying to connect the dots.

"Hunter Industries owns a publishing house. Which happens to be Alex's publisher. They had recently informed his agent that they were dropping him as an author. I imagine he wasn't thrilled about that."

"And...?" Rachael urged.

"And he wants a crap ton of money and a contract for more books in exchange for keeping the tape quiet."

"Shit, Car. That's serious," Kim said. "You should call the cops."

She shook her head. "No, I can't. If we bring in the police, the media will be all over it and everything I've been working on will be crushed. Dad will be crushed. I'll be crushed."

They sat in silence for a few minutes, mulling over the situation.

"So, Hunter Industries is involved. What happened next?" Rachael asked.

Carlie updated them on the conversations with Kurt and Mom.

"Mary Eller." Kim smiled. "A legit badass."

Rachael and Carlie exchanged a look. She may not have been Betty Crocker, but their mom was wicked smart and always a step—or ten—ahead of everyone else.

"That was yesterday morning? Then what happened? You didn't come home until today," observed Rachael.

"After that? I obviously couldn't go down and see Alex. I would have killed him. And no matter how good of a lawyer Mom is, that's something we can't do." Carlie smirked. "Kurt helped me slip out of the hotel to get my mind off things. We went to Navy Pier and just walked around and talked."

"You and Kurt, huh?" Rachael said.

"It's not like that, Rach. I don't know what Alex told him, but Kurt was different, distant. He doesn't like me anymore. At least not like that," she said sadly.

"And you?" asked Kim.

"And now I realize what a colossal screwup I am. How

huge of a mistake I made. I wish I could go back and change things, but..." She held up her hands and let them fall.

Kim slid over and wrapped her arm around her shoulders. "Cheer up, girlfriend. How could any man resist those big blue eyes of yours?"

Carlie leaned her head on Kim's shoulder and saw Rachael's eyes narrow.

"Carlie, what do you want to happen?" Rachael asked.

"I want this all to go away. And I want Kurt to forgive me."

"What happens next?" Kim asked.

She glanced back at Kim. "Next, we go to Atlanta for Bernie's fundraiser. Can you come?"

"Sure. When?"

Rachael replied, "We leave Wednesday and get back Sunday."

"Fuuuuck. I'll be in London. Annual shareholder meeting. I can't miss it," she said. "I get back to the States Saturday morning. Want me to meet you then?"

"If you can and want to, I'd love to have the support. But I understand. I know how important this is for you. Besides, the rest of the family will be there. And Kurt."

"Really? That's...interesting," Rachael observed. "Can't wait to meet him. Rick will be there, too. We'll make sure that asshole can't touch you, Car. No one messes with my sister and gets away with it."

Carlie took in her sister and Kim. Her best friends. Her confidantes.

"I love you guys," she whispered.

"Love you too, baby CarCar." Rachael smiled.

"Yeah, you're all right," teased Kim.

Carlie slapped her shoulder and held up her wine glass. "To us."

32

*S*he was going to die. Her head. Ugh. They may have outdone themselves last night. Carlie grabbed her phone and glanced at the screen to see multiple missed texts.

Made it home. Love ya, sis.

Thanks for coming over, Rach. Love you too! she wrote back.

Next was a similar chat with Kim, then an upbeat message from her boss:

Heard you made it back to town early. We got a lot of new leads already for Pendulum. Great work! Take it easy this weekend, and I'll see you Monday.

She typed out a response. *Thanks, Rebecca. Let me know if you need anything before then. I'll just be around the house and hitting the grocery store.*

Her breath caught as she read the next, this time from Kurt. *Sorry, just got this. Call me and let me know how it went.*

Carlie calculated the time difference; he was probably still asleep. Grinning to herself, she pictured him sleeping peacefully. Pictured his messed-up hair and straight, slightly upturned nose. Pictured him in his boxers. So yummy. She could probably grant him a little more beauty sleep before calling.

Ready to return to some semblance of normalcy, she washed up, then pulled on her leggings and a tank top, downed a protein bar and coffee, and went out for a good, long run.

Feet pounding out a steady rhythm, she took stock of things.

Work was good. Carlie was coming into her own. The conference was a huge victory, and she couldn't wait to see how things panned out. The matrix was not complete and would need many iterations before she felt confident turning it over to the IT crew, but it was getting there.

Kim had hardly mentioned Owen at all last night. Either things were going smoothly for the moment or she was not ready to talk about it yet.

Her sister and Rick were happy. Rachael was still obsessing over every last detail, but Carlie was encouraged that he didn't seem to be bothered by her craziness. It took a special person to put up with that. Their busy work schedules probably helped, too.

Carlie was impressed with how Mom had kept her cool and pulled out the details last night. She wished she were more like her. Her mother always held it together.

Dad seemed to be doing well. She knew her mom worried about his stress level, but he had been calm and relaxed last night. At some point, though, Carlie was afraid he would find out what happened. She did not want to be responsible for adding to his stress.

Alex. The text exchange with him was the best she could do. She couldn't let on that she knew about his deception, but she also didn't want to lead him on. After this, she could perhaps go to work for a circus doing the high-wire act. She smirked as she continued running. Bright green hair. Red nose. Balancing a long pole as she crossed high above the safety net. Good grief.

And what to do about Kurt... He occupied so much of her thoughts lately that she worried she was becoming borderline obsessed with him. She liked him. A lot. To herself, she could admit she was sliding down a slippery slope. But she had to stop there. She couldn't let herself fall in love with a man who wasn't capable of returning her feelings. Commitment. She had learned her lesson with Brent. One person's feelings and aspirations weren't enough to sustain a relationship. There was always going to be another Gina waiting in the rafters, ready to swoop in when the opportunity presented itself. Carlie refused to let that happen again.

Crossing the street to follow the path through the park, she calmed her thoughts and focused on her breathing. Ahead in the distance, a small group of joggers turned the curve out of sight. Parents and babysitters pushed strollers and watched small children rushing around the playground. Working around the curve toward the front of the park again, she closed in on the shelter house. Six weathered wooden picnic tables sat under the dark roof. A lone person sat on top of a table, watching her approach. His shape looked familiar. As she neared, the recognition escalated, and she slowed to a walk and crossed the grass to stand before him.

"What brings you here this early in the day?" she asked.

Brent smiled at her sheepishly. "This is where you like to run. I've stopped by here almost every morning this week to see if I could catch you."

Her brow furrowed. "Why?"

His gaze traveled across the park, then down to his feet resting on the seat of the picnic table. His expression when he looked back up was troubled. "I wanted to see you, to talk to you. I figured this was better done in person." He patted the tabletop next to him. "Join me?"

Four years together. Last week she would have been a mess at this confrontation and would have fled back home. Instead, she climbed to sit next to him and focused on slowing her breathing, calming her heartbeat.

He released his breath. "I wasn't sure you'd talk to me."

"I'm here. What do you want?"

"When I saw you the other day, I really wanted to talk more. I'm sorry to have sprung that on you. I shouldn't have tried to talk with Gina around. That was wrong of me. I'm sorry."

Carlie cringed as images of the two of them together flooded her mind. Saying nothing, she nodded for him to continue.

He ran his hand through his hair and clenched his jaw. She knew that look. Brent was unsure of what to do. She took pity on him and spoke up. "Congrats, I suppose. I didn't know you were engaged."

He looked at her like she was deranged. "What?"

"She was trying on dresses. At a wedding shop..." Carlie prompted.

He laughed. "She was getting fitted for a bridesmaid dress for her cousin's wedding. We're not... Oh, hell, no. She and I... We're not together like that. She's not you, Car."

No shit, Sherlock.

Strange to hear him say that, though. Toward the end of their time together, she had thought getting engaged would somehow bring them closer together. He was the symbol of the way things were supposed to work out in her life. They met in college, fell in love, moved in together. They were expected to get married and have kids. It was the American dream, right? When she caught him cheating, it was devastating but forced her to make a needed change. As much as it had killed her at the time, she knew now that it was the best thing for her. She realized Brent was a signpost in her life. He would forever be part of her. But he was in her past, not her future.

She looked across to the playground and saw the kids playing on the slide. She remembered Kurt's silly playfulness in Chicago, and relief washed over her. One chapter closed. She was over him—over Brent. Carlie would always have a soft spot for him. But she no longer felt torn in half. She was whole again.

The freedom of the moment was breathtaking. A new world of possibilities opened before her.

"I've been thinking a lot about this," Brent filled the silence. "Seeing you last week was the catalyst I needed."

Turning her attention back to him, she swallowed as she recognized where this was going. *Don't do it, Brent. Don't do this to yourself.*

"I miss you, Car. I wasn't ready before. I took you, us, for granted and lost sight of how great we were together. I was distracted. But I'm ready now. And it's you I want to spend my life with. I miss tripping over your shoes in the house. I miss your perfume, your laugh. I miss watching movies with you, making dinner together. I miss you."

"And Gina?"

"Gina and I are just friends, Carlie. God, I've been kicking myself about what happened. I swear to you I will never stray again. It's you I want."

"Brent, stop." She pushed off the table to stand in front of him. "You and I had something special. I thought you were the one. I thought we would get married and have kids, grow old together. But you helped me see that we were not *really* in love. Not the kind of love that lasts a lifetime. We had a lot of fun together, and I will always love you, but not like that."

He stared, raw emotion in his hazel depths. "Carlie, what are you saying? Please. I love you."

She shook her head, a single tear slipping down her cheek. "You're too late, Brent. And Gina wasn't the problem. *We* were the problem. If it wasn't her, it would have been someone else. We were too comfortable with maintaining the status quo. We weren't going anywhere. You don't realize it yet, but this is the best thing for both of us."

Bracing her hand on his knee, she kissed his cheek and stood back. "Listen to me. You are a good guy, and you're going to find the right person for you. It will be someone special. Someone you don't want to let out of your arms. Someone you can't imagine being without." She smiled, thinking of Kurt. "Someone you are willing to fight for."

"Carlie, I do love you."

"I know, Brent. But you're not *in* love with me. And I'm not in love with you anymore. I'll be a friend when you need one, but that's all we can be to each other."

With one last heartfelt smile, she turned and jogged away, the chains of the past falling away. Her heart hurt for him, but she felt lighter, and her mind was whirring with plans, a new goal, a new dream, coming into shape.

33

*N*ot willing to sit around twiddling her thumbs any longer, Carlie messaged Kurt. *You up yet, Mr. California?*

No response. Carlie tried not to watch her phone like a crazy person, with mild success. She even managed to shower without dropping her phone in the water. *I'm so lame.*

Her phone vibrated on the tabletop, and she raced to snatch it up, stubbing her finger against it and sending the device sailing across the room. "Gah!" she shouted, plucking it off the floor before dropping onto her bed.

Good morning, Ms. Ohio. Just getting moving. Call you after I brush my teeth.

Carlie sprawled out across the bed and watched the seconds crawl by. She couldn't believe how much she had missed talking to him.

After an insanely long three minutes, her phone came to life.

"Hi," she chirped. *Carlie, get ahold of yourself. Bring it back down an octave. Sheesh!*

"Good morning." She could hear the sleep in his voice. "How are things?"

"The same, I guess. My mom didn't have much to add. She and Larry are arranging for us to have, like, bodyguards when we go to Bernie's thing."

"Larry?"

"Mom's assistant."

"Oh. Glad to hear you'll have more people around. I don't like the thought of Alex being anywhere near you."

"Worried about me?"

"Worried about what he's going to try to do next."

"And worried about me?" she wheedled.

"And worried about you."

Satisfied, she smiled and traced circles on her bedspread. They lapsed into an easy silence.

A thought occurred to her, and she needed to deal with it before anything else could happen. "Kurt, are you angry with me?"

Pause.

"No. I'm not angry with you, Carlie. I'm angry at the situation. Fucking furious with Alex. But I'm not angry with you."

His words flowed through her mind, cooling her fears and calming her nerves. She closed her eyes, needing to hear that. "Good. Guess I'm not angry with you, either."

He laughed. "Why would you be angry with me?"

"The gym? When you practically chewed my face off."

"Oh?" He paused. "Is that how you recall it?"

She squirmed a little. "Not exactly."

"Good." She could hear his smile. "Have you heard from Alex?"

The abrupt change in topic threw her off. "He's sent a few text messages. Says he misses me."

He mumbled something she couldn't make out.

"What was that?" Carlie asked.

"Nothing. Did you reply to him?"

"Just the barest of responses. Told him I was busy here and confirmed I'd be in Atlanta next week."

"About that... It looks like I won't be your plus-one for Bernie's event," he said.

What? "Oh?" She tried not to sound disappointed.

"I had an invitation waiting for me here. I'll be there on my own invite. But I'd still like to accompany you, if that's okay?"

Don't you dare read too much into this, Carlie Eller!

"I'd like that."

"So would I."

"Did you find out when you can make it out here?"

"I can't make it out until early Thursday, so I'll have to meet you in Atlanta. Can you text me your hotel info? I'd like to get some eyes on it, maybe find a place nearby."

"Of course." She was disappointed that he wouldn't be here, but at least he would be meeting her there. "Get some eyes on it?"

"I want my security team to do a run through and keep an eye on it. Make sure Alex isn't there and doesn't get to you or your family."

"That's not necessary. Mom's got people on it already. Really, how many people do we need?"

"Please let me do this. It will help ease my mind."

"Fine. But only because you said please. I'll let Mom know."

"Thank you. I hate to say this, but I have to go. Call if you need me. And Carlie? Be careful."

"I will. See you soon."

After hanging up, she ran through the conversation in

her head, trying to decide if those were clues about his feelings or not. So frustrating!

The following days inched by. Carlie met up with Marie for lunch on Saturday and gave her the thirty-thousand-foot view of the trip. She was concerned, but not worried. Carlie might have left out the whole sex tape and blackmail portions. Marie agreed she should try to work things out with Kurt. "I still think he deserves to be slapped for violating you like that, but I'd like to meet this young man."

She grinned. Marie's view of someone violating her was refreshingly narrow. Carlie wished that was her biggest concern right now.

Work was her salvation, helping to keep the time moving. Digging into fresh data and applying it to the matrix. Debugging, making tweaks, and reevaluating. Attending sales calls and development meetings. Working on marketing strategy. Those ate up her time but, unfortunately, still allowed enough for shopping with Rachael.

"We need the perfect evening attire for you, Carlie. Quit being a downer! This is the fun stuff. Consider these gowns to be the key to turning Kurt's eyes toward you, and only you." Maybe Rachael had a point there. "As it is, we hardly have enough time for alterations. And trust me, you need to get those fitted. The waist needs to be taken in, the hemline let out, and—are you even listening to me?"

Carlie turned back to her, trying not to stare at her reflection in the mirror. She was not ordinarily one who enjoyed playing dress up, but she loved this dress. The black and silver shimmered down her figure to the floor; the low neckline was just high enough to not be risqué, but her cleavage rose to the top. Whoa. "Yes, I'm listening. Waist, hemline, yadda, yadda, yadda."

"How are we sisters?!" Rachael huffed, marching away to

talk to the salesclerk and returning with a bright red dress. "Now this one," she demanded.

"Yes, ma'am," Carlie teased, heading back to change. "I like this one, Rach. The black and silver. Good job!" she threw over her shoulder.

Rachael beamed, evidently pleased that her sister was *finally* getting into the spirit of things. "There's hope for you yet, CarCar."

They settled on the black and silver dress for Saturday and a sleek, cobalt-blue cocktail dress for Friday's dinner. The seamstress assured them the gowns would be ready, and Rachael sighed with relief. Carlie guessed that she should be relieved, too.

"Why are you so happy?" Rachael asked suspiciously.

"Because we're done, and I didn't die," Carlie teased.

"Oh, no, we're not done yet."

"We're not?"

"We need to go find the right shoes, handbags, jewelry. The dress is just the foundation for the accessories. Then there are the hairstyles, makeup, and nails to consider." She practically glowed discussing this.

"Fine. Let's go."

Carlie resigned herself to the torment. They popped in and out of so many stores she could hardly think straight. As Rachael's demands kept storeowners hopping, Carlie found a corner seat to hide in and text Kim.

S.O.S. I'm going down in the S.S. Rachael. Send help!

She got back the crying-laughter emoji face. *What's she doing now?*

Shopping. I've spent the last few evenings shopping with her. Gowns, jewelry, and everything else imaginable.

Look at you, all grown up and going to the ball, Cinderella.

Ha. Ha. At least it's a good distraction.

Have you heard from either of the boys?

Kurt and I spoke the other day. Says he isn't mad at me but at Alex and with what happened. I'm taking that as a win.

And Alex?

He's been pretty quiet. He knows we'll both be in Atlanta, but I haven't heard much on that front. I'm taking his silence as a win too.

When do you leave?

Tomorrow night. When do you head to London?

Thursday.

Carlie glanced to confirm Rachael was still engrossed in wristlets. Bah.

How are things with Owen? she inquired.

Not much to say. His birthday's coming up. Trying to figure out what to get for him.

A strip tease? Carlie added a winking emoji.

I like where you're going with this, my dear.

"There you are! What do you think of this one?" Rachael held up a dainty black wristlet.

Have to go. Project Runway has returned.

K. Bye girl. Keep me posted.

Will do.

34

*T*hey arrived in Atlanta and suffered through traffic hell to get to their swanky hotel on the north side of the city. Dad distributed room keys, and they dispersed to their rooms along the nineteenth floor, unpacking and resting before dinner. "Be on time. Five o'clock sharp," Mom warned them all in the hallway. "We will be meeting the new security team to go over some details."

Carlie finished putting away the last of her clothes and explored the room. This place was way nicer than the Chicago hotel. Clearly, Tammy had worked for her dad long enough to learn that spoiling her mother ensured a healthy bonus.

The room featured a lofty king-size bed, matching nightstands with intricately carved feet, a velveteen bench at the foot of the bed, plush carpeting, a cozy lounge chair and footstool in the corner, a heavy writing desk and office chair, an entertainment center, and a glorious restroom with a jacuzzi tub and huge walk-in shower. Luxury with a capital

L. Most hotels had similar items in their rooms, but the quality of the furnishings was unmistakable here.

She plugged in her electronics then washed up, inhaling the light fragrance of the miniature soaps with a pleased sigh. Emerging from the steamy bath, she swaddled herself in loungewear and, oddly enough, picked up her discarded shoes. Kurt would be proud, she chuckled.

A knock sounded at the door, and she ran over to look through the peephole. It was a middle-aged man in a dark suit. She didn't recognize him, but he looked harmless enough. She pulled open the door.

"Carlie Eller?" he asked.

"Yes?"

"John Wallace. Mr. Hunter asked that I introduce myself. I'm with The Guardian, alpha team leader."

"Very nice to meet you, Mr. Wallace. You're the security person he told me about?"

He nodded curtly.

"I'm sorry to be the one to break it to you, but this is probably going to be pretty boring for you. I don't expect much to happen."

"I'm here to make sure it stays that way, Ms. Eller. You might see me or some of my associates in the area. We'll be keeping an eye on things."

"Um. Thanks?"

He nodded again before turning back to the elevator... where he proceeded to stand guard, clearly not intending to move. Weird. It wasn't like they were the flipping First Family or something. Carlie shook her head and closed the door.

Minutes later, another knock sounded at the door. Blowing out her breath, she jumped up again. "Yes?" she asked an older man, stranger number two for the day.

"Delivery for you, ma'am." He held out two large boxes and a clipboard for her to sign. Hauling them to the oversized bed, she gently shook one then the other. Her dresses! She unpacked them and hung them in the closet. She had just finished when another knock sounded at the door.

Really?

She stalked to the door and flung it open. "Yes?"

A young woman stood there with an overwhelming bouquet of pink and cream long stem roses. "Ms. Eller?"

Carlie nodded, staring at the exorbitant arrangement in the arms of stranger number three.

"These are for you." She passed them off and turned, shaking out her arms in relief as she left Carlie holding the lavish display.

Well, then. Security Man, Dress Man, and Flower Lady. Got it.

Settling the flowers on the writing desk, she stood on her tiptoes to search among the tall stems for a card. Plucking it from the roses, she sat on the bed and examined the envelope, already suspecting who it was from but wishing it wasn't.

Sighing, she opened the card. It read, *Almost time. Yours, Alex.*

The flowers were beautiful, but the note was odd. And how did he know where she was staying?

She snapped a picture and sent it to Kurt with a message. *Flowers delivered from Alex.*

In the fastest reply Carlie had ever seen from him, he said, *When?*

Just now.

How long have you been there?

Less than an hour.

Don't open your door to anyone unless it's your family. I mean it.

Sure.

I mean it.

She smirked at his bossy reply. *Okay!*

Have to go. Talk soon.

K. Bye, Kurt.

Please be safe.

I will.

She tossed the card on the desk and sat back to consider what this meant. Alex had been watching her. He knew where she was. And he had sent a message that looked straightforward enough on the surface, but Carlie couldn't help but read between the lines. Almost time for what? Her mind worried over what that could mean as she dressed for dinner.

"GIRLS, Rick, this is Kevin Slater, head of the security team Larry hired," Mom announced.

"Mary, did we really need security? I don't like having people watch our every move. I hardly feel this is necessary."

Mom's expression was cryptic as she faced Dad. "I have received some conflicting information and feel better knowing there are people in place. Trust me on this one, Charles."

Dad nodded once and sat back, far from appeased, but acknowledging her wishes.

"Thank you for taking the time to meet with me. From our previous meetings, we've gathered enough information to get a team in place to keep an eye on things. I've also been in communication with Mr. Hunter's security team. Between us, I am confident in our position at this hotel. I would ask that you do not leave the hotel unaccompanied. If you must leave for any reason, at any time, please call this number and I or someone on our team will accompany you." He distributed a business card to each of the family members gathered around the table and turned back to Mom. "Ma'am, I'll have your report ready for you as discussed."

"Thank you, Slater."

They all watched in silence as he departed.

"Hunter's team?" Dad asked.

"Remember I told you I met Kurt Hunter at the conference? He was also invited this week, and his security team bumped into ours. Guess he's staying here too," Carlie said, shrugging nonchalantly.

"You *guess*?" Rachael asked.

Carlie mumbled something and pinched Rachael under the table. She jumped, then coughed.

"Dad! Did I tell you we chose a band for the reception? They are absolutely divine!" she swooned, launching into a detailed description of every song, instrument, and hair product the band was known for.

"That sounds delightful, honey," Dad said, frowning as he looked back and forth between his daughters. Mom captured his attention and the dinner resumed.

"I take it your father doesn't know," Rick murmured to Carlie.

She nodded. "I'd like to keep it that way. There's not really a halfway of knowing."

"Dad would completely freak out and give him anything he wanted," hissed Rachael. "This asshole deserves nothing. Not one penny."

"If I were in your father's place, though, I would want to

know. I would be livid if this was kept from me. I don't think you are giving Charles enough credit here."

Carlie and Rachael looked at each other, and Rachael smiled sweetly at him. "I'll take it under advisement."

Rick groaned and glanced around her at Carlie. "See what I have to deal with?"

Carlie laughed at him. "Been there, done that!"

The drama passed, and they settled into a relaxing dinner. Across the table, Mom and Dad passed endless silent thoughts between them, both able to read the other well. Carlie was correct in what she had told Brent. Her parents had a love that would last. Rach and Rick were still goofy in love, petting each other and sharing bites of food, giggling over inside jokes. Carlie sighed, knowing that love was real, and her family was blessed with it. Would it be the same for her someday?

Picking up her constantly topped-off wine glass, Carlie made a toast to the Ellers, the best damn family in the world. Her parents and sister gave her warm looks, and Rick joined in as they clinked their glasses together.

They finished dinner and too many desserts and drifted off toward the elevator together. Rachael and Rick splintered off to go to the bar, and Carlie accompanied her parents up to their floor. Once the elevator door closed, Dad leaned back and leveled a serious look at his wife and daughter. "I know something is afoot, and I do not like being kept in the dark. I'm willing to be patient and wait for one of you to tell me, but that patience will not last for long."

Carlie felt her face flush and avoided eye contact. Mom leaned her small frame into her dad's side. "Charles, if and when you need to know, I will tell you. But for now, please trust me."

He was quiet for a moment, then put a hand on the tops

of each of their heads. "If anything happens to either of you or Rachael, I will not tolerate it. I am trusting you, but please consider what I can do to help."

Her parents walked her to her door, and she turned to watch them walk to their suite at the end of the hall. Carlie waved before slipping into her room and shutting the door. Her heart was heavy as she replayed her dad's words. "I'm so sorry, Dad," she whispered.

35

𝓝othing on the television. Nothing coming across the phone. It was still early, and with the whole "don't leave unaccompanied" speech, Carlie felt irrationally imprisoned.

You guys still at the bar? she messaged her sister.

Yes! Come join us!

Carlie smiled and grabbed her bag, heading back to the elevator.

"Ms. Eller." Wallace, Kurt's security guard, nodded from his position next to the metal doors. She smiled and waited for the doors to open.

"Just meeting my sister downstairs," she explained awkwardly, unsure if she was supposed to tell him. The man nodded politely but remained silent. His eyes were on her as she slipped into the elevator. This was so over-the-top bizarre.

Exiting the elevator, Carlie reached into her bag for lip gloss and slicked some on before cruising into the bar to find Rachael and Rick.

"There's my girl!" squealed Rachael. Rick rolled his eyes

behind her and held his hand up, miming downing shots.

"Hi, Rach!" Carlie exclaimed back, not wanting to dull her luster. Her sister's petite frame was perched on a high barstool and Rick was seated next to her, his stool pulled out just enough to rest his foot on either side of her chair and drape an arm protectively around her. His posture clearly said "mine." Carlie smiled at the adorable picture they presented and plopped down in the empty stool next to Rachael.

"Something to drink?" the elderly bartender inquired.

Carlie ordered her vanilla vodka and diet, then checked out her surroundings. The bar was quiet; Wednesday night must not be a happening time. Aside from the three of them, there was only the bartender, two couples, and a lone man in a suit along the wall. She suspected he was one of either Wallace's crew from Kurt, or one of Slater's men from Larry and Mom's group. How boring this must be for them. Carlie smiled sympathetically his way and turned back to the bartender to accept her succor.

"Add hers to my tab, please," Rick said.

"Thanks, Rick."

"Thank Mom and Dad," giggled Rachael. "We're just charging it to the room."

Carlie stirred her drink with the plastic straw and thought of Alex's dislike of plastic straws. "Did you guys ever see a video about a straw and a turtle?"

Rachael curled her nose. "Ewww. Yes! It's so gross! A straw was wedged deep inside the turtle's nostril. It's so, so sad. Someone tugged and tugged forever, trying to get it out, and the poor little thing looked like it was crying in pain."

Removing the straw from her drink, Carlie sipped straight out of the glass and watched as Rach and Rick both set their straws aside. Awkward silence.

Sheesh. I'm such a conversationalist.

"Cheers," said Rick, clearing his throat and raising his drink to them. "To the most beautiful girls in all of Atlanta."

"Just Atlanta?" pouted Rachael.

"And beyond," he amended, leaning in to kiss her.

"Okay you two, get a room," Carlie laughed, nudging Rachael's shoulder.

"Have one, actually. Care to join me, Mr. Thomas?" Rachael purred at Rick.

He winked at Carlie. "Duty calls. Want us to wait for you?" he asked, pointing to her drink.

"Nah, you two go ahead. I'm going to nurse this for a while before heading back up. Besides, I'm not alone—I've got a sweet bartender and Mr. Suit over there." She nodded toward the lone man.

"G'night, CarCar!"

"Night Rach, Rick."

Carlie watched them weave their way to the elevator and head up for a night of fun for two. Turning back to the bartender, she shrugged and took another drink.

"Where's your date?" he asked.

"No date. Just me. Drinking my sorrows away," she mumbled, missing Kurt.

"Such a pretty young lady, I'm sure you have men everywhere fighting over you."

You have no idea.

"Aw, thanks."

He grinned and turned back to washing barware and helping the other couples. Carlie leaned back with her drink and considered what to do now. Sit here and drink alone? How thrilling. She checked her phone to see it was only ten p.m. Late enough to call it a night?

"Mind if I join you?"

She closed her eyes, hoping it was really him.

Turning back, she fought to not squeal like her sister just had. "Kurt! I wasn't expecting you until tomorrow."

"Surprise," he murmured, grazing her cheek with a light kiss.

"What are you doing here?"

"When you messaged me earlier, I changed my flight and got here as quickly as I could. I don't like the implication that accompanied those flowers."

"I didn't even tell you what he wrote."

"You didn't need to," Kurt said, his voice dark. "The message was clear."

"I don't care what it took, but I'm so glad you're here. I... I missed you." She blushed and took another drink. *Give him all the power, why don't you, Car. You're an idiot.*

He searched her eyes and took the seat next to hers. "You did?"

May as well go all in. "I did."

"Interesting," he said, requesting a menu and a dark beer. "Want anything?" he asked, waving the menu toward her.

Just you.

"No, I'm good. We finished dinner a little while ago."

"Here?"

"Yeah, in the restaurant. Same kitchen, same menu."

"How's the food?"

"Too good. Carb-coma good."

"Perfect."

He ordered dinner, and his drink arrived. Carlie glanced around the bar and noted the man in the suit had left. She guessed he didn't need to be here, since Kurt had arrived. It must've been one of his guys.

"How are you holding up?" he asked.

She took a sip of her drink and considered. "I'm fine. None of this feels real; it's like it happened to someone else. The more time that passes, the less real it seems."

"That's the danger, though. This is real. This is happening. And you are at the center."

"I've never liked being the center of attention," she teased. "That's more Rachael's role."

"I'm serious."

"I know," she sighed.

They sat in silence for a few minutes. "Another drink, beautiful?" asked the bartender. She nodded, and he walked away to get the vodka.

"Beautiful?" Kurt raised his eyebrows.

"Jealous?"

"Not at all. Just wondering if people fall in love with you wherever you go."

She coughed on the last sip of her drink. "Of course, they do. I just ooze sweet lovability."

He laughed and took a drink of his beer. "I believe you do."

"Here you go. This one's on me," said the bartender, smiling.

"Thank you."

"Her next one is on me," interrupted Kurt.

"If I finish this one." She tilted a sweet smile at Kurt, swiveling back and forth in her barstool.

He watched her playful swagger, his green eyes sparkling in the dim bar lighting.

"Here you go, buddy," said the bartender, setting down a steaming plate of pasta.

"Thank you," he said, turning his appreciative gaze away from her.

36

He finished his dinner, and they enjoyed another round of drinks. Carlie was cautiously optimistic, as the flirtatious Kurt had begun to reemerge. His flippant remarks made her heart beat a little faster. But she also knew that they had business to take care of.

"I met John earlier. John Wallace? He seems...nice."

He laughed. "I don't pay him to be nice. He's here to keep you safe."

"My mom's people are here, too."

"I know. Wallace sent me an update about Slater."

"This place is crawling with security. It's a bit over-whelming. Honestly, do you think anything is going to happen here, surrounded by my family, at this posh hotel?"

Kurt raised his drink and brow. "Hopefully nothing, but you're worth protecting. And your family, of course."

Warmth spread through her. "I'm so glad you're here. I really am."

He raised her hand to his lips. "Me too."

"Another round?" interrupted the bartender.

She laughed. "No, I think I'm good."

"Just the check, please," said Kurt, not taking his eyes off her. She felt the heat in his stare all the way to her toes.

They finished their drinks and strolled out to the lobby. "Are you staying here?"

He nodded. "I was checking in when I saw you." He ran his hand through his hair and looked a bit sheepish. "I hope you don't mind, but I had them put me in the room next to yours. Easier to keep track of everything that way."

"Of course," she murmured as they walked to the elevator, mentally doing a happy dance.

In the elevator, they both reached for nineteen at the same time. Their hands bumped and Carlie blushed, withdrawing to allow him to hit the button. He stood across from her, and she eyed him up and down. His wavy, dark blonde hair was just a tad long. She wondered if he had planned to get a haircut today before his original flight time. Kurt watched her, marking her progress as she examined his appearance. His mouth was perfectly sculpted, lightly lifted at the corners—one corner slightly higher than the other. Dressed in a long-sleeved, dark green polo and khakis, he looked at ease and relaxed. The elevator dinged, and she realized they had ridden the entire way in utter silence.

Wallace was still standing sentry at the elevator. He nodded to Kurt as they passed him. Kurt watched the door numbers and stopped at her door. "Can I see the note that came with the flowers?"

"Of course." She held her door open.

The heady scent of roses had infused the room. Carlie kicked her shoes off and walked barefoot to the desk where the arrangement sat, collecting the card from the table. She handed it to Kurt and watched with equal parts fascination and alarm as his warm and charismatic playboy grin turned grim.

"This is a warning, Carlie."

Suddenly cold, she rubbed her arms and sat on the edge of the bed. "Is it?"

"You should have told me what it said."

"I know."

"Damn it, this is not a game!"

"I know! Believe me, I know, okay? If you recall, I tried to tell you before." The lightheadedness took control, and her chest started to constrict. *Not now!* She desperately tried to focus on her breathing, struggling to draw a breath.

He threw the card at the table in frustration. "Did you show this to your mother or either of the security teams?"

"No," she forced out from between her clenched teeth, trying to cover the chattering. Her heart was racing as she fought a losing battle.

He sat on the edge alongside her and took her hand. "Your hand is ice cold. Are you okay?"

She started shaking, tears leaking from her eyes as she struggled to hold herself together.

"What is happening? Carlie?"

She shivered harder, and he wrapped her in his arms. "What is going on?" he whispered against her temple.

Unable to answer, she shook her head as the terror gripped her. She couldn't breathe. She couldn't stop the cold sweat that coated her skin and the shaking that knocked her teeth together.

He snagged the corner of the bedspread and hauled it toward them, wrapping her now-violently shaking body. He pulled her onto his lap and banded his arms around her, pressing her against his chest, rocking slowly as the attack wracked her body. After a time, she was able to gasp fresh air and the chills became less violent. Her body became limp, an occasional shiver passing through.

"Should I call someone?"

"No," she answered too quickly.

He set her on the bed, handling her like a fragile unknown, and walked to the restroom, turning on the bath and letting the water fill. Returning to her, he stood and eyed her, hands in his pockets.

"Truth—are you okay?"

Eyes squeezed closed, she nodded once and focused on breathing.

In and out. In and out. Focus on what you can control, Carlie.

She opened her eyes to see Kurt crouched eye level in front of her. "Panic attack?"

She nodded, tears of frustration and embarrassment welling in her eyes.

"Does this happen often?"

Carlie shook her head and lifted a shoulder. "It used to. I don't get them as much anymore."

She didn't know how long he sat with her. Eventually he wiped a tear from her cheek and hesitated a moment before returning to the bathroom, shutting off the bath.

"Come," he said.

Muscles weak with fatigue, she shrugged off the blanket, dropping it onto the bed, and put one foot in front of the other, halting in the bathroom where he waited. He met her eyes with a question in his own. She nodded, trusting him to take care of her. He gripped the bottom hem of her shirt and lifted it up and over her head. Carlie heard his swift intake of breath. He unbuttoned her pants and twirled his hand in the air, encouraging her to turn around. Kurt unhooked her bra and ran the straps down her arms before grasping her waistband and panties, sliding them down her legs. Dully, she recognized she was nude, but she couldn't bring herself to respond to it.

Behind her, she sensed his stillness. In the mirror, she saw his eyes were tightly closed, throat working, hands clenched at his sides. Her shivering had all but subsided, and she turned to him. "Kurt," she said quietly, exhausted. "It's okay. I can manage. You can go."

He opened his eyes, green fire blazing. Ignoring her comments, he took a deep breath and led her to the bath. He helped her in and watched as she sank into the warm water. Carlie closed her eyes, sighing at the buoyant effect of the water. He walked to the sink and took a glass from the counter before collecting a washcloth and bar of soap. "Shampoo? Conditioner?"

"In the shower," she replied, eyes still closed, body relaxing.

The soft thud of footsteps marked Kurt's return, followed by two hollow thumps. Curious, she opened her eyes to see that he had removed his leather shoes and rolled up his sleeves. Carlie continued to observe his movements in quiet fascination.

Kurt sat on the edge of the tub and dipped the white washcloth into the water before rubbing the bar of soap into it. Finding her hand, he lifted her arm above the water line and ran the soapy washcloth over her skin, gently scrubbing and washing away the stress. He grasped her other arm, massaging before sliding to the other end of the tub and reaching into the water for her foot. He slid the washcloth under her foot and wrapped it around the sole, sliding it up and down, eliciting a contented sigh from his patient. He smiled at her reaction, then repeated the act on her other foot before lifting her leg higher and running the washcloth up and down both of her calves.

She shivered, and he regarded her face, his eyes alive with pure heat.

He slid along the ceramic lip of the tub, returning back toward her head, and whispered, "Sit up."

Complying, she leaned forward and rested her cheek against her raised knees. He lathered up the washcloth again and moved the soapy fabric across her shoulders and down her back, rubbing her back with firm strokes. She hummed softly, and he paused, then dipped the cloth below the water's line to massage her hips and waist.

"Lie back," his hoarse voice commanded.

Meeting his eyes, she relaxed back against the tub. He lathered up the washcloth yet again and caressed her shoulders and moved down her chest, circling each breast and going lower, massaging her abdomen before swiping across her upper thighs, just grazing the curls at her middle. He continued down her thighs, rubbing the cloth in gentle circles around her skin, stopping at her knees. He wrung out the washcloth and set it aside.

"Sit up again, please," he gruffly requested.

She sat up, wrapping her arms around her knees. Taking the cup, he dipped it into the water and poured a warm trail down her hair. He moved in a steady rhythm, repeating until her thick mane of hair was thoroughly wet. The cool shampoo settled on top of her head before he worked it into a bubbly lather, encasing his hands. He dipped his hands beneath the water and rinsed them, brushing her side, his thumb grazing the side of her breast. Opening her eyes, she glanced up at him again, but his focus was solely on her hair.

Using fresh water from the faucet, he rinsed the suds from her hair, over and over again. He repeated with the conditioner, running his hands through the long silky, clean hair.

"Stay," he murmured, as though she was going to go anywhere right now.

He returned the shampoo and conditioner to the shower and moved into the bedroom. She heard the closet doors rattle, the dresser drawers sliding as he hunted.

Kurt returned to the bath empty-handed and sat on the edge of the tub. "Ready?"

Placing her hand in his, he pulled her up, water cascading down her flushed body. He brushed his hands down her body to swipe some of the excess water back into the bath, then opened the drain to let the water escape.

She stood shivering in the emptying tub while he spread a towel on the floor. He grasped her waist and plucked her from the tub, standing her on the dry towel. Another towel to dry her back, her legs, and then wrapped around to the front. He touched the folded towel to her chest and slid it down her arm before coming back to the center and working his way back down the other arm. Taking a deep breath, he stood directly in front of her and rubbed the towel against her breasts, drying the beaded water on top. He cared for each breast, wiping each completely dry before moving lower to caress her abdomen and hips. Kurt took a corner of the towel and rubbed it softly against her center, unable to keep from looking up into her face as he did so. She watched him, wondering what he would do next. He pulled the towel back and continued down her legs.

"Sit," he directed, gesturing to the edge of the tub.

If she had had more energy, she would have teased him about his canine commands, but she was too entranced to go there. So, she sat, and he worked the towel through her hair, gently squeezing and massaging.

"Comb?"

"Bag on the counter," she responded.

Kurt collected the comb and started parting her hair, easing the knots out and leaving a damp, shiny ribbon down her back. Following one last lingering caress with the towel, he pulled her to her feet and led her into the bedroom, where she discovered a shirt and underwear on the bed. He slid the shirt over her head and tugged it into place, his breathing deep. Then he knelt and touched one of her feet. She lifted it enough for him to slip her panty around an ankle, then did the same with her other foot. He worked the soft material up her legs and settled the band around her waist.

He stood in front of her, resting his hands on her hips, leaning his forehead against hers. After his breathing slowed, he scooped her into his arms and sat on the bed, cradling her. She wrapped her arms around his neck and rested her head against his chest. They sat like that for several minutes.

Eventually, he lay back and settled her against him. She snuggled against his side and felt at peace. She started to drift off but caught herself. "Kurt?"

"I'm here," he replied.

"Please don't leave me."

"I won't. Now sleep."

37

*S*he slept soundly, contentedly.

She slept against his warmth, his arm curved around her.

She slept without dreaming.

When the morning arrived, Carlie stretched and yawned, unbelievably well rested.

"I was beginning to wonder if I should wake you," she heard from across the room. Kurt was sitting at the desk, his computer set up, phone in hand.

Ignoring him, she remained buried in the plush bedding and considered last night. That bath was the most sensual thing she had ever experienced. And he hadn't even kissed her. But he had stayed.

"Good morning," she mumbled.

Shuffling to the edge of the bed, she scooted off, her feet hitting the soft-piled carpet. Carlie padded to the bathroom and shut the door, needing a few moments to wash up and gather her thoughts.

She stared in the mirror and took a deep breath. Still in the clothes he dressed her in, her hair was beyond repair.

But she didn't want to change a thing. She did finally make a concession and pulled her crazy hair back in a knot. Better.

Coming out of the bathroom, she noted Kurt was on his phone. He nodded and pointed to the dresser, where a pot of coffee stood in a halo of light. Thank God.

He seemed to be talking about one of his many businesses, so she tuned out, grabbing her own phone. She had missed a text from Kim, saying goodbye before she took off this morning. Kim had been selected to represent her company's product line at the global stakeholders meeting. That was a big freaking deal. Carlie messaged her to tell her how excited and happy she was for her.

Kurt was still on the phone, so she pulled open Instagram and scrolled through, looking to see what her friends were up to. The friends with kids were posting spring break family pictures; her friends without kids were posting spring break drinking pictures. It was a strange time of life, when the haves and the have-nots became a completely different conversation.

Her phone vibrated with a message from her dad. *Good morning, sleepyhead! We're out at the pool.*

Good morning, Dad. I'll try to wake up some more and maybe meet you out there.

He must be worried to text her voluntarily. Carlie frowned and wondered how she could ease his mind. She needed to figure out how to get through these next few days and resolve the issues with Alex. Then things would be back to normal. Or something approaching it.

Finishing her coffee as she walked around, she noted that Kurt had picked up and put her things away. She laughed to herself and pulled out a bathing suit. She held it up and shook it at Kurt. He grinned with a thumbs-up. She slipped into the restroom to change, wondering why she bothered, since he had seen it all last night. But that was different. It was...magical. Her heart melted as she thought about how he had tended to her.

Oh, Car, you are in deep, girl.

But she was starting to believe she wasn't alone in this. He wouldn't have done that and then stayed if he didn't care, right?

Dressed and ready to go, she stepped out to an empty room. Where did he go? His computer was still on her desk, but he and his phone were gone. Her phone, sunglasses, lip balm, and sunscreen were ready to go in her swim bag. She rummaged in the closet to find her flip flops and emerged triumphant with both of them. Should she wait for him? He had said his room was next to hers, but which side? Carlie grabbed her bag, hat, and room keycard and stepped into the hallway.

A suit was standing at the elevator. He nodded, and she waved back. He must know which room was Kurt's. Carlie started to walk toward him when the room between the elevator and her own opened. She jumped, surprised, and he grinned, green eyes capturing hers. "Ready?" he asked.

"Yup! Coming?"

"Yes, just give me a minute. You can come in if you want."

She followed him into his room and crossed her arms over her chest, recalling the outcome from the last time she entered a man's hotel room. She remained by the door.

Chuckling, he shook his head. "I finally got you to visit my room. Different hotel, but you're here."

She rolled her eyes, and he laughed again.

He was wearing a pair of black-and-gray swim trunks with a gray T-shirt. She couldn't wait to get him by the pool so she could see his pecs again. It seemed unfair that he had now seen all of her, but she'd only seen his torso once when he stayed with her in Chicago.

That's going to have to change, she decided.

"Ready to meet my family?" she asked.

He froze for a moment with his hand on the doorknob, then nodded. "Let's do this."

They rode down the elevator, stopping every few floors to absorb more people. By the time they hit the ground floor, they emerged with a clown-car crowd. Most went the opposite direction, but they followed a young couple and their child to the pool.

"How'd you sleep?" Kurt asked.

She blushed and smiled. "Really well, actually. You?"

"I was a little uncomfortable for a while, but eventually fell asleep. Some chick was snoring next to me, so I had to adjust to that."

Laughing, she slapped his arm. "I don't snore!"

"What makes you think I was referring to you?" he teased.

They were still laughing as they entered the pool deck. She spotted her parents and Rachael near the deep end.

"Mom, Dad, Rachael—this is Kurt Hunter. Kurt, my family."

They all greeted each other politely, and Carlie looked at Rachael. "Where's Rick?"

She blushed and winked. "He's still in bed."

Mom watched Kurt with interest as he and Dad discussed some of their mutual connections. "So that's him?" Mom whispered.

"Shhh! And yes," Carlie replied.

"Very handsome. And he has a great track record with business. No current active relationships on record." She ticked off on her fingers.

"Mom! Did you...?"

"Baby, you know your mother is nothing if not thorough. When one of my girls shows an interest in someone, I start digging. This one gets a tentative green light from your mother."

"Tentative?"

"Tentative. I have yet to see how he is around you."

"And how did Brent and Rick stack up?"

"You see which one is still around? That's no accident. Brent was not mature enough or capable of standing up for you. Rick is...Rick. He makes your sister happy, and they are good for each other."

"Mother!" gasped Rachael. "You ran a report on Rick?"

"Of course." Mom shrugged like it was asinine to even be asking.

Grumbling, Rachael stomped over to her lounger.

Carlie laughed at both of them. "How's the water?"

"Still a little cool in the shade, but feels nice in the sunny areas," Mom said as she sat back on her own lounger.

Carlie dug in her bag for the sunscreen, loaded up, then sat on the chair while she waited for it to soak in. "Mom?"

"Mmhmm?"

"I got flowers delivered yesterday. A huge bouquet of roses. From Alex."

She sat up at attention. "Here?"

"Mhm. Before dinner."

Mom's face paled. She grabbed her phone and sent out a text, magically summoning Kevin Slater.

"Honey, why don't you go talk with your dad and Kurt?"

"Don't you want to know what the note said?"

She looked at Carlie, waiting.

"'Almost time. Yours, Alex.'"

"What does that mean?" she asked.

"Your guess is as good as mine. On the surface, it's almost time to see him at Bernie's. But did he mean something else? I don't know."

Her lips were pressed in a firm line. "Go rescue Kurt from your father and give me a few minutes with Slater." She glanced at Rachael and caught her eye. "You too, Rachael."

Her sister groaned and followed her to the covered table, where Kurt was talking with the one and only Charles Eller.

38

"...On the flight to Chicago. We were sitting next to each other," Kurt was saying as she arrived.

Carlie slid onto the wooden bench beside Kurt. He smiled—the most nervous specimen of a smile she had ever seen from him—clearly getting grilled by her dad.

"Were you now?" her dad responded, greeting Rachael as she sat next to him.

"And he was incredibly annoying," Carlie teased.

"I was not!" he huffed.

"What were you doing at a marketing conference?" her dad asked.

"Excuse me?" Kurt asked, confused.

"I didn't know Hunter Industries was directly involved in digital marketing."

"You're right, not directly. But show me a business today that isn't involved in digital marketing. It's the primary vehicle for driving business for the majority of our holdings."

"That's true enough."

Carlie coughed. "So, Dad, Bernie said he knew you when you were younger. How did that come about?"

While Dad toyed with his mug and reminisced about his early career days, Carlie watched Kurt out of the corner of her eye. He was looking at her dad with open intent, listening to his stories and laughing at the mishaps that invariably accompanied all aggressive growth operations. Rachael joined in, and they all looked at ease with each other.

Carlie glanced over her shoulder at her mom, still deep in conversation with Slater. His face was passive, but his hands were tapping notes into his phone. Her mother must have sensed her watching because she sent a cursory smile. Carlie hesitantly smiled back and returned her focus to the laughter at the table.

The guilt was starting to weigh on her. If it weren't for her behavior in Chicago, none of this additional security would be necessary. Mom and Kurt had both had their work completely interrupted by her actions. Frowning, she debated what she could do to fix this. How could she get things back to normal?

Kurt leaned against her, tearing her from her thoughts, watching her with concern. "Penny for your thoughts?"

She put on a false smile. "They're not worth that much."

He watched her for a moment, assessing, then shook his head. "You know you can trust me, right?"

"I know," Carlie responded. "I just don't want to add to your stress."

He reached over and squeezed her hand. "You don't need to worry about me."

"Rick!" shouted Rachael, standing to wave him over.

Carlie's future brother-in-law strolled over, stopping to greet her mom, who shooed him along to join them.

"Good morning, babe," he said, dropping a kiss on top of Rachael's head. "Morning, all."

"Rick, this is Kurt Hunter, my friend from the conference."

"Nice to finally meet you. I'm a fan," Rick said.

Kurt looked up. "Thanks. I'm a fan of yours. Rachael was telling me about your practice. You're a vet?"

"Yes, that's actually how we met." He smiled fondly at Rachael. "One of her dogs was injured, and I helped piece her back together."

"If it weren't for Rick, my Olive would never have survived." She gazed at him with adoration. "And Martini would be all alone."

He gripped her shoulder and leaned down to whisper in her ear. She blushed and cleared her throat.

"Rick is going to make a fine husband for my Rachael," Dad nodded, raising his coffee cup to them.

"Thank you, sir." Rick smiled, resting his hands on Rachael's shoulders.

"Who's up for a swim?" Rach piped up.

"You kids go ahead. I'm going to finish the paper and drink my morning meds," Dad said, adding more coffee to his cup from the silver carafe.

Carlie kissed his cheek. "Love you, Dad."

"Love you too, Carlie-Q," he returned with a soft smile. "Now, go have fun and leave this old man to his paper."

"Carlie-Q? That's cute," Kurt said, treading water as she dipped her toes in the pool. Rachael and Carlie sat along the ledge, and Rick was swimming laps.

Rachael giggled. "Better than some of the nicknames I've given her, right, Stink Bug?"

Carlie rolled her eyes. "Heaven save us from clever older sisters."

Rachael laughed heartily, then turned to Kurt. "When did you get here? We weren't expecting you until later today."

"Came in late last night to find Carlie drinking her worries away at the bar by herself. Guess I just missed meeting you."

"Oh, well, I'm glad she had some company."

Carlie watched Slater disappear into the hotel and turned to her mother. "Joining us?"

"In a bit. I need to relax here for a minute," her mom said.

And there went the guilt, ratcheting up again. Carlie sighed and leaned against Rachael.

"You okay, CarCar?"

"I'm fine."

Kurt and Rachael exchanged a look, and Rachael shrugged her off her shoulder. "You need to shake out of this. The last thing we need is for you to go all dark and emo on us."

"Emo?" Carlie laughed.

"Goth," Kurt suggested.

"All right, you two, that's enough!" Carlie shoved at her sister, pushing her into the water.

"Ahh—" the petite blonde's scream cut off as she dropped beneath the water's surface. She popped back up and glared at her younger sister. "That does it!" Rachael grabbed Carlie's ankle with a devious smile and flopped her into the water next to her.

Carlie emerged laughing and splashing her.

"That's better." Rachael grinned.

Rick joined them, catching Rachael by the waist and eyeing Carlie and Kurt. "So, what's the deal with you two, anyway?"

Her heart stopped, and she stared at her future brother-in-law. Carlie recalled asking him the same words regarding her sister last summer at the start of their whirlwind romance. "What?" Carlie said.

Kurt arched a brow and remained quiet.

"Rick, this is not the time or place for that," admonished Rachael. She sent Carlie an apologetic look.

He turned to Kurt. "Look, man, I like you, but Carlie's my sister now, and I want to know what you're doing."

Could she just disappear now? Oh, dear God. Carlie should have been more worried about Rick than Dad.

"Right now? I'm trying to help her. Make sure that son of a bitch doesn't ruin her future," Kurt at last responded in a low voice. "Other than that, I'm going to have to defer to Carlie."

Carlie's eyes widened and she quickly smoothed out her face.

"Defer? What kind of crap is that?" Rick tossed back at him.

"That's enough, Rick." Carlie glared at him.

"Okay, okay. I just want to make sure you're not getting taken advantage of. Again. You don't have the strongest track record, Carlie."

"Jesus, Rick! That's enough!" Carlie exclaimed. She swam to the ladder and climbed out, pissed off and not wanting to hear more of his judgement.

"Cool it, Rick," Rachael murmured.

Kurt followed her with his eyes, his jaw working, before turning back to Rick. "I just met her a week ago. I am going to protect Carlie, make sure she isn't hurt. Beyond that, I'm not saying a word until she does. Satisfied?"

What did that mean?

Rick weighed Kurt's words and nodded. "For now. But if

you hurt her, you'll have to answer to me. And a whole host of other people."

"Understood."

"If you two are done with this primitive display, I suggest we figure out what we want to do today before we spend the rest of the day fighting," Rachael said, diffusing the situation.

"Your father and I are going to the museum after lunch," said their mother, walking over to the pool's edge. "You're welcome to join us."

"Pass," frowned Rachael. "We could go shopping?" she suggested hopefully.

"Hard pass," Carlie called over from her chair. "I've had enough for a while."

"Mini golf?" asked Rick.

Carlie grinned. "I'm in!"

"Sounds like a plan," said Kurt.

"Just do me a favor," said Mom. "Bring Kevin or one of Kurt's people with you."

39

*A*fter swimming through lunch, they split up to get ready. "Meet at four?" asked Rachael.

"Sounds good," said Kurt, heading into his room.

"Pretty convenient that he's right next to you, Carlie," observed Rick.

Carlie shrugged and opened her door. "I didn't arrange it."

Rachael tugged at Rick's arm. "I think she's had enough of you for now. Let's go."

Dropping her swim bag on the bathroom floor, Carlie stepped into the shower and twisted the water on to heat up. A cold shower floor was no way to start a shower. Snagging her laptop, she cranked up the audio and swayed to the music, stripping down before losing herself in the steady stream of hot water and the sounds of Coldplay.

Turning down the music and dressed again in a baggy shirt and her favorite flannel pants, she opened her email and scrolled through the messages. The sense of playing hooky was strong, knowing everyone else was hard at work in the office, and she was sitting in the lap of luxury, nursing a touch of sunburn across her shoulders. Chicago did have one thing on this place, though—she missed the stocked mini fridge.

Carlie called down for bottled water, a chicken Caesar salad, and some soft drinks before lying on her back and grabbing the phone to check her texts. The first gave her pause.

Did you get the flowers? Alex messaged.

She glared at the beautiful monstrosity.

Yes, thank you. You shouldn't have.

Dinner tonight?

Carlie huffed aloud. *I'm sorry, but I already have plans with my sister.*

Why do I get the feeling you're avoiding me?

Sighing, she frowned at her phone, uncertainty slowing her response.

I'm busy, Alex. I wasn't kidding before. There's a lot going on.

Too busy to explore things with me?

TBH, I'm not sure I'm ready for a relationship right now. With you, she amended to herself. *And you pressuring me isn't helping.*

You owe it to yourself, to me, to play things out, he wrote back.

She rolled her eyes at the phone. Not a goddamn chance in hell.

A knock sounded at the door, and she jumped, convinced he was standing at her door.

Where are you? she messaged Alex, a cold chill gripping her.

In my room. Want to meet?

Relieved, she opened the door to find her room service delivery. Thank God. She directed them to the desk and signed the receipt, sending the young man on his way.

Opening a cold water, she drank deeply and collected herself.

I'm actually getting ready to leave. Have to get going.

Carlie, you're being unreasonable. Say yes, come to dinner with me.

I'm sorry, but I have to go.

No reply. Somehow this unnerved her more than the rest of the conversation.

She picked at her salad and debated what to do. She checked her phone. Still no reply. Calling in reinforcements, she messaged Kurt, *Need to talk.*

Moments later, a knock sounded at the door. "It's me," he said from the hallway. She opened the door, then returned to stare at her salad. She picked out the chicken and left the rest on the plate.

"You could just order grilled chicken," he commented, noting her lunch.

She sliced up the next chunk of breast and tossed him her phone, opened to the text thread. He scanned it quickly, frowning as he reached the end. "I don't like this."

"I don't either, but what can I do?"

He walked over and took a bite of her discarded salad.

"Please, help yourself," she murmured, her thoughts distracting her.

He glanced at her with a crooked grin. "Someone should eat it."

"What's going on with your end? Has he contacted you again?"

Kurt picked up the napkin and wiped his mouth, chewing while he considered what to tell her. "He's been sending an email each day, nothing but a number in the subject line. Counting down to Saturday."

"He hasn't breathed a word about it to me. But he's upset." She paused. "Does he know you're in Atlanta?"

"Maybe? But I doubt he knows I'm here with you." He took another bite of salad. "This is good. Sure you don't want some?"

"I'm not that hungry."

"Don't let him get to you. We're going to figure this out. In the meantime, finish getting ready, and we'll head down to the bar. You could use a drink."

"I THINK they play that to make you drink more," she said, referring to the terrible instrumental music over the bar's sound system.

"Once the music starts sounding good, you know you've had enough," Rachael said, nodding in agreement while she sipped on her iced tea.

Swirling the ice in her drink, Carlie watched Kurt and Rick walk back from the lobby. "Closest place is about a ten-minute walk. But the place they recommend is about a twenty-minute drive," said Rick.

Carlie waved dismissively. "You guys decide."

"How many of those have you had, Car?" Rachael inquired.

"Not enough to make the music sound good." She smirked, downing another gulp.

Kurt glanced between them and rolled his eyes. "I'll call for my car."

They signed the tab, and the girls stopped to freshen up in the ladies' room before emerging into the full force of the unclouded Atlanta afternoon. As the sun beat down on them, Carlie was grateful they would be going the air-conditioned route.

A black SUV with dark tinted windows idled on the curb in front of them, and the valet tossed the keys to Kurt. He walked her to the passenger door, ushering her inside. "Thanks," she murmured, sliding into the car.

Rachael and Rick hopped into the roomy second row, and they were off. A sedan merged into traffic behind them, one of the security guards at the wheel. She had no idea anymore who belonged to which security team. John Wallace, Kevin Slater, Guardian, suits, elevators. It was too much.

"Nice car," Rick interrupted her thoughts.

"Thanks. It's a company car."

Carlie smiled at Kurt's answer, recalling the same response in Chicago.

"Which company?" she asked.

"Does it matter?" he repeated with a teasing smile.

"You have a place out here, Hunter?" asked Rick.

Kurt caught Rick's eyes in the rearview mirror. "Yes, but it's a bit of a drive from here."

Interested, Carlie looked at him. "What business do you have in Atlanta?"

He glanced at Carlie then studied the road for a moment before responding. "I own a private security firm here and a few other investments."

"A private security company? Would it happen to include John Wallace?"

He nodded. "The Guardian's one of my more recent acquisitions. We offer top, confidential security options for visiting dignitaries, officials, and high-profile events."

"Is this car theirs?"

"Yes, nosey," he responded with a quick glance.

Publishing, communications, IT, security... He was a little all over the place. How did he keep track of it all? What was the connection?

"How long have you owned The Guardian?" Rachael asked.

"Since Friday."

Carlie's eyes grew round as she considered this. "You just went out and bought a company?" she asked, incredulous.

"The previous owner was looking for a buyer, and the company aligned with my interests."

"Which interests are those?" Rach asked.

"Safety," he replied, turning his head to look meaningfully at Carlie.

Oh.

Carlie fidgeted in her seat, trying to comprehend his decision. She studied his profile. "Why?"

He reached for her hand while he drove, squeezing it. "Besides being a solid business with a good reputation and excellent revenue potential, it seemed like the best way to get reliable eyes around the area from experienced professionals who know the town."

"Impressive," Rick approved.

Very.

40

"*W*hich color?"

"Green," Carlie said, thinking the color of the ball was a poor substitute for her favorite shade of green.

Outfitted with putters and balls, they lined up at the first hole. "What are we going to wager?" asked Rick.

"It's miniature golf," Carlie pointed out. "You want to bet on that?"

Rachael laughed. "Yes, yes, he does." She blushed.

"I'll take your word on it," Carlie teased her sister.

"Let's play teams, boys against girls," suggested Rachael. "Winners choose the prize."

"You're going to regret that decision," said Rick, wrapping his arms around her and kissing her neck.

"Don't be so sure, hot stuff. You may recall I wiped the floor with you last time we played," Rachael teased.

Carlie turned to Kurt, raising her eyebrows in question.

"Prepare to go down, Eller women," Kurt said roguishly. He fist-bumped Rick, then stepped back, bowing with flair. "Ladies first."

"Shit just got real." Carlie teed up, determined to win.

A little over an hour later, Rick held up the scorecard. "And the final score. Ladies, a very respectable 119. Men...115. Prepare to meet your doom, baby," he said, holding the card just out of her reach.

"Give me that card!" Rachael squealed. "There's no way!"

"We're putting an asterisk on this," Carlie complained. "You fudged the score."

"Read it and weep, girls," Kurt laughed, leaning his hip against the putter return box. "We got you fair and square."

"Complain all you want, Rachael, but you're mine," Rick said.

She theatrically swooned and latched onto his arm, pulling him away.

"And that makes you mine," Kurt said, no longer laughing as he brushed a stray hair behind her ear.

Awareness pooled in her stomach as he looked into her eyes, holding his hand out to her.

"Does it?" she asked, attempting for coy, but sounding breathless even to her own ears.

He nodded as he reeled her in. "It most certainly does."

"And what prize are you going to claim?"

He drew her even closer, and her breath caught.

"You two coming?" hollered Rachael from the parking lot.

"Are we?" Carlie whispered.

He bent down and grazed her lips with his own before standing upright and leading them back around to the car.

"That was the prize?" Carlie asked.

Fire smoldered in his eyes, and a mischievous smile pulled at his sensuous mouth. "No."

"Oh."

Strolling back to the car, Carlie waved at the guard alone

in the lot. "That must be mind-numbing." She gestured to the sedan.

"We all have parts of our jobs that are less than ideal. I'd venture he'd rather be sitting there than running after someone," said Kurt.

"Where to next?" asked Rachael.

"Dinner?" Carlie suggested. Her stomach was grumbling.

"I could eat," said Kurt.

"BBQ?" asked Rick.

"Yes!" Rach and Carlie said in unison.

Rachael and Carlie's parents met them for dinner, and they feasted on pulled pork, ribs, and fried chicken.

"How am I ever going to fit in my wedding dress if I continue to eat like this?" moaned Rachael.

Carlie licked the sauce off her fingers, and her mom tossed her a moist towelette. "Carlie, really." Her mother frowned at her.

Shrugging, Carlie tore open the wrapper and went to town trying to get all the sauce off her fingers and under her nails.

"You missed some," laughed Kurt, dabbing her chin with his napkin. He leaned closer. "And I don't mind if you lick your fingers," he teased.

Tossing the napkin atop the heap of bones in front of her, she sighed happily. "Just size up, Rach. It'll be fine."

"Please, that's not going to happen," she grumped.

"When is the wedding?" asked Kurt.

"August," she replied.

"Four months should give you enough time to recover from this meal."

Laughing, she shook her head. "Oh, this is just one of many. Hang around for a while, and you'll see!"

Carlie picked up her water and drank. "She's not kidding. We like to eat."

Dad winked at Rick. "It's a good thing you girls found men who don't mind a woman with an appetite."

"Daaaaad," moaned Rachael.

He laughed and turned to Carlie. "Tell me about this dinner tomorrow."

"I don't know much about it. All I know is what you told me. And Saturday is a benefit for Bernie and his wife's inner-city reading program."

"That seems like a good cause," said Mom.

"Bernie and I spoke about some of their foundation's projects," Carlie continued. "I think we should get more involved in some kind of more formalized corporate giving. I was going to talk to you and the Brians about it at the office, Dad."

"Sounds interesting. I'll ask Tammy to put something on our calendars."

Happy and full, Carlie sat back and listened as Rachael and Dad discussed the catering for the wedding. Rick tried to maintain the appearance of being interested in the discussion. She smiled at his struggle. Mom ordered another bottle of wine and everyone relaxed, chatting about topics big and small.

When they emerged from the restaurant, Mom and Dad said their good nights and left the foursome to go unwind at the hotel. They considered a local bar but ultimately decided against it, returning to the hotel for the convenience. The hotel bar was decent—even if the music wasn't stellar. They passed through the humming lobby, oblivious to the world around them. Carlie was happy and relieved to slide into a seat between Rachael and Kurt.

Awaiting their first round of drinks, she swayed back

and forth to the instrumental overhead and leaned into Kurt's side. He wrapped an arm around her back and loosely hugged her to him.

"This explains a lot," came a deep voice over her shoulder.

Carlie froze, shock and fear coursing through her. "Alex?" she gasped.

"I didn't expect to see you here, Hunter," he said, ignoring her.

Rachael turned around and eyed him warily until Rick moved between her and Alex.

"A word, Carlie?" Alex demanded, grasping her shoulder firmly.

"I don't think so," said Kurt, knocking Alex's hand off her shoulder.

Alex glared at him then turned his focus back to her. "Carlie?"

She took a deep breath and nodded at Kurt. "It's okay. I'll be right back." Maybe she could end things here and now.

"Carlie, don't—" Kurt started.

She slid out of her seat and patted his shoulder, cutting him off. "Five minutes," she said, then walked to the lobby, Alex stalking behind her.

"Car?" called Rachael.

Carlie waved her hand at her sister and urged her to stay. All was well.

"What the fuck is going on here?" he growled as she sat in a lobby chair.

"Nothing," she said. It wasn't any of his business.

"Why is Kurt here?"

"Bernie invited him here this weekend, too. He's interested in the charity work."

"That's not what I mean, and you know it."

Carlie looked down at her clasped hands and considered which card to play.

"I know, Alex. I know what you did," she said quietly.

"Shit. Carlie, that has nothing to do with you. That's between me and Kurt."

She blinked at him, disbelievingly.

"Nothing to do with me?" she asked, her voice rising. "You shot a fucking video of us together and it has nothing to do with me?"

"Calm down, Carlie. No one else is going to see it. It's just a bargaining chip."

"That's what I was to you? A bargaining chip?"

"You know damn well that isn't true. This," he said, gesturing between the two of them. "This is special. This is love, Carlie. I love you."

She stared at him in shocked silence.

"You don't even know me."

He snorted and rolled his eyes, clasping his hands over hers. "I know you. We belong together."

Looking over his shoulder, Carlie saw Kurt and Rick standing in the doorway to the bar, both ready to charge at the slightest provocation. She shook her head at them and stood up, pulling her hands from Alex's grasp, crossing her arms to clutch her elbows. "Alex, you are crazy. You don't love me. Do you hear yourself?"

"Carlie, don't. Don't walk away from me." He loomed over her.

"I'm sorry, Alex. We should never have..." She stopped, embarrassed. "I'm sorry. It's over."

"You're going to regret this," Alex muttered darkly. Carlie felt a cold chill move through her at the words but shook it off and walked away to the safety of Kurt and Rick. Security entered the lobby from different directions and remained there, watching Alex until he left the hotel.

"I need to go. Now," she said to Kurt, still gripping her elbows and trying to keep from shaking. He nodded and returned to the bar to collect her things and settle the tab.

"I've got this. Go," Rachael said, shooing him away. "Rick, go with them."

41

*K*urt was busy on his phone as they rode up the elevator. He glared at the screen, and a decidedly frosty air settled around him.

Regaining her cool, Carlie stood in the corner behind him and Rick, the two of them forming a solid wall between her and the elevator door. "You guys, this is ridiculous. I'm fine. I just don't feel like hanging out in the bar right now."

Neither even bothered to acknowledge her.

She blew out a breath, pissed at the entire situation. How dare he! Alex was delusional. Love? Yes, the best way to show that was clearly by shopping around a tape of the two of them!

The elevator dinged and opened to their floor. Kurt and Rick stuck their heads out—she had no idea what they expected to find, considering they all watched Alex leave the building—and stepped out, waving at her to follow. "Did I miss something? Are we in Vietnam?"

Rick scowled at her. "Rachael is worried, so I'm worried. What happened down there?"

Kurt had yet to talk since they had left the lobby. She

stared at him while answering Rick. "I don't know. Alex is crazy. He thinks he loves me."

No words to follow that.

Carlie dismissed it. "He's gone now. I just want to be alone."

"I don't want you to be anywhere alone right now," Rick stated. "I'll send Rachael up to stay with you."

"No. You two should go have some time together. Unwind, forget this happened."

He snorted. "You try telling that to Rachael."

"I'm staying," Kurt broke his silence. "Go back downstairs, Rick. Make sure Alex doesn't return. My security team and your family's staff are gathering now to split up shifts to watch all access points. This will not happen again," he vowed, looking at Carlie.

Rick nodded. "Don't leave her alone, or I'll never hear the end of it."

"I don't intend to."

"Hello? Standing right here." She waved, feeling invisible. "I think you two are taking this way too seriously. He's gone."

"For now," Kurt said flatly, giving her a chill.

"Goodnight, Car. We're right downstairs, and we'll be back up soon. If you need anything at all, or if Kurt has to leave, you text me or Rach. We'll be right there," Rick said.

This touched her. "Thanks, Rick. Tell her I'm fine and make sure she has a strong drink before coming up. And actually, there is something I could use... Think you could send up a bottle of wine or something?"

He nodded. "On it."

They watched him disappear into the elevator. Kurt held out his hand for her keycard. She relinquished it, figuring it was useless to argue. He was on a big, bad macho kick. Might as well let him do this.

Carlie leveled a look at the elevator. "Where's the suit?" she asked, noticing the absence of their breathing statue.

"In the lobby. The teams are meeting there now. Weren't you paying attention?"

"Guess I didn't put two and two together."

He grunted as he opened the door. They walked into her room, and he checked the bedroom and bathroom before turning back to her. "I need to grab a few things from my room. Wait here."

She smirked as the door closed behind him. That whole "don't leave her alone" thing hadn't lasted very long. Carlie laughed and walked to the restroom to wash up, leaving the door ajar so she could hear when he returned.

Moments later, the door opened and closed again. She peeked out and caught his sleek blonde figure prowling across the room with a bag. Relieved, she shut the door and changed into her comfy pants and a clean tank top.

Returning to the bedroom, she watched as he shuffled through his bag and removed a holster and firearm. She sucked in her breath and stared at the weapon, her wide eyes drawn to how deftly he handled it. "What is that for?"

He continued to check his weapon, then set it aside.

"Kurt," she said more firmly. "Why do you have that? I don't like guns—do you even have a permit for that thing?"

He sat on the corner of the bed, an amused smile warming his face. "I've gone through extensive training. And yes, I have a permit." He paused, his smile dissipating. "Carlie, you are not taking this seriously. Please, for the love of God, think about what's happened. What frame of mind Alex is operating in. This is not normal."

Carlie wrapped her arms around herself and sat next to him. "You're that concerned?"

"I'm more concerned that you're not concerned."

They sat quietly, lost in their thoughts. A knock sounded on the door, and she jumped, letting out a small yelp.

Kurt chuckled. "At least it looks like you're more alert now."

After confirming the visitor through the peephole, he held the door open. Rachael stood there with her arms loaded. "Rick said you wanted a bottle of something. I grabbed a couple options," she babbled as she eased in, settling several bottles of wine, a corkscrew, and large glasses on the desk.

"Thanks, Rach."

Rachael turned to wrap her in her arms, concern written across every inch of her face. "You're okay, CarCar?"

"Of course I am. And I'm about to be even better," she said, lifting a bottle of Riesling.

Rachael smiled. "I figured that would be the one you'd want. It seems to be your breakup bottle. Not that you broke up or anything... That cretin. But I wasn't sure what you'd want," she rattled on, glancing at Kurt.

"You're staying here tonight?" Rachael asked Kurt.

He hesitated only a moment. "I am."

Nodding to herself, she took a deep breath. "Take care of my baby sister."

"I will."

She smiled and sniffed, her long blonde hair screening her face. Clearing her throat, Rachael shook it back and met her eyes. "Love you, Carlie."

"Love you too, Rach."

～

CARLIE DROPPED the empty wine bottle into the metal wastebasket. A dull thud rang out from the thick glass. "More wine?" she asked, opening the bottle of merlot.

"No, I'm good with this."

Carlie carried her glass over to the fluffy lounge chair in the corner, crossing her ankles on the ottoman. "Tell me more about you. Your family."

He looked surprised by the question. "My family? It's just me and Mom. My dad died when I was a baby."

"Oh. I'm sorry." Her mind flitted to the hug she'd given her dad earlier. She couldn't imagine.

Swirling his glass, he stared into the liquid pool. "I don't remember him. Mom and my grandmother talked about him sometimes, enough that I've adopted some of their memories, but otherwise I don't know much about him."

"You mentioned cousins and other kids back in Chicago?"

He smiled, sweeping his hair back off his forehead. "You remembered. Yes, my aunts and uncles were always around. I spent a lot of time with them and my grandparents while Mom worked and did what she had to do to make ends meet. She never had it easy."

"And now?"

"Now, she can take it easy." He smiled fondly before finishing the last of his wine. "I like taking care of her, making sure she knows how much I appreciate all the sacrifices she made for me."

Carlie thought about how he took care of her at every turn. "Your mom is lucky to have you."

"I'm lucky to have such a great mom," he replied.

They lapsed into a comfortable silence, and he clicked on the television, finding a music station the bar would be envious of.

"That's nice."

"The music?"

"Mmhmm," she hummed along to the slow rock, taking another sip of wine.

He stood and put his empty glass on the dresser, then crossed and knocked her feet off the ottoman, sitting in their stead, legs braced on either side of her own. "I had fun today," he said. "You know, before…"

"Me too." She smiled dreamily, relaxed and happy to have his company.

"But you know you still owe me."

"Owe you?"

"Mini golf," he confirmed, resting his hands on the outsides of her knees.

Oh.

She studied him, his startling green eyes and shaggy blonde hair, his slightly upturned nose, those perfect lips. Men weren't supposed to be described as beautiful. But he was. Heartachingly so.

"And what do you intend to claim?" she asked, her breath catching as his hands caressed the worn flannel, inching higher up her legs.

"In a word?" He lifted his brow, a devilish smile playing around his lips. "You."

"Oh," she breathed.

He leaned forward from his low perch and slid his hands higher up her thighs and around to her sides, tugging her forward on the seat until she was barely sitting on the cushion, effectively trapped between him and the furniture. He ran a hand up her side and brought it to the back of her neck, pulling her the rest of the way to meet him in a warm, gentle kiss. As he settled his mouth over hers, Carlie sighed as a knot unwound in her, warmth spreading to her fingertips and down to her toes.

Releasing her lips, he cocked his head and smiled, then stood abruptly, shoving the ottoman back with his leg. He deposited her wine glass next to his and pulled her to her feet. Trailing his hands down her arms, he threaded his fingers through hers and slid their joined hands up his chest and over his shoulders. Depositing her hands about his neck, he settled his hands on her hips, and they began to dance, swaying to the soft music floating from the television. Adele gave way to Lonestar, and Carlie melted as Kurt sang along, his chest rumbling against her cheek. "Every time our eyes meet, this feeling inside me is almost more than I can take."

He gazed down into her eyes, and she was lost. "Carlie, I want..." He swallowed thickly and restarted. "Do you think we can try this?"

She was thrown by the question. "What are you asking?"

"I want to be with you, and not just for the night. I don't know what we'll do tomorrow or the next day...but I want to find out. If it's what you want, too."

42

"What about Alex? Doesn't that bother you?"

Stupid, stupid, stupid, Carlie!

Kurt froze, and his lids dropped before he shook his head, swaying again to the music as he met her eyes. "I don't like that you slept with him. I hate it, actually. I hope to God I never feel that way again. I told myself to stay away from you, to walk away, to move on. But that didn't work out so well." He smiled, dipping her over his arm.

He swept her back up, and she laughed as he spun her around. "Kurt, I really, really like you. But you could have anyone you want. Why me?"

Leading the dance, swaying back and forth, he weighed her question. "You listen. You don't let who you are interfere with who you want to be—your hopes, your dreams. You're kind and clever. You're shy, but brave. You take my breath away every time I see you, and you don't even know you're doing it. My whole life I've been waiting to find someone who would see me for who I am and not what I could do for them. I've been waiting to find you, Carlie. You ask for nothing and offer everything without a second thought. I have never wanted a woman so much in my life."

Dazzled. That was the only way she could describe it. He was dazzling her.

Could she trust him? Surely, when he thought it through later, he would realize. He would wonder... Carlie stepped out of his arms and took a deep breath. She had to lay it out. "Before anything else happens, I have something to say. It's not easy for me to say this, but I don't want you to think that I am the kind of person who hops from bed to bed."

He started to interrupt, but she held her hand up to silence him. "I can count on one hand the number of men I have been with. Before Alex, the last person I was with intimately I dated for four years, we lived together. I caught him in our bed with one of my friends last summer, and that was the end of that. Then, with Alex... Well, you know what he did." She searched his eyes, willing him to understand what she was trying to say. "I don't want to fall for you and be crushed again. I can't go through that again."

"I won't hurt you, Carlie," he whispered, pulling her against him. "I swear it."

Head tucked under his chin, she inhaled his scent, recalling how he had been there every time she needed him. Even when she didn't want him to be. He never pushed her or made her feel guilty for her own misdeeds. Maybe she was the one who shouldn't be trusted? It was up to her. She pulled in a ragged breath. "I believe you," she whispered, pulling him down for a kiss.

His mouth crashed down on hers, and she surrendered, wrapping her arms around his neck and clinging to his shoulders. He parted her lips, his tongue firm and demanding, sweeping throughout her mouth to seek every corner.

Carlie moaned against his mouth, and he caught a hand behind her knees, scooping her up into his arms. He cradled her, never breaking the kiss as he waltzed them to the huge bed. She couldn't get enough of him, of this.

Kurt laid her across the bed, his fingers collecting a lock of her hair, which he waved beneath his nose. "I've dreamt of you most nights since we met." He grazed a hand along the side of her face, his thumb rubbing lightly across her swollen lips. "Your sassy dismissal of me on the plane, imagining other ways things could have played out in the gym." She chuckled, both amused and embarrassed at the way she'd treated him.

"No matter how much I screwed up, we somehow ended up here," she wondered aloud. "Together."

He captured her lower lip, then lifted his head long enough to tug her tank top over her head. "Sit up, Carlie," he whispered. As she complied, she shivered, recalling those same words in the bath. The mattress dipped as he knelt on one knee and reached around to unclasp her bra, letting the ends fall to her sides. He sat back on his ankles and dragged one strap down her arm before walking his fingers across her chest, circling around and between her breasts. His fingers snagged the other strap, sliding it down and slipping it off her arm. "So beautiful," he whispered to himself.

She smiled, biting her lower lip. He watched her mouth, and her tongue darted out to wet her lips. He clasped her head between his hands and drank deeply, the kiss drugging them both. Dropping his hands to her sides, he hooked her waistband and tugged, pulling her up against him.

Anxious to feel him against her, she grasped her pants and shimmied them down her legs. A wolfish smile lit his face, and then he made quick work of his own clothes.

Unbelievably fine and sculpted. She admired his body, unable to stop the possessive smile as he piled their clothes against the wall before climbing back onto the bed and stretching out next to her. He ran a warm hand across her midsection, tracing the muscles of her abdomen and marking a burning trail through the path between her breasts. He continued up to caress her collarbone and neck, finally leaning across to devour her mouth again.

Not to be outdone, she slid her hand over the back of his head and down his neck, tracing light patterns across his shoulders and back with her nails, varying the pressure. He hissed before moaning as her hand dropped lower, massaging his lower back, teasing the firm muscles below. "Carlie," he groaned, trapping her teasing hands in one fist, and planting them above her head. Her wandering hands out of the way, he buried his head in her neck, kissing from shoulder to ear. She shivered as he bit and sucked at the sensitive skin, thrilling at his explorations that eventually reclaimed her mouth. She tried to pull her hands free to caress him, but he smirked and shook his head. "Not so fast, girl o' mine," he teased.

Laughing, she nipped at him, and he responded with a nip of his own, tugging at her lip. He nudged her legs apart and settled between them, dropping his head to trail hot kisses lower. Carlie closed her eyes, focused on the heat and guessing at the path he would follow as he licked the soft skin at the top of her breasts, teasing and tasting her flesh as he worked his free hand lower, grasping and massaging her hip. He teased her nipple before taking her breast deep into his mouth. Carlie gasped and arched into him, shocked at the intensity, the need. Kurt's hand shifted from her hip and traced along her stomach, coming to a stop at the junction of her thighs. He hesitated, and she breathed, "Yes," urging him to touch her. She shivered as his mouth moved its attention to her other breast, while his fingers simultaneously slid back and forth, teasing. He groaned as he found the way wet and welcoming to him. He teased and toyed, one finger circling and tracing her entrance. "Kurt," she gasped, squirming against his mouth and hand.

"The things you do to me," he moaned, freeing her hands so he could trail lower. His tongue burrowed and swept across her skin, his teeth scraping. His hand continued to tease and torment her, his other hand grasping her hip, then sliding under her leg.

"No more than you do to me," she said, running her fingers through that shaggy tangle of blonde hair as he moved lower to her waist. He turned his shoulder beneath her thigh and hooked her leg around him. He glanced up at her face as his fingers continued to work through her heat before he dropped his head to lick her most secret place.

"Oh, my God," she gasped. He brushed her peaked sex with his thumb and licked deeper, sucking and twirling. He lifted her other leg and moved his hands under to shift her where he wanted her. She flung her arms out, grasping handfuls of the sheet.

His body worked in rhythmic pursuit. Moving a hand between them, he pinched and rolled, rubbing and caressing her sensitive clit, while his tongue delved deeper. A bonfire burned within her, insistent and relentless. He slid a finger in her, his mouth inching up to take over the ministrations on her tight bud, licking and suckling as his experienced hand worked its magic. She squeezed her eyes closed and focused on the white fire, the tendrils tightening, wrapped so that she could barely breathe. She gasped as he slid a second finger into her, the pair stretching and moving, curving to hit her just so, all the while his tongue lapped and teased. Crying out his name, her legs flexed and tightened around his shoulders as her body unraveled, fire storming out from her core. "Oh, my God," she panted, the waves of blissful heat stealing her breath.

Before she recovered, he was already sliding back up her body, capturing her breast in his mouth and sliding his fingers in and out, drawing out her release as her body continued to pulse and shudder around him. Clutching his shoulders as he returned to her, she wrapped her legs around him, capturing his hand between them. She wanted him, needed him. "Condom?"

He pushed off the bed, returning a moment later. She heard him rip open the package, and then he was pressing her body down into the mattress. She reached for him, wanting to claim him in return. He moved between her legs and worked his hand down, pressing into her again, priming and stretching her. She ran her palm up the side of his face, sliding the errant blonde locks back from his forehead so she could see his face. His fervent green eyes were filled with so much passion that she closed her eyes to the burning intensity. "Carlie," he whispered hoarsely. "Open your eyes. Look at me, baby."

One look and she was captured, heart and soul. He braced his hands on either side of her, and she felt him press, rubbing up and down, teasing her. She reached down to guide him home, exhaling as he eased in, then pulled back. He slid back in, stretching her even more. Carlie moaned as his body continued the dance, surging in and out, filling her. She wrapped her legs around his waist to urge him on. Kurt leaned down to kiss her, then watched her eyes as he impaled her again. She sighed with pleasure, his weight on her, his body taut and his thick heat pulsing in her. She held onto his shoulders as he began to thrust slowly, then changed his tempo, moving faster and deeper, before easing off again and teasing in and out. Her mouth traced his shoulder and neck, earning her a growl from the back of his throat.

"Kurt," she moaned. He cut off the moan with a passionate kiss, stealing her breath as he filled her over and over. Reaching up, she grasped the headboard as the ride turned harder, his body slamming into hers. He angled her hips and continued to hammer into her, finding her sensitive spot. She gasped and bit down on his shoulder as he kept going, the fever blazing between them. He grunted, and his breaths were shallow and rapid. Her own body trembled, and the pressure climbed until there was nothing else, no one else. He moved deeper and crushed her mouth with his own, his tongue flicking and caressing in time.

Oh, God. Oh, my God.

Her body began convulsing, wave after wave of release, as she came apart beneath him. Still he continued, pumping faster, until he slid his arms under her back and gripped her shoulders, driving deeply into her one last time, groaning as his body was both rigid and pulsing.

They stared at each other in silence. He trailed a finger down the side of her face, then rolled to place her on top of him, and she snuggled against his chest. Arm curled around her, he held her close and caressed her back and hair.

Neither of them made the slightest effort to move, both quiet and content. He trailed a hand up her arm, raising gooseflesh. She stretched her neck back to look up at his beautiful face and found him watching her. He slid his hand up to sweep her hair to the side and wove the tresses around his fist. She closed her eyes and relaxed into him.

"This is nice," he murmured.

"Mmhmm," she replied.

"Are you cold?"

"A little," she admitted.

He sat up, still holding her to his chest, and stretched for the blanket at their feet. He pulled it up and tucked it around them. She sighed, enjoying the sensation of her softness pressed to his firm chest. Carlie ran her fingers through fine bronze chest hair, tugging gently.

Kurt chuckled and captured her hand, holding it flat against his drumming heart. She focused on the beating, each thump a caress.

"Kurt?"

"Hmm?"

"I live in Ohio."

"I know."

"You live in California."

"Sometimes."

Contemplating this, she puzzled over what kind of future they could possibly have.

"Carlie?"

She glanced up, noting the line of concern burrowed between his eyes.

"I won't give up on this. And neither should you. We'll find a way."

She nodded as he pressed a kiss to her forehead. "Try to rest," he teased. "I'm not sure that I've fully collected on that bet yet."

Laughing, she tried to settle her persistent thoughts. So much had happened. She attempted to organize them into buckets, find the path through.

First, Kurt. Wow. If this wasn't love, she was well on her way there. He was passionate and kind, generous. His life was fascinating and, she admitted to herself if no one else, his protective possessiveness was a turn-on. He was smart, funny, and driven. And he was not after her money. She couldn't believe they were lying here together. She smiled and considered what tomorrow might hold.

Second, Alex. She wanted to believe today's confrontation was the worst of it. But she wasn't stupid. He still had that damn recording. She would have to talk to Kurt about it, and soon; time was running out. She kissed Kurt's chest. Anything Alex-related could wait until tomorrow.

Next, Mom and Dad. Mom was in on this already. But how could she keep Dad from feeling hurt? She knew he'd eventually find out what was happening, so she would have to find some way of fixing things with him.

Rachael and Rick. She had spent some time around Rick off and on over the last few months, but this trip had cemented him as part of the family. He was one hundred percent committed to Rachael and was becoming a real brother to her. This latter part was unexpected and made her weepy happy.

Kim. Oh, she needed to text her. She wondered how Kim was faring in London. *Please let it be amazing and perfect for her.* With all the abandonment and shit in her life, Kim deserved this victory.

Brent. Carlie didn't know what the situation was with Gina, if they were just fuck buddies or what, but she hoped he would find someone who made him feel like this.

She made a mental list of what she needed to do in the morning, before glancing back up at Kurt.

"You're supposed to be sleeping," he said with an amused twinkle.

"I know," she replied, slipping her hand out from

beneath his, trailing it down his chest and sliding the back-side of her hand against his firming erection.

"Maybe I can help you relax a bit more?" he tempted, already turning to slide his hand up her waist before framing the side of her face.

She surrendered, and they let their bodies commit to each other.

43

----

*I*t is a ropes course, but instead of ropes, they are power lines. I need to hold the upper line and walk along the lower. It's not difficult. The towering power lines snake their way among the thick tree trunks and sturdy treetops, and I easily coast from branch to branch, feet grazing the line beneath me and hands loosely tracking the black cable above. I continue this way for some time, vaguely aware that others are spread across the aerial course, similarly traversing the forest.

A breeze blows in my face, bringing the first stirrings of unease. Ahead, I can see an opening in the trees. There's a gap between this side and the next wooded area. I can do this.

I steel my nerves and grasp the upper wire, my feet shuffling along the line waving loose from a thick oak branch to span a small glen. Looking down as I cross, I note a large pond surrounded by gravel before the landscape transitions to grass and wildflowers. If I fall now, I could perhaps splash into the pond. But if it's not deep enough... I intuit that I would not survive.

Weak with relief, I reach the trees on the other side and continue with ease.

A shout echoes through the wood, but I am unable to see anyone through the dense leaves. They don't sound like they're in trouble, so I continue, focused on my mission. I'm not sure where I'm going, but going back is not an option.

The leafy maples, oaks, and elms of the deciduous forest transition to pines. Their sharp, sticky branches poke at my hands, pierce holes into my sleeves and pants. I try to brush them away and keep my eyes on the power lines. I have to keep going, stick to these lines.

The wind picks up again, heavy with exhaust and blacktop fumes. My heart races, knowing this may mean the end of the trees. My fears are multiplied as I see the power lines continue across a vast open space. The poles and lines sway in the wind, crossing high over an interstate. The cars blur by at high speeds, and my stomach clenches, knowing there is no escaping my fate.

My fingers are slick with sweat and tree sap. I wipe one hand at a time on my pants, holding tight to the line above my head, my feet motionless until both hands have a solid grip. I close my eyes and face into the wind. Another shout, and I turn toward it, noticing a similar line running parallel to my own. A woman slides forward, her power line a concave ribbon between the two poles. How low can it go? How can she possibly climb back up to the next pole?

I wipe my forehead against the tattered remains of my sleeve and pray for the courage to continue. There is no going back, and with one wrong step I will plummet and be crushed—if not from the fall, then from the speeding cars and semis. How did I end up here?

The woman is still on the downslope. She's nearing the midpoint. I have yet to cross into this new opening. I'm terrified, but there is no alternative. Edging my foot forward, I toe the line. Stopping my feet, I trail my hands forward, then freeze as a stiff wind blows across the way. I gasp and bury my face in my shoulder, holding tight. *My hands hurt and my forearms burn from the death grip.* Just wait this out, it will get better.

After an eternity, the winds die down, and I take a deep breath, starting the slow shuffle forward. I no longer see the stranger across the way. I don't know what happened to her.

Steeling my nerves, I tell myself it doesn't matter how I came to be here. I just have to keep going. No matter where it takes me. There's no escaping this path, these high wires. The moment I began to climb, my path was laid out. The terror in my stomach doesn't diminish, but I know it will soon become my new normal. I must keep going.

I must keep going.

SHE AWOKE TO A DARK ROOM; the sun had yet to rise. Kurt was sleeping soundly next to her. Carlie was wide-awake, alert, filled with adrenaline and the fading vestiges of terror.

Focus on what you can control, Car!

Deep breaths. In and out. In and out. In and out.

Sitting up, she tried to calm herself. She slipped off the bed and into the restroom, collecting her discarded tank along the way. Tugging it over her head, she freshened up before sitting on the edge of the tub. This was where he had first touched her. That bath. Smiling at the memory, she soaked in the way he made her feel. Valued. Treasured. Special.

So, what was with the dream? Why the anxiety? Was this about her and Kurt? Or Alex? What was her subconscious trying to tell her?

Stop it, Car. You're driving yourself crazy over a stupid dream. Sometimes a dream was just a dream. She had probably seen a brochure or something about a ropes course and her wackadoodle brain had dialed up this skyborne episode.

Shaking herself, she eased across the room to grab her phone, checking the time as she returned to the restroom. What time was it in London? Almost ten. Kim should be up.

Hey, girl! How's London? she texted Kim. She chewed her fingernails and waited to see if Kim was watching her phone.

To pass the minutes, she flipped through apps and checked Facebook. The glamorized lives of friends greeted her. What would Facebook be like if people posted their mundane everyday moments instead of these glossy versions of themselves?

What are you doing up so early? Bad dream? messaged Kim.

She loved Kim. She was not bothered by Carlie's dreams and panic attacks, having helped her through more than she could count. Most people outgrew this stuff. Since they continued to plague her, Carlie had tried to educate herself and find ways to make sense of them. It didn't always work, but it helped.

Kind of. It was weird. I was walking on electric wires and got stuck having to cross a highway.

Any idea?

Fear of change? Carlie speculated. Her mind tugged at a memory of her contemplating a circus life. That was probably part of it.

Hmm... You all right?

Yeah, just wide-awake. She added the eyerolling emoji.

Glad to hear from you. This trip is unreal. There's a group of twenty of us from our offices around the world. Pretty cool.

Did you do any touristy stuff?

Not yet. We're doing that after today's shareholder meeting. Palace, Big Ben, double-decker bus, the works.

Meet anyone interesting? Carlie had to tread lightly here, but she held onto a secret hope that Kim would meet someone to make her realize what she had with Owen wasn't enough.

A couple people, nothing too wild. How's Atlanta?

How's Atlanta? Hmm. She tapped her fingernail against the tub lip and tried to figure out what to say.

Kurt is here. I am really into him, and I think the feeling's mutual.

Really? Kim added the heart eyes emoji.

Really, really.

Niiiiice. Bout damn time. Did Rachael give you her "I told you so"?

No. Not yet, at any rate.

Excited for the dinner? What are you going to do when you see Alex?

Wellllll... about that.

She filled Kim in on the previous evening's drama, and her friend proceeded to curse him in multiple languages.

What are you going to do? Kim asked, once she'd exhausted the global supply chain of insults.

I don't know. Hopefully, he won't show.

And if he does?

If he's there... I'll figure it out. And stay close to Kurt.

Be careful, Car.

I will.

They signed off, and she sighed, feeling a little more at peace.

"What are you doing?"

She glanced up at Kurt. His hair was a mess, and he was leaning his incredible naked body against the doorframe. Her mouth dried, and she had to look away before answering.

"Just finished texting Kim, seeing how she's doing," she replied. "She's in London."

"And Kim is...?"

"My best friend. You'll meet her. She's crazy and wonderful."

"She's the one with the boyfriend drama you mentioned in Chicago?"

"Yeah. How'd you remember that?" She was surprised. And impressed.

He smiled and drew her to her feet. "Go lie down, I'll be right there." He pointed her out to the bedroom and washed up before rejoining her.

Carlie burrowed beneath the blanket and sighed. He returned, wrapping a steely arm around her waist. She snuggled closer into his warmth, and they drifted, catching more sleep before facing the day.

44

"*E*arth to Carlie, come in, Carlie," he whispered, pressing gentle kisses along her neck.

She giggled and stretched before opening her eyes to a crystal green heaven, filled with humor and hunger.

"Good morning," she murmured, blinking up at him.

"Yes, it is," he said, sliding his lips down her neck to kiss her collarbone before continuing lower. She squirmed, his warm mouth heating through her tank top and doing funny things to her sleepy head.

"Can we just stay here forever?" she whimpered.

"Maybe not forever, but definitely another hour," his muffled voice drifted up from her navel.

"What time is it?"

"Almost nine thirty."

Damn. "Kurt?"

"Mmhmm?"

"We need to get up." She sighed but made no effort to move away.

"Do we?"

"Yes... I have to meet my mother and—Oh!" She gasped as he caressed her tender clit.

"Your mother?" he prompted innocently, continuing to work his fingers in wicked ways.

"My mother?" Carlie echoed, at a loss as he teased and played with her.

"You have to meet your mother?" he chuckled, kissing her stomach beneath the hem of her tank top.

"Yes," she moaned. "And yes."

He drove a finger into her, sliding in and out, and her breathing grew erratic as he added a second to the mix, sliding deep and massaging, caressing. He kissed lower, his tongue searching for her covered bud. Finding it, he lapped at it without mercy, his fingers tormenting her. She squirmed and moaned, pulling at him until he slid back up to her, reaching for the nightstand. "We'll need to find a store today," he laughed as he tore open the package. She reached for him, helping slide the rubber down his shaft. He held his breath, no longer laughing. His calculated expression made her suspicious. A startled squeal erupted out of her as he flipped her over onto her stomach. He grasped her hips and lifted her higher, his fingers sliding into her warmth, teasing her.

As the desire and anticipation ramped up, Carlie moaned his name and reached for a pillow, holding onto it as he kissed her shoulder and arched over her back before slamming home, filling her in one strong stride. He held tightly to her hips, pulling back before surging forward again. She panted as his movements quickened, her body moving in time to meet his. Grasping and pulling at her, he charged in even more deeply. Her eyes clenched shut as she tried to keep a hold on sanity. He pumped into her, his balls slapping against her erotically. He reached his hand around to fondle her, squeezing her breast before moving lower, rubbing and teasing her clit, eliciting a moan.

Pace steady, he tormented her, holding her right at the edge. She bit the pillow and stopped trying to hold to reality. Grasping the bed rails above her, the heat flamed through her body, and she shuddered, squeezing and convulsing around him, gasping as the orgasm swept her away. "Yes, that's it, baby," he panted, groaning and pushing even deeper, finding his own release. "Fuck," he groaned, collapsing against her, his breath harsh in her ear.

Spent and breathing heavily, Carlie closed her eyes and enjoyed the press of his hot, sweaty body against her own. He pulled back and out of her, sliding the condom off and tossing it aside before dropping next to her and closing his eyes, his chest still rising rapidly.

He blindly reached for her, pulling her onto his chest. Content to rest there, she relaxed and let his breathing soothe her, her own calming with his.

"This is heaven," Carlie whispered.

"You're heaven," he replied, kissing the top of her head.

"I do need to meet my mother this morning," she sighed moments later.

"So I gathered," he said, his arms tightening around her. "Where are you going?"

"Breakfast, then the spa. Mom's booked us for manis and pedis before we get our hair done."

He frowned. "Where are you going?"

"I don't know," she shrugged. "Are you worried?"

He kissed her forehead. "I'll text both security teams and see who can escort you. I'm sure it'll be fine, but I'm not about to let you go without them, especially when we don't know where Alex is."

She kissed his chest and snuggled into his protective embrace.

After quick showers and changing, Carlie watched Kurt make phone calls and conduct business at the desk. The man was a machine, keeping track of so many threads. She shook her head in wonder.

Grabbing her laptop, she settled into the corner chair to catch up on her email before food and pampering. Some notes popped up from Rebecca about Pendulum issues. She opened her test site and played with it, trying to replicate the problems. Unsuccessful, she noted that it would have to wait until she could see it for herself at the office on Monday. She closed her computer with a frustrated sigh. She hated having something left open like that.

"You okay?" Kurt called from the desk.

"Yeah, just some work stuff that I can't figure out from here. How do you manage it?"

"Delegation," he said. "I hire the right people who are smart and focused on our shared vision. I trust them to resolve issues and to elevate those that I need to tend to. I learned early on that I can't micromanage and expect to succeed. In general, my associates perform better when they have room to take calculated risks and make decisions on their own."

She couldn't imagine handing off her matrix to someone else to develop. But she knew she would have to do that eventually. It wasn't like she wouldn't have other projects.

Carlie left her laptop on the ottoman and stood behind him, wrapping her arms around his neck. She kissed his cheek, and his smiling green eyes lifted to her. "Am I invited to breakfast?" he asked.

At her definitive nod, he shut down his laptop and rose, pulling her into his arms. She hugged his waist and inhaled his scent, humming with satisfaction. She loved that he seemed to always want to be touching her. "Breakfast is a yes for both of us. Pretty sure we've burned enough calories overnight to require sustenance," she teased him.

He laughed and grabbed his things. She paused when she saw the holster and gun were no longer on the desk but said nothing. If he felt it was necessary, she'd let him do what he needed to do.

They walked to the elevator, and Carlie messaged the family, letting them know they were on their way down for breakfast. Rach replied that they were already on seconds. Figured.

"Are you going to keep your room?" she asked, then mentally slapped herself. Too much too soon.

Surprise flashed in his eyes. "Should I not?"

Trying not to show how flustered she felt, she turned and shrugged. "According to you and Rick, I'm not supposed to be left alone right now..."

He laughed. "Well, I don't plan to spend much time in there. But won't you want your own space?"

"Right now? Not particularly."

"Ms. Eller, are you asking me to move in with you?" he drawled with a twangy southern accent.

She was pretty sure he could hear her eyes rolling. "Not after that," she laughed.

He held up his hands, full of faux offense. "Ms. Eller, you wound this old man."

The doors opened to the lobby, and she stepped out, turning back to him with her hands on her hips. "Make your own call, Old Man Hunter."

"Well, now, I never turn down a beautiful damsel in distress's passionate plea," he twanged.

"Good Lord." She laughed. "Do what you want," she

tossed over her shoulder and walked toward the breakfast room.

He snagged her hand, hauling her back to him. "Carlie," he breathed. "I would like nothing better than to spend every moment here with you." He pressed a kiss to her lips before releasing her. "Will your family mind?"

She smirked. "I'm twenty-four years old, Kurt. I lived with my ex for four years."

"I'm thirty-one, but I still don't like to upset my mother without cause. Your point?"

"I don't think it's any of their concern," she stated.

"Seeing as how I would like to stick around for a while, if you don't mind, I'd rather not piss off your parents."

How adorably, unexpectedly old-fashioned. "I don't think they care, but do what your conscience requires."

She felt his eyes on her as she joined the family. Glancing over her shoulder, she saw him watching her speculatively. He shook his head and caught up with her.

45

With a hearty family breakfast, then the spa, the hours passed quickly. Security ended up not being an issue since the spa was in the hotel. So nice. Aside from some general comments about Kurt and how much they liked him, her family didn't ask about their relationship, and she didn't offer up details.

When they returned to their rooms to dress for dinner at Bernie's estate, Carlie was disappointed to find her room Kurt-less. Frowning, she wondered if he had decided to return to his room. Maybe he thought they were moving too fast. She turned to her closet and pulled out her cocktail gown, excited to see Bernie again and learn more about his charity work.

Zipping up her dress, she spied the silver heels Rachael had insisted would set off the cobalt blue fabric. Carlie touched up her makeup and spritzed on a light trace of perfume before donning her earrings and bracelet. Assessing the final ensemble in the full-length mirror, she was pretty happy. The stylist had swept her honey hair into an intricate updo, with soft caramel tendrils framing her face. The satin halter dress hugged her curves. She fingered the shimmering high neckline. The silver heels did add a nice pop of brightness to the overall look. She just hoped she didn't fall on her ass.

She straightened up the vanity and tossed a few items into her bag while she wondered again where Kurt was. In his room? She didn't want to pout, but she couldn't help but feel slighted by his choosing to stay there.

Pull yourself together, Car! You sound like a lovesick teenager!

There were still twenty minutes before it was time to meet in the lobby. Carlie grabbed her phone and messaged Rach.

Meet in the bar?

Sorry, girl. No can do. Still working on my face, replied her sister.

She tried Kurt. *In your room? I'm ready and thinking about heading down to the bar. Join me?*

No response. Frustrated, Carlie snagged her wristlet, hauled open the door, and headed down alone. She refused to feel like a prisoner in her own room. Stepping into the hall, she froze at the vision awaiting her.

His blonde hair was trimmed and styled back, and he wore a sharp black tuxedo with a cobalt-blue vest and silver pocket square. *Oh, my.* She sucked in her breath and stared.

"Sorry," he said, closing the distance between them. "I tried to beat you back to the room, but the traffic..." He trailed off, stopping to take in her look for the evening. "Carlie. You are stunning."

"You're not so bad yourself." She kissed him on the cheek. He offered his arm, and they headed to the elevator. "The colors. How did you know?"

He looked sheepish. "I called in a favor from Rick."

"You two made up?"

"He's a good guy. We hung out for a while when you girls had your salon time."

They staked out some seats, and the bartender glanced her way and stared. Carlie blushed and fiddled with her evening bag. Kurt cleared his throat. Loudly. He wrapped an arm around her seat, and she noted the similarity in his posture to the way Rick had been wrapped around Rachael. She loved it.

Carlie ordered a glass of shiraz and sat back to sip on the spicy red, watching Kurt through her lashes. He was so striking. He had gotten a haircut, his wavy hair stopping above his collar. His eyes were lighter with his hair darkened and slicked back. Turning toward her with his bourbon, he stared at her, commanding her full attention. It was no hardship on her part; she could stare at him all night.

"I know you planned to arrive with your family, but I was wondering, hoping actually, that you would come with me. As my date?"

A giddy flutter bounced about in her stomach. She was about to reply when a voice behind her piped up. "She would love to, right, Car?"

Carlie glared at Rach. "Mind if I answer?"

She chuckled and waved magnanimously. "By all means."

Turning back to Kurt, she took his hand. "I would love to."

He exhaled, relief crossing his features. It was touching. Perhaps she wasn't the only lovesick teenager.

Taking the stool next to hers, Rachael ordered a chardonnay and a bourbon for Rick. "He's on his way," she said. She smirked at Kurt. "Heard you two had quite the afternoon."

Carlie glanced from her to Kurt, her unspoken question hanging in the air.

"Did you?" he muttered, taking a sip of his drink.

"Mmhmm," her sister confirmed. "Some stylish conversations?" she hinted.

He looked away then back at Rachael. "I need to remember that what I tell him makes its way back to you."

"Yes, you do." She winked. "But don't worry, I'm in your corner on this one." She turned to watch Rick stroll in.

"Is someone going to tell me what this is about?" Carlie grumbled, looking from innocent face to innocent face.

"No," said all three in unison, before succumbing to giddy laughter.

"Fine," she said, frowning at all of them.

"Don't worry, Car," Rachael stage whispered. "It's a good thing."

"If you say so," Carlie said.

Later, Carlie's family departed in the first limo, then Kurt handed her into the second. "I thought you preferred to travel low-key," she commented.

"Your mom arranged these." He shrugged. "But I don't mind. I was hoping for a few minutes alone with you."

"Really?"

"Yes," he said, kissing her softly and sliding a large, flat rectangular jewelry box onto her lap. "For you," he whispered.

She stared down at the baby blue felt in surprise, afraid to touch it. "Why?"

"Why not?"

Carlie bit her lower lip as she opened the box. A breathtaking diamond and blue sapphire pendant winked at her, a silky silver chain disappearing behind it. "Oh!" she gasped, her hand fluttering to cover her gaping mouth.

"Do you like it?"

She couldn't answer. She fingered the face of it, tracing the brilliant, gleaming stones. "It's gorgeous," she whispered and turned her wide eyes back to him. "But it's too much, Kurt. I can't accept this."

He shook his head with an adorable boyish smile. "It's yours."

She shook her head, unable to grasp this.

"Please," he begged. "I want this for you. Will you wear it?"

Carlie stared into his eyes, knowing she was hopelessly in love, with or without the jewels. She nodded not for the gems, but for him. She would wear it for him.

Lifting the box from her lap, he removed the necklace and twirled his finger to have her turn around. He settled the heavy necklace on her chest and clasped the delicate chain. His fingers slid up the side of her neck, brushing aside a curling tendril of hair to kiss the exposed skin.

"Kurt," she breathed, turning to look up at him.

He sat back and took in the effect. "It's almost as beautiful as you."

She fingered the gift, tears swimming in her eyes. "Thank you. I love it."

And I've so completely fallen for you.

He wrapped his hand around hers, they relaxed into each other.

"I was thinking about something you said earlier," he said, glancing out the window. A slight frown marred his face.

"What?"

"Am I too old for you?" His hand clenched around her fingers ever so slightly as he asked, and Carlie fought to avoid laughing.

"Why would you think that?"

"You called me old. I am seven years older than you. Is that too much of a difference?"

This time, she did laugh. "Old Man Hunter? That bothered you?"

Kurt looked uncomfortable. She leaned against his arm and twisted her hand in his grip to thread her fingers through his. "I was teasing you, silly. But I am not teasing in the slightest when I say no, you are not too old for me. You are perfect."

She felt his lips press to the top of her head and smiled, tickled that he would ask her that. It showed a surprising vulnerability on his part, and it confirmed that he was not thinking about a short fling.

The limo turned down a wide street with tall walls and private gates sectioning off the elite estates. They approached a tall, ornate black gate, two men flanking the opening. The limo driver slowed, and then they were on their way again, rolling down a smooth driveway. An impressive masonry structure rose in the distance, and as they drew closer, she could make out the limousines lined up around a spectacular fountain. *Wow.*

Their turn arrived and the door was opened from the outside, a gloved hand escorting them from the car to the elevated stonework terrace by the front door where her family waited. Rachael was practically bouncing. "Let me see it, let me see it," she squealed. She started toward the approaching couple, but Rick held her arm, keeping her at his side. She pouted up at him, then recovered and waited.

When Carlie came up the last step, her sister's restraint disappeared, and she slipped out of Rick's hold and bounded over. "Oh, it's perfect! I wasn't sure about the color when Rick told me. You never know how cobalt is going to work with other blues, but it's perfect! And look at the quality of the cut..." she rattled on, holding and turning the necklace to capture the light in it.

"Carlie, Kurt," greeted her mother. Carlie smiled and kissed her offered cheek, then turned and embraced her dad. "You look dashing, Dad!"

"As do you, Carlie-Q. Kurt, glad you're here. Let's go in," he said, ushering the group to the open door, where their security team waited in the shadows.

They entered a cavernous foyer, bright with candles and crystal chandeliers, and were led to a formal sitting room—though no one was sitting. A glamorous crowd mingled, quietly judging and snubbing each other while nodding appreciatively at the talented pianist coaxing melodies from the baby grand. A server passed by with a gilt tray of champagne flutes and martinis. Carlie selected a glass of champagne and sipped, letting the cool bubbles slide down her throat. Her fingers periodically reached up to caress the necklace, and she caught Kurt watching her do so, a satisfied smile curving his lips. She winked at him before turning to greet yet another person her father had led to her. Kurt was likewise surrounded by a stream of interested parties, and they found themselves separated quickly.

"...and I told him that we would need to bring the whole division stateside if we're going to make that deadline." A woman cackled next to Carlie. Rachael smiled gamely at her, encouraging the stories, laughing with verve, and working her magic. Carlie found these conversations tedious and underwhelming. She didn't know how her sister managed to look so fascinated. Stifling a yawn, Carlie turned to skim the crowd, which was maybe thirty or so people. She noted with relief the absence of a particular tall, moody writer. Setting down her empty glass, she sidled up to her mother.

"Is he here?" her mother inquired.

Smiling, Carlie shook her head no. Mary visibly relaxed. "Thank goodness. One crisis averted. Have you seen your father?"

"He's over by the window, reliving old times with Bernie."

She chuckled. "I should go make sure he doesn't revert to old times."

Uncomfortable with such formal environments, Carlie tried to remember why she had been so excited to come here. She would do much better with a larger crowd, where it was easier to lose herself at the edges. Forcing a smile, she zigzagged through the tuxedos and gowns, nodding and laughing at bad jokes along the way. She took a deep breath and slipped into the vacant foyer. Kurt tracked her progress and followed, grinning. "I just met the Governor," he said. "He's trying to sell me on moving some of our key operations to the state."

"Really?"

"I had to excuse myself before he started asking for campaign contributions." He chuckled. "What are you doing out here?"

She blushed. "I don't do well with crowds."

He held his arm out to her, looking for all the world like a prince. "Would it make a difference if I told you there's no one here who compares to you?"

Butterflies everywhere. Carlie patted his arm and smiled into his face. "You flatter me."

"It's the truth, Carlie," he said, bending slightly to kiss her cheek.

"I do need to go freshen up," she said, looking around and catching the eye of a man nearby.

"Ma'am?" intoned a white-gloved butler.

"Restroom?"

"Right through there." He gestured to a short hallway.

"I'll be back in a minute." Carlie kissed Kurt's cheek before she turned down the wood-paneled hallway.

Alone at last, she sighed and braced her hands on the counter in the spacious sitting room that opened into the restroom. She stared at her reflection, feeling out of her league. This was crazy. This wasn't her. But it was clearly the kind of world Kurt had to woo and interact with regularly. If she was going to make things work with him, she would have to find a way to fit in, be pleasant, be sociable and dashing. Be more like Mom and Rachael. Touching up her powder and lipstick, Carlie practiced her smile, praying it didn't look as fake to the others as it did to her.

"You look beautiful, Carlie," said a terribly familiar voice.

Dropping her cosmetics back into the handbag, Carlie choked down her anxiety and turned to face him. "What are you doing here?" she asked, glancing at the closed door to the hallway, praying someone would come in. Alex stood alone, dressed winningly in a simple black tuxedo.

"Invited, same as you. Remember? We agreed to meet here."

"But that was before..." She trailed off, not wanting to discuss yesterday's events.

"Before you betrayed me with that pompous rich boy?"

Betrayed him?

"Alex, if you recall, you're the one who betrayed me." She heard the door open and felt a swoosh of relief. She started to turn to the newcomer, but his words caught her attention.

"No, that's not what happened. But let's not discuss that here."

At his nod, a cloth dropped over her mouth and an arm closed around her waist. Carlie struggled, trying to tear at the mystery person, scrape at their white-gloved hands. She pushed harder at the arm, but the grip was undeterred. A sharp stab of pain lanced her upper arm, and she fought harder. A sluggish heat started to seep through her limbs. Her vision blurred, her eyes watering. *This can't be happening!* She screamed, but the sound came out as a whimper, muffled by the rag over her mouth. If she could just make it back out and down the short hallway.

Her legs weakened, and soon she was sliding to the floor. She was vaguely aware of being scooped up, looking into a face she had once thought more handsome than any other. Her vision narrowed and despair crashed over her.

Everything disappeared; the world was dark.

46

*S*he was alone in a dark hotel room. A soft light glowed under the door. She patted around herself and realized she was on a bed. She was barefoot. She was wearing a fancy dress. The surrealness of the situation struck her. What happened? What did this mean?

Oh, God. This is not a dream.

Sitting up, she edged off the bed, her feet soundless on the cold barren floor. Carlie knew she wasn't dreaming, but everything was soft and hazy. The world had turned into a dreamscape. A small bathroom opened to the side, and she slipped in, quietly closing the door. There was no knob, no lock, just a hole where one used to be. Carlie stuffed a washcloth into the hole and flipped the light on, eyes wincing and head screaming at the bright glare. A glance in the mirror showed that her hair was half fallen, makeup smeared across her face. She looked dopey. Her necklace was gone. Turning to the side, she saw a dark bruise forming on her upper arm, an angry red splotch in the center. What the...?

She removed the hair clips and shook her hair out, alleviating the tension from the tightly pulled hair. Her head still pounded, and she sat hard on the toilet lid, trying to figure out where she was and what she should do now.

The bedroom door opened, and a moment later the bathroom door crashed into the wall. "What are you doing?" Alex demanded.

Carlie blinked at him. "I... I don't know." She was honest.

He gestured to the bedroom. "Finish up, then get out here."

No alternative solution presenting itself, she numbly did as he directed. She washed up, scrubbing at her makeup, trying to ease the burning in her eyes.

Alex sat fidgeting on the edge of the bed, wearing a peculiar smile as he watched her approach. Slowly, Carlie walked right up to him and looked deep in his eyes. He leaned forward in anticipation.

She let her arm fly and her palm connected with his cheek, the sound echoing in the small room.

"The fuck, Carlie?" he barked, capturing her hand as it arced through the air to land a second slap and flipping her onto the bed. He covered her with his body and pinned her arms to her sides. She struggled and tried to use her knees, her feet, anything to throw him off. He grinned, his sheer physical size not budging under her assault. "You're just turning me on now, sweetheart."

Carlie froze. What the actual fuck.

He saw her confusion and pressed his advantage, dropping his head to lick the side of her neck. His knee dug between her clenched legs, forcing them apart to press closer to her. This could not be happening.

"Stop, Alex. Stop it!" she screeched. She squeezed her eyes closed, praying this was a nightmare, that she would wake up and be at home. But his mouth moved, and he suffocated her, abusing her mouth, his hand tearing at her breast, his hip digging into her. Desperate, she bit down on his lip, hard. His head jerked back, and he swung his hand, backhanding her across the cheek. Her eyes burned; her skin stung. She could taste blood in her mouth.

"That's enough," he growled.

He stormed out of the room, slamming the door behind him. Carlie heard the lock engage and knew she was trapped.

Trembling, she fought the waves of panic. If she remained quiet and calm, she could think through this. But her fear wouldn't subside; her chest continued to tighten, and her hands became icy. Panic rising, she counted to ten and tried to focus on her breathing. In and out. In and out. In and out. *Focus, Carlie. What can you control?*

She pictured Kurt, imagining she could feel his arms around her, soothing her. She dragged in breath after painful breath.

Regaining control of herself by degrees, she sat up again and nursed the side of her face. It stung, but she would survive.

Think, Carlie, think!

There had to be a way out. She rushed to the window and pulled back the curtain. She gasped at the view. The room had to be at least twenty flights up. There was no fire escape or platform outside the window. They were in a high-rise, somewhere downtown. She assumed it was still Atlanta. Not familiar with this area, she couldn't even speculate where she might be.

Tiptoeing to the door, she pressed herself to the floor, looking out where the light spilled in. All she could see was beige carpet and the side of a blue chair or sofa.

Carlie checked the furnishings, the holes where a television must have been screwed into the dresser top, the walls. Everything was basic, nothing fancy. No phone lines or internet connections. She wondered where her phone was, if it was lost for good. God, her mother would kill her if she ever found out that worry had crossed her mind now. Returning to the bathroom, Carlie tapped on the walls, praying someone would respond.

Nothing.

More dead ends.

Returning to the confines of the bedroom, she looked under the bed and in all the dresser drawers, the closet, wondering if there was anything she might use, anything at all.

Exasperated, she stared down at her finds: two wooden hangers, a notepad of paper (no pen), a mini bar of soap, two washcloths, and a hand towel. If she were MacGyver, she could figure something out, build a freaking rocket ship or stealth weapon. But she had nothing. She grunted with frustration, tears tracking down her face.

What was she going to do?

Ripping the bedspread off, she wrapped herself in it, insulating with additional layers. She curled up on the bed and lay down, the remnants of whatever they had injected her with draining her remaining balance and alertness. She closed her eyes and clung again to the memory of Kurt, his arms around her, his smile, his way of making her feel safe. Where was he now? Had they figured out what happened? He and Mom were probably meeting with their teams and the police. Dad likely knew everything now. Rachael was probably freaking out.

The tears continued to run down her face. The pressure, the guilt, the overwhelming unfairness of it all. She punched the pillow, angry and frustrated. Why was this happening?

She thought back over the conversations she had had with Alex in Chicago. Before. Were there things he had said that hinted at this crazy person underneath? Nothing came to mind.

Who had been with him in the washroom? Someone was helping him. She recalled a white glove—similar to the ones worn by the butler and the usher who had assisted her out of the limo. One of Bernie's people, then? Was Bernie involved? God, what had she gotten into?

No, Carlie. Bernie is not involved. Stop this!

But he did invite them all. And he knew Alex. And his staff wore white gloves.

She was losing the battle to stay awake and welcomed a brief escape from this latest development. Thankfully, no dreams marred her sleep.

Minutes, hours—she didn't know how long—passed. A body joined her on the bed, warmth pressed to her back. Carlie didn't move, staying wrapped up in her cocoon. If she just pretended to still be asleep, then she wouldn't have to deal with it. After a while, the body left, and relief loosened her limbs.

An argument in the Blue Chair Room broke through the silence. Two voices. She recognized Alex, but the other voice was unknown to her. It must be White Glove Man. Alex wanted to leave, take her somewhere else. The other voice said to stay here, see what they could get now. This was promising. If they were just trying to ransom her, they would not harm her. Right?

The entrance to the hotel room opened and closed—someone had left or entered? She pressed her ear to the door, listening for signs. A refrigerator opened and closed, something rattled. The sounds drew closer, and she backed away, jumping onto the bed. Her door opened, and the light flared to life. She blinked at the brightness and saw Alex in the doorway. He held out a bottle of water and a bowl of granola. "Glad to see you're up. I was worried we'd given you too much. Eat this, you'll feel better."

She stared at him, unmoving. He shook his head. "I'm not the enemy, Carlie."

Turning away from him, she heard the dishes connect with the dresser's top before the door and lock clicked firmly.

Her stomach growled and she inspected the food, rationalizing that he had no cause to harm her. Her hunger satisfied, she paced the floor, mind analyzing and dismissing each possible escape attempt. There had to be a way.

A phone rang in the next room, and she jumped. What would happen if she started screaming, yelling for help? Would it work or make things worse? But what if the caller was the partner who had just left? She strained to hear any conversation, but the phone just rang and rang. No one answered it. Damn.

Sitting on the bed, she stared at the hangers. There had to be something. Some way. And now there was only one person in the next room.

Alex.

Who still wanted her.

A knock sounded on the door, and she wondered at the change in tactic. He wasn't barging in this time? She bundled the pair of wooden hangers under the blanket and looked at the door, debating, thinking. A ghost of a plan started to take shape in her mind. But she'd have to work quickly.

When she didn't respond, he opened the door, filling the

frame. "Carlie," he said, entering the room and closing the door behind him. "This has all gone wrong. We need to talk. You need to understand what's happened."

"Then talk," she said.

He sat on the bed to face her. His dark hair looked disheveled, and there were dark circles under his eyes. She could see his throat working as he swallowed. "First, I'm sorry for making up the story about the tape. There is no video."

She balked. What?! "Are you serious? Why does Kurt think there is one?"

"I was very convincing. I played a bit of audio from something else."

She wrinkled her nose. "Why?"

He ran a hand through his dark hair. "Writing is my life, Carlie. It's what I do. I've published amazing analyses, received glowing praise. The books I write are changing things. Bringing the country back to our roots, reestablishing our core values. This is the start of a future where we are not killing each other, where we honor and respect each other. This is how we make the world great again."

"And how does kidnapping and extortion play into this great new world?"

"It is a small price to pay to get to the next level. Once you understand, you'll join me, be part of this." He mumbled something unintelligible. "Besides, you were supposed to choose me. It was going to be perfect. I'd get the money and contract from Kurt, then you and I would be together."

She frowned and asked what had been bothering her. "Why? Why did you go after Kurt and not me or my family?"

He reached out and touched her chin. "I thought about it, but as we got closer to each other, I realized I didn't want to mess that up. Kurt, though, he has the money and the connections. It's better this way. Fate brought us together, Carlie, and dropped Kurt in here to make sure of it."

Ignoring his madness, she pressed on. "What on earth made you think telling him you had a tape of me would affect him?"

Alex's mouth turned to a sneer. "Don't you know anything? He's a momma's boy and a freaking cub scout. Not a chance in hell he'd pass up an opportunity to help a damsel in distress."

Her face must have shown her puzzlement, because he grunted and laughed bitterly.

"All the humanitarian shit he did with his ex? The interviews where he goes on and on about his mom and how he takes care of her now? He can't help himself—he's weak when it comes to women and people in need. But I didn't count on him fucking telling you about it. So pathetic."

Being a good person made someone weak? Pathetic? Alex was out of his mind.

She shook her head. "Do you hear yourself, Alex? Do you honestly believe what you're saying? This. Will. Not. Work."

His eyes gleamed. "It will. It's already working. That flashy necklace of yours is going to pay off some debts and give us some breathing room to start the next chapter."

Son of a bitch.

She pressed her eyes closed.

Deep breath, Carlie. Keep calm.

"And what's the next chapter?"

He grinned broadly. "I get my book deal, and we get married. This will set us up for life. We'll tour the country, change the world. Together."

Jesus. He seriously believed this.

Tread lightly, Car.

"And my job?"

"You don't need a job. You'll stay by my side. With my books and your family's money... We'll have a great life, Carlie. You'll see."

"I love my job, my life. I want to stay in Ohio."

He sneered. "No one wants to stay in Ohio. Think of the places we'll go, the things we'll do. New York, Seattle, Chicago—the place that brought me my Lois Lane."

Clearly, reason was not going to work. Suppressing a shudder, she knew what she had to do. "And you'll be my Superman?"

His smoldering look was all she needed to know this was the right path. "Yes." He crawled across the bed to her, smiling.

"And you'll protect me?"

"Of course," he said, edging closer.

She gazed up at him through her lashes, trying to emulate her sister's perfect pout. "And you'll love me?"

"I already do," he growled.

She crooked a finger, drawing him closer so she could push him down on the bed. She slid the blanket off to the side and sent up a silent prayer. Carlie took a deep breath and climbed on top of him, straddling him. "And you'll please me?" she whispered, leaning down, letting her hair wrap around them both, blocking his view of her hands.

Alex caught his breath, reaching for her. He grabbed the back of her neck, hauling her to him. She kissed him. She kissed him with all the passion she felt for someone else. He groaned, and his body grew rigid, responding to her. She worked her hips back and forth across him and sat up to tempt him further, riding him slowly, grimacing as she recalled the similarities to their walk in Chicago. He closed his eyes and dug his fingers into her hips, pulling her against him. The dark blue fabric of her dress strained across his waist, his erection stabbing through the layers of clothes. He groaned, demanding more. She hid her smile.

"Shhh! Can they hear us?" she whispered.

"Who?" he panted. "We're alone, baby. Just you and me. No need to be quiet."

His neck rigid and hands coiled around her hips, he grasped her face, drowning out further conversation. He sucked at her, pawing in desperate arousal. She needed to get his hands off her. She pushed him back down, giving him her best temptress smile. "My turn," she demanded.

He grinned and crossed his hands behind his neck. "Ride on, baby."

Carlie made a show of settling over him again, raking her nails down his chest. His breathing was strained and he was enthralled. But he was still watching her too closely.

Shit, shit, shit!

Trailing a hand to the side, she closed her fingers around the bundle hidden under the blanket, inching it closer. He was rocking rhythmically, and she focused on keeping the pace steady, desperate to not draw his attention elsewhere. She threw a nervous glance at the door, praying he was telling the truth, that there was no one else out there.

Now or never, Car.

Please, let this work.

Sliding her free hand down his chest, she brought both hands to rest on his waist, unbuttoning his pants. "Fuck, yes." He grunted, eyes still wide open. There was no going back now. After a brief hesitation, she unzipped him and slid a hand between them, grasping him. She rose up higher on her knees, teasing him with a view of her skirt rising.

"Close your eyes," she purred.

He did.

Swallowing her disgust, she stroked his length, gliding up and down as she slid the other hand back to the bundle at her side, her plan B. She wiggled the bundle to make sure it was free of the blanket. "Carlie," he gasped. "Jesus, I love you."

Casting one last look over her shoulder to calculate the distance, she moved. Raising one leg and gliding it along his thigh, she slid back and slammed her knee into his exposed genitals. He howled, instantly balling up, and she threw the unneeded hangers at his head as she flung herself off of him and ran to the door. She slammed the door closed and scrambled to lock it, then took off for the front door.

"You bitch!" he snarled, slamming against the door. The frame shook, and she bolted, fleeing into the hallway. She had hoped he would take longer to recover. Frantically surveying her surroundings, she spied a stairwell a few doors down. She ran like hell.

Her bare feet slapped the cold, gray concrete in the dark stairwell, which reeked of cigarette smoke, and she raced down the stairs, heart pounding in her chest. She had only gone two flights down when she heard a door crash into the wall above her.

"Carlie!" he bellowed. "Stop and get back here right now, you fucking whore!"

She fought the absurd desire to laugh. *Oh, yeah. Like that's going to happen.*

She tried the door at the landing. Locked. No exit. Fuck. Trying not to succumb to panic, she raced down the stairs, praying for an escape.

The door at the next landing was slightly ajar. She tried to pull it shut behind her, but it wouldn't close. *Please let him pass. Please let him pass.* She didn't wait. She rushed down the hallway and searched for any sign of life. The elevator looked too far away. She knew she couldn't wait for it without being found. An empty room service tray sat outside a door. She knocked on the door. "Please, please help me," she cried urgently. Carlie waited as long as she dared, then moved on to the next door.

Please, someone answer.

She had raised her fist to pound on the next door when a confused woman opened the door by the discarded tray.

"Help me," Carlie repeated, tears running down her face. Casting a terrified glance over her shoulder, she saw the stairway door hadn't moved. Yet. She couldn't imagine what he would do now if he caught her.

The woman in the doorway considered her for a long moment, then beckoned her into the room.

47

"*P*hone?"

She nodded to a hotel phone on the table. Carlie grabbed it and dialed 9-1-1.

Hurry, hurry, hurry.

The line connected with the dispatcher at last, and she begged for help, giving them her identity and location. Carlie glanced out the window and saw a horde of police cars already at the far side of the parking lot.

"What the...?" she questioned.

"Carlie!" a voice boomed down the hallway. "I know you're here." Shaking, she dropped down in the corner, silently begging this stranger to not give her away.

"Carlie! Where are you?"

He began banging on doors in the hallway, each thud echoing in the barren space. "Where is she?" he demanded, yelling at a stranger unwise enough to answer their door.

She took a deep breath and stood. Carlie couldn't let this happen. No one else was going to get hurt for what had transpired between her and this madman.

"Honey, I don't know what's going on, but I would sit back down if I were you. Do not go out there."

Carlie blinked at the well-meaning stranger with the southern accent. "What floor is this?" Carlie asked.

"Fourteen."

She moved back to the phone and called the front desk. "This is Carlie Eller. Tell the police I'm on the fourteenth floor. Please hurry."

Alex continued roaring down the hallway, slamming doors and yelling for her. Her mind flashed back to Donkey Kong, imagining he was a deranged gorilla. Seemed appropriate.

Carlie's gracious hostess, a woman who looked around her mother's age, disappeared into her bedroom. She couldn't blame her. And she couldn't let Alex hurt these people. She tiptoed to the door and leaned against it. Listening, waiting, praying. *Please let the police get the message in time.*

He was yelling at someone across the hall. She could see the struggle through the peephole. It was a terrified elderly woman. *No!* She could not let him do this.

Taking a deep breath, she unlocked the door, stepping into the hallway.

"I'm here. Let her go."

He dropped the old woman to the ground, who stared wild-eyed before rushing into her room, locking the door behind her.

He took a long step and grasped the top of Carlie's dress. The fabric gave way, tearing across her chest. She didn't even blink. "You. Fucking. Bitch," he spat before slamming her back into the wall. He pulled her closer to his torso, then slammed her back again, her head ringing. "You will beg for forgiveness before I'm done with you."

"Put. Her. Down," came a calm, accented female voice behind Carlie.

Carlie tried to turn her head to confirm who it was, to warn her away, but she couldn't move. He ignored the voice, wrapping his hands around her throat.

"Alex," she gasped. "Please." She felt a tear slide down her face, her head spinning from the blows and her constricted throat.

"Too late for that," he snarled, squeezing his hands tighter.

"I said, put her down, asshole," the stranger said more firmly.

Carlie's vision began to waver, and she clawed at his hands, desperately trying to get a breath.

"Close the fucking door and get out of here," Alex said over his shoulder, dismissing the woman.

A gun cocked, and Carlie's already wide eyes widened further, straining as she tried to retain her grip on consciousness. Alex heard it, too, swearing as he dropped her in a heap to swing at the good Samaritan. Knocking the gun from her hand, he flung her backward into the hallway, her body sprawled out, unconscious. Turning back to Carlie, Alex grabbed a fistful of hair and hauled her to her feet, before trapping her arms at her sides. "We're not done here," he snarled, glancing up and down the hallway. Coming to a decision, he picked her up and dropped her over his shoulder. The little breath she'd managed to draw into her burning lungs was forced out in a whoosh. A clearly insane corner of her mind imagined she was now a large wooden barrel about to be tossed by the giant gorilla.

The stairwell door burst open, and Kurt was there, running toward them. "Stop right there," Alex screamed.

Bending briefly, tilting her world, Alex crouched and stood back up with the discarded gun.

Kurt froze, eyeing Alex and his fireman's hold on her. "Let her go, Williams," he said in a deadly calm voice. "It's over."

Maniacal laughter jostled her. Alex glanced down at her discolored face, then back at Kurt. "You're right. It is over. You move, and she's dead."

Movement from the floor drew Carlie's eyes. The Southern woman stirred behind Alex's back, still sprawled on the floor between them and the elevator. She was muttering incoherently. Alex glanced at her dismissively, then turned back to Kurt.

"Put her down," Kurt ordered. His voice rang with authority.

"She's coming with me. You lost, Hunter. Again," he sneered as he inched backward down the hallway.

The woman kicked out, jarring Alex's knee forcefully with her heel. Losing his balance, he dropped Carlie to the side, her head crashing into the wall, and Alex staggered back.

Kurt wasted no time. He dropped to his knee, aimed, and fired low, away from Carlie, catching Alex in the thigh. Stunned, Donkey Kong turned and fell to the floor, trying to grasp Carlie's leg. She scooted out of reach, putting any distance between them she could, before her new friend stepped forward and kicked him in the face.

"Lowlife," she growled, clutching her reclaimed gun in her hand. "You should know better than to come after a woman in the South. We all carry, asshole, and we don't go down easy." She kicked him in his wounded thigh. Alex groaned and clutched at the leg, blood running down his face and limb.

Carlie fell to her knees, stunned, still gasping for air and unable to look away from the growing pool of crimson on the floor being fed by Alex's leg.

The elevator door rattled open, and police poured out, surrounding them and cuffing Alex.

Kurt rushed forward and sank down next to Carlie. "Towel?" he begged of the day's savior.

She disappeared into her room and returned with a lavender bathrobe. "It'll be too big on her, but it's better than a towel."

Barely holding the dark at bay, Carlie stared mutely, unable to move. Kurt slid her forward and wrapped the robe around her, pushing her arms into the sleeves and pulling it closed around her.

"She's in shock," said the EMT. "She needs medical care."

The paramedics brought up a stretcher, and Kurt brushed them aside, lifting her in his arms to lay her on the lightly padded bedding. "I'm coming with you," he said, clutching her hand.

They emerged from the lobby. Reality kept fading in and out, and nothing made sense. Sounds and faces echoed in her head. Police swarmed the place, taking statements and holding back the press. Carlie closed her eyes against the flashing lights, calming when she felt Kurt squeeze her hand again.

"It's over," he whispered, brushing her hair back, tears bathing his face. "I've got you."

48

"What time is it?" Carlie coughed, her throat burning from the effort.

"Almost midnight," came her father's steady voice.

The hours of interviews, assessments, and more than a few tearful reunions blurred together. Still nothing made sense. She shook her head and groaned as pain raced through, nausea roaring in its wake.

"What happened?" It hurt to talk, but she needed to know.

He sighed and put down his paper. "When you didn't return, security locked down the residence and started combing the grounds. They discovered one of the event staff was missing, a guy by the name of Parker Dalton, and they began hunting him down."

His voice coming from afar, her dad continued the story, telling her that the key breakthrough had arrived when Alex's accomplice tried to pawn her unique necklace. The shop owner sent in a photo and description of the piece to the police, and Kurt's local team picked up on it immediately. Parker got nervous at the delay and took off. The security team caught his trail and tailed him back to the hotel, where they apprehended him before he could get into the building. Kurt's investigators had been questioning Parker and Mom's crew had been questioning the front desk when her 9-1-1 call came through.

"Kurt took off for the stairs, not yet knowing which floor you were on. He was a man obsessed, honey. Once you phoned down and said fourteen, Wallace texted him and the rest... Well, you were there."

She recalled the doors locking from the inside. Thank God that door wasn't able to lock. If Alex had managed to lock Kurt out, if Kurt hadn't stopped him... She shivered and shut down that line of thought.

"The other people on the floor? There was an older woman across the hallway. And the woman with the gun. There were others, too."

"They're all okay, Carlie-Q."

"The woman who helped me?"

He chuckled. "Karen. She stopped by here, fairly determined to see you. I gave her my card and she assured me she'll be in touch. Quite a spitfire. She refused to be seen by the doctor."

Carlie smiled, grateful for that fire. She almost didn't ask the next question, but she had to know. "Alex?"

"He was treated for his gunshot wound and is being transferred to a secure facility." His mouth pressed into a flat line. "We will see that he is convicted and sent to prison. You don't have to worry about him anymore."

"Kurt?"

He sighed. "He was questioned and released. He's okay. I made him go get some food a little while ago. He didn't eat or stop at all since you were taken."

She'd caused so much pain. "Dad, I'm so sorry about all of this. Everything."

He looked down at his hands and shook his head. His voice was full of emotion when he said, "I wish you had trusted me from the start... This was not your fault, baby." He walked to her side, wrapping his arms around her. When he straightened up, tears swam in his eyes. Grabbing a tissue, he dabbed at the tears streaking down her face.

"Love you, Dad."

"Love you, too."

Dad stepped back, revealing Kurt standing in the doorway behind him. Carlie caught her breath, and her dad turned. He smiled and collected his newspaper. "I believe I'm in need of some fresh air." He tapped Kurt's arm with the paper on his way out.

"Hi," Carlie said, her voice gravelly.

"Hi," he replied.

They watched each other for a moment, and then she broke into a smile. "I knew you would be there."

He smiled back. "You were doing pretty well without me, though."

"No. I wasn't," she whispered, her voice wobbly.

Kurt eased onto the bed at her side. "Doctor said you could go home tomorrow," he murmured, picking up her hand and tracing the IV in her arm.

"Good."

"Carlie... I..." He stopped, taking a deep breath. "When you were gone, when I realized... Shit. I was terrified. I didn't know what he would do to you. I failed you."

Her heart broke at the pain and torment in his words. "You didn't fail me; you saved me. I'm so sorry to put you through all of this. I don't blame you if you want to leave..."

She stopped, swallowing hard. "I never meant to hurt you. Again."

Kurt sucked in his breath, then wrapped his hand around hers. "Damn it, Carlie, I'm not going anywhere. I love you."

"You do?"

"Yes, I do."

She closed her eyes, tears falling.

"I know, it's terrible timing. You are in a hospital bed, for God's sake. And I don't expect you to say anything." He held his hand up to her face, cupping her cheek and wiping her tears with his thumb, and said it again. "I love you, Carlie."

She pressed her hand against his, holding it to her cheek. "I love you, too."

He kissed her gently, and she sighed. She was finally kissing the right man, the man she loved.

"Now will you tell me what all this muttering about Donkey Kong was?" he asked.

As much as it pained her, she laughed.

49

*T*he following week was a blur. Carlie had been worried she'd be overwhelmed by press and media, but she was largely left alone. She suspected her parents and Kurt had something to do with that. Whatever or whoever was responsible, she was grateful.

Kurt stayed at her side, attending to her every need. After a few days of this, Carlie had to shoo him away; she knew he had to see to his mounting pile of work. Eventually he relented, as long as Kim or Rachael vowed to not leave her unaccompanied while he flew back to California for two days. Carlie felt guilty disrupting everyone's lives, but she was also relieved, not ready yet to be left alone to face her thoughts and memories.

The next day, a knock sounded at the door. Kim hopped up, running to answer. Carlie heard Kim murmuring to the visitor. "Car, I think you'll want to see this person." She grinned, nodding over her shoulder before ushering the guest into the room.

"Bernie!? What are you doing here? In Cincinnati? In my apartment?"

"Why do you think? I'm here to see you, Ms. Eller. Though I must admit, I was worried you would not admit me."

Kim hovered in the background, covertly picking up dishes and discarded belongings. Kurt had been gone for less than twenty-four hours and Carlie had already made a mess. Kim caught Carlie's eye. "I'll be in the kitchen."

Bernie groaned and sat on the armchair across from her. The bags under his eyes appeared to be heavier. "Why would I refuse to see you?" Carlie asked, genuinely confused.

His eyes were troubled. "It was my party, my staff. If I had known..."

"Mr. Bartlett—Bernie, Dad and Kurt told me how great you were. You offered to cover everything. Why would I hold any of this against you?"

He clutched the arm of the chair. "My dear, that does not negate the fact that it happened in my home. Helen and I are devastated."

She tried to put herself in his shoes. What she would have felt. How mortifying it must have been. How she would also be driven by the need to apologize, to be forgiven. Smiling at his grandfatherly face, Carlie endeavored to set his mind at ease. "I am fully aware of the situation and what and how it happened. And I forgive you and Mrs. Bartlett completely. You will always be welcome in my home."

He humbly accepted this. "I must confess that I am still in shock. Alex always seemed like such a bright young man. For him to behave so abominably is beyond my understanding."

Thinking back to the rambling apologetic note she had received from Allie Williams, Alex's sister, she had to agree.

"I've been told he will be institutionalized for a while before being transferred to a prison."

"There is sometimes a fine line between brilliance and madness," he mused aloud.

She steered the conversation to something worth talking about—Bernie's charity event and the work they were doing. He was delighted to talk about it and extended an open invitation for Carlie to join their board. She was strongly considering it, though it was a bit intimidating.

"You have a great deal of good to do in this world, Ms. Eller. You have been blessed with a sharp mind and generous resources. I hope if you do not take me up on my invitation, you at least allow me to invade upon your world from time to time to tempt you to do more good work."

She was flattered and humbled by his offer, and suspected her world was going to change in many ways after all this drama.

Kim rejoined them and discovered Bernie was acquainted with her father. "The Senator and I have had a loose association over the years. We don't always see eye to eye, but I believe he means well," he told her gently, aware of their estranged relationship.

Kim blinked at the statement and nodded, refusing to be drawn into a discussion about her dad. Carlie couldn't blame her for that one. It was a taboo subject, one sure to make Kim clam up.

When Carlie lost the ability to smother her yawns and her fatigue became obvious, Bernie stood and clasped her hand. "Young lady, I want to thank you for making this old man feel better about a horrific event. You have my respect and my gratitude. Should you ever need anything at all, you have but to ask. And I will be in touch."

Kim walked him to the door and was still chatting in the doorway when sleep claimed Carlie.

50

"*I* can't believe you're leaving," cried Marie.

"Just for a month, Marie," Carlie said, hugging her dear friend and trying not to get any hair dye on her sweater. "We'll be back before you know it."

"But look at what happened when you went away for a week!"

Carlie laughed at her obvious dismay and smiled. "Granted, that was quite a week, but it's not something that will ever be repeated."

"At least you did end up catching that nice young man," she said, gesturing to the waiting area. Kurt sat chatting with Rachael in the waiting area. He had insisted on coming with Carlie to meet her "other mom."

"Why California? It's too far away, too trendy." She frowned. "You'll come back eating kiwi and drinking coconut water."

Carlie smiled to herself. "Marie, I already eat kiwi, and I promise not to develop a love for coconut water. And I will be back," she added.

Carlie waved to Kurt, and he rolled his eyes, holding up

an issue of *Modern Bride*. Rachael didn't have a subtle bone in her body.

"I still don't like it," the stylist mumbled.

"Marie, would you want me to be with someone who didn't introduce me to his mother?"

Marie sniffed, not answering.

"Wouldn't you want your sons to bring their girlfriends by long enough for you to get to know them?"

She still didn't answer, but her lips twitched, giving away her internal conflict.

"Marie?"

"Fine! You win. Go to California, but you come back here. Don't you go filling that head of yours with California dreams."

Carlie laughed at her, eyes full of love. "Yes, ma'am."

"Now, are you sure you don't want a new style?"

She rolled her eyes. "No, thank you. Just a trim."

Some things never changed.

ABOUT THE AUTHOR

Kathryn Halberg is the contemporary romance author of The Eller Series, including the upcoming *Lost and Found, The Eller Series Book 3*. She is a weaver of words to help you feel connected to the world around you. Often found with a large mug of coffee in hand, her nose is perpetually in her laptop or smartphone, working round-the-clock in social media or writing. She holds a Bachelor of Science from Towson University in Baltimore, Maryland, and a Master of Business Administration from Wright State University in Dayton, Ohio. Kathryn resides in Ohio with her husband, their houseful of boys, and her lone female companion, a sweet, elderly lap dog named Chelsea Bell.

Connect with Kathryn online.
Social media: @KathrynHalberg
Website: KathrynHalberg.com

Enjoy *Hidden Agenda*?
Please leave a review online.

Get more of The Ellers!
Find Rachael's story, *Animal Attraction, The Eller Series Book 1*, on Amazon or other retailers. Watch for Kim's story, *Lost and Found, The Eller Series Book 3*, coming soon!